T0078415

TWIN CONSPIRACIES

TWIN CONSPIRACIES

Like Mother, Like Son

A Novel

Lori Sanders

iUniverse

TWIN CONSPIRACIES
LIKE MOTHER, LIKE SON

*This is a work of fiction. All of the characters, names, incidents, organizations, anddialogue
in this novel are either the products of the author's imagination or are usedfictitiously.*

iUniverse books may be ordered through booksellers or by contacting:

iUniverse
1663 Liberty Drive
Bloomington, IN 47403
www.iuniverse.com
1-800-Authors (1-800-288-4677)

ISBN: 978-0-5954-3852-5 (sc)
ISBN: 978-0-5956-8448-9 (hc)

Print information available on the last page.

iUniverse rev. date: 12/28/2018

To my soul mate

Many thanks to my wonderful friend Robyn, who always made time for me and my creative quest. Your input was invaluable.

Many thanks to my amazing husband who always encourages me to follow my dreams and always believes in my ability to fulfill them.

CHAPTER 1

▼

Roberta planted her cherry red stilettos firmly against the tattered linoleum floor. She stretched her short arms forward and tightly gripped the old, dusty handgun between her palms. A smile adorned her wrinkled face; her deep stare focused on her abusive husband. Her finger snapped back on the cool trigger, catapulting death toward the only man she had ever loved. His ocean green eyes widened as he witnessed this preface to his unexpected demise. Confusion and doubt plagued his handsomely tanned face. His head jerked backward, and his hands frantically grabbed for her as he took his last few gasps of breath. Roberta stood unfazed by his wasted attempt at retaliation. With the pleasurable smell of gunfire looming in the stale air, she watched her husband's burly body plummet onto the slightly discolored kitchen tile. The thud of his fall echoed, and his corpse bounced slightly before inevitably coming to rest.

The punishment for his crimes finally had a beginning and an end. He now knew what it was like to fear for one's life, just as she had for over twenty years. His name was Charlie, and after tonight, he would never be able to harm her again. Although the assassination transpired in a matter of seconds, she had taken a well-deserved snapshot of the shiny bullet moving through the still air, the sleek, soft-nosed tip entering his thoughts, and the first spew of blood shooting out of his punctured brain. She granted herself a long, better-late-than-never exhale, and glanced over at the tacky calendar hanging on the side of her lime green refrigerator; May 8. A smirk of satisfaction crossed her lips.

The descending sun warmed her leathery skin as it shone through the open slats of the off-white venetian blinds. Freedom captured her thoughts.

"What now?" she wondered.

With no escape plan and no getaway car full of money or clothing, there was only one solution.

"Who's gonna ask questions; who's even gonna know he ain't around?" she asked herself. "It don't matter none, anyhow. They all know he's a pig and that he takes off and comes back when he's done being sexed up by cheap whores. I just ain't gonna say nothing! It ain't like disappearing is out of character. He left on one of his 'business trips' and never came back. I guess my new role is that of poor, abandoned wife left to deal with my crummy life. 'Poor Roberta,' that's what they'll say. If they only knew the truth, they'd be saying, 'Good for you, Roberta; good for you.' At least now he'll be remembered as the bastard he was, a guy that left his old lady for cheap thrills."

She wasn't sure who she was trying to convince with her one-sided debate, but it kept her mind occupied while she went into the bedroom in search of a cigarette. She took her sweet time, stopped to pee, and then took a good, long look in the mirror. For the first time in years, she liked who she saw staring back. A woman who didn't take no shit, a woman who righted a wrong, and more importantly, a woman who was now a widow.

"Back to business," she said with relief as she sauntered back into her kitchen.

"Roberta, what the hell is going on! What happened? Who did this? Are you all right?"

The back door of the kitchen stood wide open, and a pleasant breeze smelling of blooming flowers danced through the crime scene. Sam stood just a few feet away from Charlie's damaged body and the handgun lying on the cluttered counter. Roberta stood strong, gazing deeply into her neighbor's stare. She couldn't come up with a quick story to exonerate herself from the bloody mess that slowly stained her floor.

"Damn it, Roberta, what have you done?"

"Sam, you know how he was!"

"Sure, I know he was an ass, but that is no reason to blow his brains out!"

"He just went off, Sam. He was out of control. All because he don't like what I fixed for dinner. I had to protect myself. It was me or him."

Roberta watched her neighbor glance over at the undisturbed stove.

"Sam, it was self-defense! I ain't got nothing to be ashamed of! He shouldn't have put his hands on me! Plus, he was all over me about what I was wearing! Tried to tear my shorts right off me! Who the hell is he to tell me what to wear? You know him, Sam; he wants me to put on some oversized sweater and baggy sweat pants!" Roberta ranted.

The body remained on the floor, dividing them. The odor of Marlboro filled the air as Roberta took long, heavy drags.

"I know he probably deserved it, but the law isn't going to see it that way," Sam said.

The silence screamed. Sam took a regretful look at the corpse. Charlie's empty eyes gazed toward the ceiling, and his mouth remained open as if in the midst of a powerful yawn. Blood leaked from his forehead and had already begun to stain portions of his black hair. Sam looked away before stepping around the growing puddle of blood. Despite the crime and despite the troubles that lay ahead for them both, they were in it together now.

CHAPTER 2

▼

Dillon Andresen gave his petite bride a quick peck on the cheek before dashing out of his luxurious three-story home as if Satan himself was not far behind. With dark, wavy hair slicked back behind his ears, he ran to his car carrying a travel mug in one hand and a black leather briefcase in the other. Although Jag had been secretly observing the lovebirds for almost three months now, the mere sight of Dillon still caused a tornado of rage to take off inside him. Jag despised watching his subject live out a successful life. Knowing self-confidence was oozing out of every athletic pore in Dillon's body exposed Jag's own feelings of inadequacy, but it also doubled as his driving force.

"It won't be long now, Dillon," Jag said cunningly from across the street.

"I'm gonna punish you for what you did to us. It's about time you knew how the other half lives!"

Like clockwork, Jag watched his twenty-four-year-old rival drop down into his silver BMW at precisely 7:50 AM. With a clenched jaw, Jag absentmindedly cracked his knuckles.

"So predictable!" he thought.

Dillon's adoring wife waved good-bye from their front porch just as she did every morning. The combination of her strawberry blond locks and charmingly crooked smile mesmerized Jag. He often fantasized about what it would be like to touch her and to feel her body pressed up against his.

"He don't deserve you!" Jag mumbled to himself, "and he ain't gonna have you for much longer."

From the first moment he'd seen her step out onto that porch all those days ago, Jag knew Dillon's wife was a woman of intrigue. Ultimately, she was the kind of woman every man wanted after the days of partying and one-night stands ended and the days of settling down began. Her name remained a mystery, but for now, to him, she was his Angel.

Within the hour, she emerged from the house and skipped down the front steps. She was dressed in a skirt made of dark denim that hugged her subtle curves, and the casual strut of her slender body stole his sense of purpose. One after the other, her sexy legs disappeared into her midnight blue Lexus, and the sound of the car door slamming shut jolted Jag out of his trance.

"Snap out of it, Jag. Damn! Remember why you're here, what you're gonna get out of this. Focus, man! Focus!"

As Jag watched her drive around the corner, he turned off the soothing chaos of Aerosmith, slid a single key off of the dashboard of his rented Ford Explorer, and headed on foot to the back of the ritzy home. For the first time since he had arrived in Bend, Oregon, Jag was venturing out of his safe vehicle and into the upper-class neighborhood that housed his target. His hand quivered with each heavy step as he trudged across the freshly cut and manicured lawn. He turned sharp down the path that paved the side of Dillon's home before approaching the glass door that stood between him and his future success. As quickly and as quietly as possible, Jag opened the door with the key his partner had provided him, stepped inside, and then closed the door behind him. He was faced with what appeared to be a fancy dining room. The aroma of fresh-brewed coffee greeted him as he stood still and took in the unfamiliar atmosphere around him. Crystal vases and decorative plates lined the shelves of a huge, antique-looking hutch accessorized by an enormous gold-laced chandelier. There were also hideous paintings hung along all four walls, but from his research, Jag knew that the uglier the art was, the more expensive it turned out to be. The rest of the house, however, offered a feeling of excitement and warmth. Pillows and lush furniture accessorized what appeared to be the prime living space with reds and oranges; dark woods laced glass-paned cabinets and side tables; and the electronics were clearly the best of the best. Jag couldn't imagine what it would be like to live in such a place. It was the complete opposite of his humble home in Emmett, Idaho.

Ashamed by his distraction, he pressed on with the task at hand and began snooping in a room that could best be described as an office. Jag shuffled carefully through a stack of papers that neatly covered a heavy, well-crafted desk; he collected bits of information that would give him as much access to Dillon's world as possible. *Purchased house in 2003, monthly mortgage payment: $2,235, SSN: 535-54-8880, … bank account number: 5863-2221-02.* Stumbling across a cell phone bill perked his interest. He quickly folded it up and inserted it into his notebook. After taking a short break in a soft, brown leather chair, he attempted to open the drawers of the sturdy desk, only to find them locked.

"Damn it!"

A large, dark-framed print of a map of the world caught Jag's attention. It was blanketed with pushpins that seemed to be color coded and arranged with a purpose, or even more likely, with an agenda. Jag took a step back to admire with disgust what he assumed was a record of all the places Dillon had embezzled money from.

"Your past will be catching up to you very soon, you son of a bitch," he whispered to himself.

By order of his partner, Jag's next order of business was to insert a small camera on the inside of two specific lampshades. One that sat on the desk in the office and the other that was positioned on the main living area's chandelier. Jag was a little bit insulted that his partner wanted to keep an eye on his progress, but knew he could never say it out loud. He needed to obey just as he always had. Jag then traveled from room to room noting the details of his targets' lives: what kind of coffee they drank, what music they listened to, and even what they kept in the medicine cabinet. Slowly and quietly, his heavy boots carried him up the carpeted steps. A bedroom was directly ahead of him, and the mere sight of it forced shivers up and down his tall, muscular body. He envisioned her, his Angel, lying on the queen-sized bed, curled up on her side, wearing a content expression and nothing else. He could almost feel her thin fingers running through his brown locks. Just then, ten soothing chimes of a clock halted his fantasy and reminded him that it was time to go, at least for now. Angel's schedule was too unpredictable to linger any longer; plus, he had to report his findings to his partner in crime. A partner who would be happy to know that Jag was one step closer to an infiltration.

CHAPTER 3

▼

Lanie Andresen returned home from her productive day at around 5:30 PM after completing a monstrous project for work. The arches of her size-seven feet ached from standing in her favorite red and white pumps for way too long. She gladly tossed them, along with everything else she had been wearing, into a messy pile on the speckled-green bathroom tile. One inch at a time, she immersed her narrow body into a hot, lavender-scented bubble bath as she thought about her life. She was only in her early twenties, but she had accomplished so much already. Her career was on the right track, she had a comfortable lifestyle, and she was married to a man who was tall, dark, and handsome and who loved her for all that she was and all that they were together. The water continued to rush into the porcelain tub as she took several deep breaths. Fragrance soothed her senses, as if a blossoming garden surrounded her. Beads of water danced across her shoulders and down her toned biceps. She had been married for eight months now, and her new commitment brought with it a new level of appreciation for things like aromatherapy, yoga, and the importance of spirituality. This was not the kind of spirituality a person gains sitting in a pew with hundreds of robotic attendees, but the kind a person gains from centering their mind, body, and soul with the universe. She was a new woman with new goals. Her life was unfolding just as she had planned.

As Lanie strolled down the long, chandelier-lit staircase, her gaze fell on the brilliantly framed picture of her and her husband as it hung on the fawn-colored wall at the end of the staircase. Dillon had only been her boyfriend at the time the photo had been taken. She remembered that trip well, not because of the ambience of Napa Valley or the conversations they'd had, but because of the spout of violence they'd encountered while there. They had been walking down a cobblestone street in the crisp spring air and sipping hot chocolate, while exchanging an interesting dialogue about their future. They had stopped to sit on a park bench, when a man wearing a blue mask approached them. Within seconds, the intruder had cracked Dillon over the head with a steel pipe before disappeared into the park with Dillon's wallet in tow. Dillon was left lying on the ground with blood secreting out of the back of his skull, and Lanie remembered all too well the sound of his moans as he struggled to push himself up off of the cool grassy field. A chill went down her spine just thinking about that day. She abruptly pushed it out of her mind and strolled into her lavish kitchen. Her eyes fell on an expensive bottle of Sauternes resting in the top layer of the wrought iron wine rack. It was given to her on her wedding day, along with a romantic letter from her groom, "A sweet and rare wine for a sweet and rare lady; both will only get more precious with age." Thinking he was due home within about an hour, she took the opportunity to set up a seduction of her handsome six-foot-two husband. It was Friday night; they both had been working very hard and desperately needed a release. Time was not always on their side because of their busy schedules, but tonight would be different. Tonight would be about limitless passion.

Lanie sprinkled freshly picked rose petals on a red, satin blanket that she had spread out across the living room floor. She crafted a low-key fire in the rock fireplace and made sure her husband's favorite soul CD spun in its player. A silky, yellow negligee outfitted her otherwise naked body as she set the bottle of unopened Sauternes on the hall table with a note of her own. "A sweet and rare wine for a sweet and rare man, both only getting more desirable with age." She was hoping he would remember that it was the same bottle of wine he had given her years back as she placed the wine in a silver ice-filled bucket and set it on the entryway table where it wouldn't be missed. She lay by the fire, slightly exposed, waiting for her lover to arrive.

"Oh, you look so beautiful with the firelight shining off of your supple skin. You are such an angel, my Angel," Jag softly whispered. "Dillon don't deserve you," he blurted out as he watched the scene of seduction unfolding from inside his car on the camera's small receiver.

CHAPTER 4

▼

Sam had only known Roberta for about two months, yet there they were, standing within view of Charlie's forty-five-year-old body as his freshly spilled blood lingered on the kitchen floor. The scene was tainted with bloodshed from a man who deserved a lot more suffering than he had endured from that single bullet, at least according to his wife.

After spending two hours plotting how to cover up the messy crime, they felt the best course of action was to simply bury the body out behind the house once darkness fell. They didn't see how the plan could fail; no one would be around to see them dig the deep grave or to watch them push and pull the heavy body across the property.

"Not too close to the house, Sam! Dead or alive, that bastard gives me the creeps. I wouldn't put it past him to crawl up outta that grave and pop me a good one for what I done," Roberta said.

"Don't be ridiculous. He's dead. You put a bullet into his head, remember! This is real life, Roberta, not some scene in a horror movie. Death is real! Do you even realize what you've done? What consequences could be in store for you? For us?" Sam asked.

Roberta glared at Sam.

"You're supposed to be my friend, Sam. Don't talk to me like he did! Look where that got him!" she said, sternly.

"I'm sorry, but this whole ordeal is way over the top for me! I am here for you, okay. He won't be able to hurt you again. We'll get through this ... together."

Roberta looked at Sam with adoration and felt safe and comfortable once again. Her ears welcomed the kind words, and she hoped things would be different from this point on. She now had someone to share her secret with, someone to understand her crime, and someone to celebrate in her victory.

"Sam?"

"Huh?"

"This is a special day, a day to always remember. I will never forget what you're doing to help me out."

They continued to shovel, changing shifts whenever the other needed a break. Sam was uneasy about the entire string of events that day, and felt engulfed with guilt for participating in such a horrific episode.

"Why is Roberta so at ease with all of this? Surely she has to feel a little bit of remorse or sadness for what she has done. She is acting as if we are gardening or something!" Sam thought with confusion.

Roberta expelled a new memory with each thrust of dirt. "This is for when ya locked me in the closet for hours, and this is for when ya slept with that red-headed slum dweller from across town."

Finally, by a half past two, the freshly dug grave was ready to swallow Charlie up whole.

"He deserved this, Sam. Keep telling yourself that. You're doing the world a favor, helping to rid it of scum. I was only defending myself. I'm the victim here—it ain't Charlie!" Sam halfway nodded.

They walked back up to the house where Charlie was still lying in the exact spot where he had been murdered over fourteen hours earlier. The only difference was that now an old, red sheet covered him up just in case anyone popped in to say, "Hey." Roberta knew she had a better chance of winning the Idaho State Lottery than she had of finding an unexpected visitor at her door, but Sam insisted nonetheless. One after the other they entered the kitchen. The scent of gunpowder and stale cigarettes had been replaced by an overpowering pungency of fecal matter. Disgust and fear swallowed Sam as Roberta casually sauntered over to Charlie and ripped the sheet right off him. The sheet must have been stuck against the crusted wound because once it was pulled from the body; blood began to trickle out of the curdled bullet hole. His skin had lost the healthy redness that usually embellished his whiskered cheeks, and paleness plagued him. Clumps of squishy brain matter stuck against his left temple and piled up inside his ear. Sam sprinted out the back door and vomited uncontrollably. Chunks of refried beans and corn hit the ground, adding disgust to an already unbearable situation. Roberta kicked her feet up onto the table and waited patiently in the kitchen for the intermission to end. The sight and smell of her husband's body didn't faze her. In fact, she welcomed the view, welcomed seeing him in this vulnerable state—helpless and incapacitated on all possible levels. Now she was the one calling the shots, making the decisions, and reaping the benefits of cruelty. Ten minutes passed before Roberta put out her well-deserved cigarette. "Sam, come on! We gotta finish this! It'll all be done soon. Pull it together!" She hollered from her seat.

Soon after, they positioned Charlie face up on the stained, red sheet after rolling his two-hundred-and-fifty-pound body over twice. Sam's shaking hands grabbed a hold of the bottom portion of the sheet while Roberta handled the top, claiming she wanted to look into her husband's eyes every step of the way. They began the strenuous journey toward the freshly dug grave that sat only about two hundred feet from the rear of the house. Sam concentrated on the crickets chirping, the leaves on the trees rustling in the slight breeze, and the smell of bark that laced the grounds to avoid the reality of what was actually happening.

BAM! The body plunged into the ground's cavity.

Vomit tried to make its way back up Sam's throat.

"We're almost done now; let's just finish so we can get the hell outta here! Come on, Sam; quit being a softy so we can be done already! We can grab some chow. All this hard work's making me hungry. Ya hungry, Sam?" Roberta asked.

Silence and a glare was all the response Roberta needed to know that she should stop talking and press on with business. The gaping grave was plugged shortly after, and Charlie was no more.

"Tomorrow, I'll sprinkle some seed down. Pretty soon, it'll be just another plot of land. You and I will be the only ones who ever know about this unmarked grave and about Charlie lying just a few feet below us. Right, Sam?"

Sam quickly nodded and then departed without uttering another word.

Meanwhile, Roberta flipped open a Heineken, placed a meat lover's pizza into her gas oven, and waited for her snack.

CHAPTER 5

▼

Dillon pulled into the driveway, worn out from his long day at the bank. His usual fast-paced step had slowed to a lazy saunter as he approached his home on Rosewood Street. The clock in his BMW read 8:45 PM, and guilt entered his thoughts, at least for a moment. He had just had a discussion with his wife the day prior about making it home on time every now and again. Tonight clearly wasn't one of those nights. There was a light on in the living room, which led Dillon to wonder if Lanie had waited up for him. As soon as he entered their abode, he knew that she had. Flickering candles illuminated the hallway, revealing a bottle of wine floating in a bucket of melted ice. The smell of smoldering wood drifted throughout the house. Both of their faces registered regret, but for very different reasons. He dropped to one knee, kissing her on the lips passionately. "I'm going to take a quick shower and meet you back down here in fifteen minutes. I'm so sorry. You look beautiful," he uttered and waited for a reaction. She offered a half smile and nodded to imply that she, once again, understood.

Soon after, he returned downstairs extremely tired from his day, but eager to find that extra spring in his step so he could romance his wife the way a husband should. They began their evening sipping wine and discussing the happenings of the day. Lanie told him about the successful research she had completed and how beneficial it would be in aiding the poor and hungry in west Africa. She had a strong role in coordinating the disbursement of medical supplies and food to various countries, and she always put strong determination into ensuring that her job was carried out successfully. Her official title was International Support Manager, but she portrayed herself as just another cog on the wheel. Hiding behind a fancy title was not her style, and she always said that each member, starting with the mail clerk and ending with the founding president, were all of equal importance. Her work touched the lives of thousands and stretched out to dozens of countries around the world. That alone seemed to be more important to her than any amount of money she could ever earn while tending to the less fortunate.

"I am always so proud of you," Dillon said. "But when are you going to get that well-deserved raise? Have you talked to Mr. Sharply about paying you what you're worth yet?"

Lanie wondered how her lying there half-naked had somehow led to a discussion about money. Words felt like her enemy. She grabbed Dillon's face with both hands and pressed her lips hard against his. Their conversation ended, just as she had anticipated. They kissed erotically for the perfect amount of time before he grabbed her hair and used it to yank her head back. The tug was just hard enough to shoot her arousal level up a notch before he aggressively kissed her neck. His hands ran their course across her body, feeling every curve more than once. He reached for the bottom of her nightgown and pulled it up over her tousled hair. Her bare breasts were briefly revealed to him before his tongue danced across them.

Nausea consumed Jag as he watched the two together, but oddly enough he couldn't take his eyes off of them. The man who had ruined his life was now making love to the woman he wanted, better yet needed, and Jag was left out in the cold, just as he had always been.

"Enjoy these next few days, Dillon. They'll be your last!" Jag mumbled with fierce confidence. "Soon, it will be you and me, my Angel. You and me and a whole lot of Dillon's money," he said from his vehicle while continuing to watch their bodies colliding.

CHAPTER 6

▼

It didn't take long for the new widow to gobble up every speck of pizza before licking her fingers and placing her chipped ceramic plate into the sink. Although crawling into bed sounded like the perfect ending to a perfect day, Roberta decided that she had a much more vital and monumental task to tackle first. While looking down at the pool of blood that had recently provided the gift of death to a man who made her feel like she was in her own special kind of hell, she shook her head with a sigh. It was as if she had casually noticed an insignificant mess such as a dropped bowl of spaghetti or spilled orange juice.

The gore was still wet, and the stench held its own, but Roberta's senses weren't bothered. She pushed a bleach-laced mop back and forth over Charlie's last pieces of existence until the mop was too drenched with death to be effective any longer. Her cycle of rinsing and mopping and rinsing and mopping began. Each rinsing included a detailed watch of the expelled fluid splashing into the sink, swishing around the basin, and falling into the depths of the drain. Roberta considered this ritual to be symbolic of what had been and what was still to come. Her husband, as well as his memory, was being removed from her life, washed away from existence, and sent to the rot of the unknown. Only then, when this task was complete, would her house and her life be left clean, untainted, and back in order.

Her fresh start would bring with it a conscience that was cleared by a motive that would humble even the harshest of minds. It wasn't long before her floor was completely rid of human smears and back to its initial state. She finished up with a sponge, erasing the spots and splatters that kissed the walls and table legs throughout the room. By 6:00 AM, Roberta had completely covered her tracks.

As her many hours of "good deeds" came to an end, she finished her day off with a long, hot shower before climbing into bed. The rankness of her husband burned her nostrils as she crawled between the sheets.

"Damn it! Charlie ain't gonna creep his way into my first sleep as a single woman," she uttered with irritation. Roberta pulled the sheets off the bed and calmly placed them in the washing machine with plenty of soap and hot water. While dressing the twelve-year-old mattress with a new set of bedclothes, she could hear the faint sound of agitation from the laundry room. It calmed her. It was just another reminder that she was washing away the old to bring in the new. It only took Roberta a matter of minutes to drift into a state of unconsciousness.

Running ... running ... as fast as her bruised legs could carry her through the woods, Roberta dodged branches, roots, holes, snakes, and the swooping of black crows that were surely out to aid her predator in her capture. She struggled for breath, gasped for air, and prayed from the depths of her soul for endurance to carry her away from the continuous threat that encircled her.

Mysterious shadows in the moonlight were the only apparent forms to be seen. Above her were silhouettes of long-winged birds and swinging tree branches edged with thorns. In her peripheral vision, she saw wild animals with fierce, sharp teeth and small troll-like figures. They were immobile, as if watching her running in place, waiting patiently for her to accept the inevitable outcome of surrender. The worst, however, lagged behind her. An occasional glance backward revealed snapping tree limbs, crunching leaves, and the sound of panting. She heard, felt, and smelled the evidence of an entity following her every maneuver, but she was unable to see the entity to support her theory. Evil swarmed all around, encircling her with confusion. She wasn't going to give up, but she also had no idea how to escape this crazy and unbelievable curse. Despite the long, quick strides she maintained in her fight for an escape, the evil surroundings remained the same. The same wicked shadows, the same paths, and the same horrific feeling of her inescapable demise stuck with her. Her eyes widened with shock and panic as she heard her undetectable pursuer reveal himself to her.

"Roberta ..." he taunted in a long, drawn-out voice. "Where are you going? Why are you running? You killed me ... remember? What are you afraid of now, my sweet and loving wife? I can't hurt you anymore. My death was supposed to set you free ... remember? Don't you feel free ... Roberta? Free from pain, free from guilt, and free from the destruction you insist I brought to your life? How can I hurt you now? Am I even real? Am I really as dead as your friend Sam claims? You can't hide from a ghost, from your past, or even from your own state of mind. Running from the demons in your head, your own inner world, is a never-ending and impossible task. I beg you to stop! I just want to talk to you … just talk. I love you, Roberta Lynn, with all of my heart."

"No! Go away!" she screams.

Her foot jams under a twine of root that stretches across her wooded path. With arms flailing, she hits the ground with a strong and unstoppable force. The wind is knocked out of her for a brief moment. Struggling to free her ankle from the elements of nature, she sees the shadows and hears the voices drawing closer and closer. Trying to escape with what little strength she has left in her one-hundred-fifty pound, five-foot-five-inch body, she looks up and sees the bloody face of the man she'd murdered just hours before. As large drops of blood drip slowly onto her cheek from the man-made hole in Charlie's head, Roberta wails out a frightful and drawn-out scream.

Her head instinctively snapped up as she profusely began wiping the blood off in quick, harsh strokes. She looked at her palm expecting to find a slick, red coating but instead discovered a glaze of sweat. She looked to her right and then to her left, her eyes blinking hard as she recognized the surroundings of her bedroom. Her sheets were soaked with sweat and urine. Her peaceful night's sleep had turned into a reunion with her dead husband.

CHAPTER 7

▼

"Twenty-eight, twenty-nine, and … thirty," Jag counted breathlessly as he completed his last set of pull-ups at the YMCA. He was too focused to even notice the racket of techno blaring from the overhead speakers as he wiped his moist forehead with the palm of his hand. He had been working out consistently since his quest began; as a result, his physique had changed dramatically. The skinny, insecure boy he had once been had morphed into the strong and intimidating man he always wanted to be, at least on the outside. His size and shape as well as his mental state were extremely important factors if he was going to pull off the most interesting and risky part of the inventive plan. He was only human, however, and he felt a good sense of guilt about what he had in store for Dillon. However, a belief in his own good intentions overshadowed his occasional desire to retreat. He wasn't a mean-spirited man; in fact, he was just the opposite. He was a man of compassion, one who valued the importance of honesty and unconditional love. He knew the difference between good and evil and believed in righting wrongs. He believed he was a warrior, attempting to change an undeserved fate that cursed his life.

Jag dried himself off after his thought-filled shower at the club and returned to his damaged Oldsmobile. Although the blue leather seats were worn with holes and scratches, and the dash sported a large crack, he felt more comfortable in it than in the fancy rental he used for his stakeouts. A long forty-nine miles stood between the YMCA and the place he temporarily called home—a two-star motel just twelve short miles from Dillon's immaculate world. The motel stood in a part of town that held no intrigue for a prominent man in polished Prada shoes.

Jag dreaded each trip back to the motel from the gym. There was too much time to think, too many thoughts invading his concentration.

"Jorgie is a loser; Jorgie is a geek; Jorgie is a beanpole whose name should be freak!"

The cruel words echoed in his head as he drove down the dusty dirt road. He could still hear the childish laughter of the kids as they chased him; he could still see the hateful grins piercing through him just before he turned to run. "Jorgie is a loser; Jorgie is a geek; Jorgie is a beanpole whose name should be freak!" Sometimes, handfuls of rocks and mud would rain down over his gaunt body as he ran as fast as his weak legs allowed. Other times, the kids would tackle him to the ground or pin him against a tree while throwing kicks and punches in his direction. As a child, he often wondered why kids were so mean to him when all he wanted to do was make friends, but as an adult, he knew that he simply made an easy, unresisting target. It only made it worse that Jorge's stone-washed pants never reached the tops of his generic shoes or that his mother was referred to as the town whore.

"I ain't running no more!" He said loudly to himself, while continuing to drive. The name Jorge represented a time and place that needed to be forgotten, an identity that was accompanied by misery and misfortune. Jag, on the other hand, was all about confidence and having the courage to run toward something instead of away from it. Although his new name was only about as old as his quest, he believed that his Jag-like qualities had always been there, hidden deep within. A few deep breaths steadily moved through his chest to slow his speeding pulse. His patience wore thin. His desire to take the next step suffocated the voice of reason that begged him to wait behind the scenes a bit longer. It was time. He just knew it was time. Tomorrow, he would make one last trip inside the Andresen's house as an outsider, and the following day would mark the start of new beginnings. He turned his Oldsmobile into the littered motel parking lot and parked. A surge of eagerness blasted through him. He tossed his keys onto the bolted-down nightstand and dialed the number of his trusted partner.

After three rings, a voice answered, "Hello?"

"It's Jorge. Tuesday's the day. I will need you to be here by 3:00 PM sharp so we can be good and ready when it all goes down. Can ya do that?" Jag asked.

"I'll be there!"

Jag and his accomplice spent a good thirty-five minutes while going over the particulars of the plan, ensuring that no details were left unreviewed. It was foolproof, or so they thought.

CHAPTER 8

▼

Clad in her baby blue cotton tank top and matching shorts, Lanie rolled out of bed with thoughts of freshly brewed coffee. Rain danced softly on the shingled roof. Dillon exited the bed and entered the bathroom to begin his morning hygiene routine. The strong, good-looking, dark-haired man dressed himself in a custom-tailored charcoal gray suit, which he complemented with a striking blue silk tie. The smell of expensive cologne lingered in the large master bedroom.

"You are looking *good*, my friend!" he said with a wink of arrogance directed to the hunk staring back at him in the full-length mirror. Thirty minutes from the time he'd rolled out of bed, he was traipsing down the staircase, just like every other morning, rushing around and preparing himself for another long day at work.

As she watched the raindrops descend around her, Lanie lounged on the covered back porch and silently sipped her vanilla-bean coffee. She heard the familiar sounds of bustling about in the house and wondered, as she often had, if her husband ever really felt relaxed. Lanie reveled in each morning's tranquility, enjoying her cup of coffee in the same white wicker chair she always sat in. The coffee mug heated her delicate hands. Thoughts of her day and her future danced through her simple mind. Lanie and her husband were two very different people who shared a unique love, and that was enough for her, at least for now. Once the last drop of coffee trickled down her throat, back into the house she went to give her husband a good-bye kiss. As she leaned in and pressed her plump lips against his, she smelled the familiar tang of his citrus cologne.

The reality of the rainy day enticed Lanie to stay within the confines of her inviting home, but loose ends at work needed to be tied up. The radio blasted a funky, upbeat song. She threw her top and panties onto the fabric-covered bench that edged the foot of the bed before she covered her healthy shape with a white terrycloth robe. Her pure green eyes took a glance out her recently cleaned bedroom window; she was hoping for an indication that sunshine would visit her quaint neighborhood. Disappointment set in as she snapped back to thoughts of her upcoming day. She closed the drapes before dressing herself in dark Levis and a trendy floral blouse.

CHAPTER 9

▼

"Hundreds of flowers blooming on a perfect spring day
Drops of moonlight lighting a lost child's way
The colors of a rainbow illuminating the freshly washed sky
Enough faith in a heart to never have to ask why
That's what you are.

A field of daisies touched by a gentle warm wind
An honest embrace felt by a true friend
The wonderment of dolphins frolicking in the ocean
Two lovers dancing in perfect harmonious motion
That's what you are.

Strange and different like a fish out of water
A day that's too hot and only getting hotter
An unfinished painting that will never be perfected
A flawed diamond that the buyer rejected
That's what I am.

A piece of a puzzle that doesn't quite fit
A struggling artist who is ready to quit
A heart that's been broken and yearns for a mend

A new boy at school that no one will befriend
That's what I am.

The miracle of birth after hours of pain
The rewards from hard work you eventually gain
The toughened spirit that failure creates
The gifts gained from life when your course deviates
That's what we are.

The comfort received after a bad dream has ended
The calm you feel before a storm has descended
Goodness and badness combined into one
Creating uniqueness when it is all said and done
That's what we are.

You are the essence of all that is pure
And I, the disease, searching for a cure
I need you in my life to salvage the true me
To find my true soul, a part no one can see
And in return, I will fill your life with joy
I will treat you as my queen, never as my toy
I will take away the badness, destroy the evil villain
The man you thought you knew so well, the man we call Dillon"

"I think I will call this one, 'Collaborations of Love,'" Jag thought before writing the words on the top of his ode to Angel.

Poetry was one of Jag's passions. It brought out the true and tender side of him, a side that was personal and private, a side that expressed his real self. And that self needed to be protected from the ridicule of others. It was no secret that vulnerability was a weak characteristic for any man, so his sensitive side remained bottled up until a thrust of inspiration forced him to release it quietly in his book of poetry. Whether motivated by hatred or love, greed or perseverance, the poems easily flowed from him in forms of rhyme or song.

Despite the lack of a single spoken word, the real Angel had emerged onto the pages of an eight-by-ten-inch notebook. Not the immaterial facts of her favorite dinners or which college she went to, but facts that reached beyond the shallow hollows of habit. Her personality radiated from all directions: her body language, her style of dress, the way her house was so fresh and comfortable, and even in the way she kissed her unworthy husband good-bye each morning. Actions always spoke louder than words, and he felt that her goodness and purity screamed from every slice of life that she lived. Distracted by the sound of a car engine turning over, he looked up to find Angel pulling out of her driveway. The clock in the dash had ticked away for over two hours, and finally, the coast was clear. As he watched her turn the corner onto a neighboring street, his heart began its sprint.

"Time to roll," he thought.

He opened the vehicle's door and proceeded to the house to complete his day's mission. The key turned. The door clicked open. Once again, he entered a place so opposite his usual environment he could almost compare it to a parallel universe. After removing his large, blue tennis shoes and placing them near the exit, he ran directly to the upstairs bedroom, snatched the items of importance, and abruptly shoved them into his vinyl knapsack. He took a short pause to gaze out the streak-free window he'd just seen his Angel peering from. A calming, deep breath introduced him to a refreshing, clean smell in the room, and a smile interrupted his stressed expression as he unintentionally envisioned her taking the shower she must have recently taken. Splashes of pale greens and purples highlighted the cream-colored room, and more ugly art hung perfectly centered on the walls. He wanted to remember everything about this moment. It marked the last day of standing on the sidelines, the last day he would be on the outside looking in. With his bag in hand, he returned to his silver Ford and headed back to the simple motel.

CHAPTER 10

▼

Ring … ring …

"Hello?"

"Hi. This is Mr. Chaptner; may I please speak with Charlie?"

"Charlie? Uh, he ain't around. Who's this again?" Roberta spoke nervously. "Are you a friend or something?"

"Well, yes, you could say that, but I also work with him at the job site. I've been worried about him for the past couple of days. Is he all right?"

"Now is as good of a time as any," Roberta thought to herself. "Come on; tell him Charlie disappeared; that he left like usual; that you ain't sure when he'll be traipsing back home, if ever."

"What was your name again?"

"Ken, Ken Chaptner."

"Well, Ken, he left the other night, and I ain't seen him since."

"Left? Left for where?"

"Just left! Took off! Split! Headed for greener pastures! It ain't like it's the first time. I'm sure you're used to his disappearing acts."

"I'm not sure what you mean … disappearing acts?" Ken said, confused.

"Well, it don't take no brain surgeon to know what disappearing means. He left, and I don't know where he went. Do you get it now … Ken?" Roberta asked with sarcasm.

"So he left? You have no idea where he is? And you don't know when he will be back? Am I understanding you correctly?"

"Oh, for crying out loud, I don't know what else to tell ya. Like I said before, he just does this sometimes. I can't do nothin' about it. I really don't feel like explaining why my husband skips out on me, especially to a man I don't even know. Speaking of which, I ain't never heard him mention you before, Mr. Chaptner. You say you work with him?"

"Yes, ma'am."

"Uh huh, well, your name don't sound familiar to me," Roberta rudely snapped.

"I've worked with him for many years and consider him my very best friend. He would have told me if he were just leaving. It all sounds pretty out of character for Charlie."

"Don't you dare suggest that you, a strange man I ain't heard of knows my husband of over twenty years better than I do! I got things to tend to. If I hear from him, I'll let him know you was looking for him. Good-bye now, Mr. Chaptner!" And with that, Roberta slammed the phone down in irritation.

"Acting like he don't know the way Charlie was. The nerve! What, does he think I'm stupid or something? I'm sure Charlie really painted me something awful. What a jackass!" Roberta paced for a few seconds before she picked the phone back up and dialed her friend.

Ring … ring … ring … ring …

"Barker residence, can I help you?"

"Hey, Sam, it's Roberta. Some guy from Charlie's work just called looking for him. The bastard, some guy named Ken, acted like Charlie was some kind of saint, and he was all concerned about his whereabouts."

"What did you tell him?" Sam replied in panic.

"That Charlie took off. That it was nothing unusual and not to worry. He acted like it was such a shock that Charlie hasn't been showing up for work. Plus, it was some yahoo I ain't never heard of. I know everyone Charlie works with, and this guy ain't one of them. It must have been one of his drug buddies; they call sometimes, you know, pretending to be all nice and wholesome."

"What if it was his work, Roberta? What then? People are going to start asking questions!"

"You worry too much, Sam; there ain't no question I can't answer. I just have to stick to my story of him running off. Anyone who really knows him won't give it a second thought. His buddies won't do nothing; they call the cops, and they run the risk of getting themselves busted for whatever they're messed up with. No blues will be showing up here. I'm sure of it. So, what are you up to today?"

"I'm just laying low and working on my book."

Sam had been a journalist for a national newspaper, but had dreams of becoming a successful published novelist. That dream is what led Sam to the town of

Emmett, Idaho, a quiet and uneventful place. Giving up the hustle and bustle of the big city and quitting a job that demanded a minimum of sixty hours per week was only the first step. It was going to take sacrifice, dedication, and a complete lifestyle change to succeed. Free time and a fresh environment would hopefully prompt a strong level of creative thinking, and even more importantly, a future book deal. Unfortunately, this supposedly uneventful town had led the aspiring author down a dangerous path: aiding and abetting a criminal, conspiracy to cover up a murder, and obstruction of justice. All the makings for a good fictional story, but completely disastrous for a real life.

"I need to get going, Roberta. I have a lot of work to do."

"No problem. I got things to get to anyway. I'll talk at you later."

"Good-bye," Sam said. "I hope to never hear your voice again!" Sam continued after hearing the click on the other end of the line.

CHAPTER 11

▼

The day had finally arrived, and Jag was positioned near the parking lot of the bank that Dillon could easily call his second home. The back of the building conveniently bordered a large grassy field, giving Jag little concern for spectators. Jag waited diligently for the bank to turn its lights out and close down for the evening. Soon, the bank tellers and loan officers would clock out and head home to their families. This option no longer existed for Dillon.

Tick, tick, tick, tick, tick …

Five o'clock came and went as Jag listened to the passing of time. The second hand of his thrift store watch seemed to scream at him. Because of his nervousness and sweaty palms, he took deep breaths to calm his palpitations. He knew the plan by heart, repeated it over and over in his head, and hoped and prayed for a quick and successful outcome.

"Why are you so nervous?" he snapped. "Just calm down. It'll be over soon. Just breath. In and out; in and out. Focus on one thing at a time. Shut down your emotions. Come on now, you've done it all your life!"

Tick, tick, tick, tick, tick …

Each passing minute felt like an eternally ticking time bomb. Minutes seemed like hours, hours like days. While longing for the moment when he would be able to look back on this day and smile, he continued his painstaking duty. He was definitely in a hurry to be done with it, but at the same time, he didn't want the precise moment of truth to arrive. After today, Jag knew there was no going back. Impatience streamed through his veins.

"You can do this. You can do this. You can do this," he reassured himself. "Stay calm, and remember why you're here. You can do this. Relax. Remember what you will get in return. Remember that you're the good guy. 'I am the good guy!'" he told himself.

Jag's self-proclaimed pep talk did little to ease his mind or calm his jitters. A chug of Jim Beam sailed down his throat. The clock showed 6:15 PM. The waiting was killing him; not knowing when Dillon would step out of the back entrance of the bank continued to spike his nerves.

"Damn it! When is he going to come out?" Jag wondered.

Meanwhile, his collaborator sat quietly in the dingy motel room skimming an entertaining article about the upcoming county fair. The room was poorly lit, and the drapes were drawn so that only a small stream of light peeked through. Partner X wasn't the least bit anxious. In fact, "happy" was a more appropriate word to describe the emotion back at the motel. Jag's partner was eager to finally see Dillon.

The coconspirator put down the paper and looked at the clock. "Ain't gonna be long now."

A quick glance around the room confirmed that the accessories needed to complete the job—two plastic syringes carefully filled with clear fluid—were still present.

"This is gonna be so easy," X's head shook with confidence. "So easy."

Cars could be heard entering and exiting the parking lot. A man was yelling at a woman about money, and someone else was listening to the Eagles. It was refreshing to hear life continue on with chaotic normalcy in an environment representative to what X was accustomed. Plus, the commotion itself was a valuable contributor to the plan. It was a necessary and beneficial partner, and it was right on cue.

Knock, knock, knock.

X's eyes widened. "No call? He was supposed to call."

X peered out the peephole with slight concern. A slender man stirred from side to side on the other side of the door.

Without opening the door, X responded, "Yeah?"

"Uh, your month ended last night. If ya want to stay, you'll have to pay. I ain't running no shelter here." The man hollered back thorough the door.

"Uh … yeah, all right. Jor … ahh … The renter ain't here right now, I'll pass the message. Don't worry. He's good for it. I'll have him see ya when he gets back."

"Yeah, okay. He's paid good so far. Just let him know I's here and to come see me when he gets in," the motel manager instructed.

X sat down on the bed, relieved that the visitor had come and gone before the drama began. X clicked the television on, and again waited. The official mastermind of the entire ordeal lounged safely in the confines of the motel room's four walls, while Jag put himself smack dab in the middle of danger.

CHAPTER 12

▼

The metal door opened. Jag watched Dillon pass through the threshold of his insignificant little life and into a zone of danger. The moment that had taken forever and a day to come had finally arrived. Jag grabbed the knapsack from the passenger seat and swung his heavy, black leather boots out the driver-side door. It could have been the Jim Beam, or possibly the sight of his rival, but his confidence level abruptly rose to that of arrogance. His strides were wide and strong. He strutted toward the parking lot and continued to stare at his unsuspecting target. Dillon turned after locking the back door to his mistress and made a beeline for his classic BMW. Jag heard the sound of the car alarm being deactivated as Dillon scurried toward the passenger-side door to dump his flashy briefcase. The parking lot was fairly well lit with an iridescent glow beaming from two street lamps. Dampness coated the air, and the wind was nonexistent. Dillon circled around to the driver-side door, apparently unaware of Jag's approach.

"Hey, dude, am I glad I finally found somebody!" Jag hollered from a distance. He continued his approach. Dillon stood, annoyed.

"It is amazing how deserted this town gets once the sun starts to go down. Can I trouble you for some assistance?"

"I'm in a hurry," Dillon said firmly, barely looking up to acknowledge the stranger's presence.

Jag's voice spoke louder the second time he attempted to distract his prey.

"It'll just take a minute. Maybe I could use your phone right quick? My car broke down just over yonder."

Dillon leaned against the open car door while tapping his index finger hard against the roof of his car. He shook his head back and fourth in irritation.

"I need to call for a tow truck, and the phone over there in that booth is out of order. Plus, I'm late getting home, so I want to let my wife know what happened and that I'm okay. You know how women can get all out of sorts when they worry."

Jag was hoping the wife card would get Dillon's attention and stop him from entering the vehicle.

Jag made one last attempt. "What do ya say? Can I make a quick call?"

"I have to get home myself. Sorry, but I have a wife waiting too. I just don't have time for this."

"Once a bastard, always a bastard!" Jag said loudly.

Now within arm's reach of Dillon, Jag removed his black stocking hat, unzipped his fully closed coat, and stared his opponent directly in the eye. Dillon, taken aback, remained speechless. He stared in disbelief, astonished by the mere sight of the person he saw standing before him. Jag reached into the open bag and pulled out a heavy, blunt object.

Dillon protested, "What the hell is going on. How …?"

CRACK!

Dillon took one devastating blow to the side of the head. His muscular body collided into his own car before sinking to the cold pavement in the parking area. Jag raised the metal pipe high and slugged Dillon again and again and again with unrestrained force. With each blow, Jag attempted to hit the same ruptured wound. Swiftly, Jag gripped Dillon under the armpits and dragged him across the pavement to the other side of the BMW. The vigorous dose of adrenaline that pumped though Jag's veins allowed just enough of a boost to enable him to lift Dillon's limp body off the pavement and to thrust him into the leather passenger seat. Jag slammed the heavy door, walked around to the driver's side of the car, and picked up the dropped car keys off of the concrete. He tossed his bag of necessities onto the backseat. With only inches separating the two of them, Jag stared at the unconscious body and took a moment to grasp what had just happened. The man he had hunted, the man who had taken away a life of prospect, the man who had been too busy to let a stranded man use his phone, was now hunched in despair with no way out. The tables had turned; karma had come back around full circle. Jag pulled out his weapon and clobbered Dillon one last time out of sheer hatred. Blood continued to ooze out of his rival's head, and his body remained pathetically slumped over his own lap. He reached into the pocket of Dillon's tailored suit and removed the cell phone to make the all-important call to his partner.

"I have him; we're coming!" he said, before he snapped the phone closed.

The pair pulled out of the parking lot and took a left onto Fawn Drive. The car handled like a dream, and for the moment, Jag was experiencing a day like no other, one that included him playing the role of husband instead of predator. He imagined that he was leaving his successful job promptly at 4:00 PM. He would call his Angel to let her know he was on his way home to her.

He would ask if she wanted him to pick anything up on the way home, and she in return would say, "All I need, all I will ever need is you in my arms, so hurry home, sweetheart."

He would smile and blow her a kiss through the receiver, and she would lovingly reciprocate. He would make his usual stop for flowers at the corner of Elmira and Third Street. He'd enter the shop with comfortable salutations for its owner.

"Evening, Terrence, it's a beautiful night out there."

"You said it, Jag. Say hello to the missus for me."

"Will do, see ya next time."

He daydreamed about how perfect it would be to actually pull into the driveway of their home with a beautiful bouquet of roses in hand. Goose bumps glazed his skin as he pictured her standing at the double-door entrance with a smile on her face. Her hands would wave excitedly.

"Hey there, I missed you so much today."

"Not as much as I missed you," he would reply as they embraced on the wraparound porch. His imagination ran wild as he continued to fantasize about spending the rest of the evening making passionate love to her. While caught up in thoughts of erotica, Jag realized he had gotten an erection from the mere thought of being near his Angel.

"Damn it! What are you doing? This is the most important day of your life. Don't get distracted by her again!" Jag knew all too well that she clouded his concentration.

"One more day. Just one more day. Then you can think about her all you want!"

For now, arriving at the motel with a clear head was top priority. There could be no talk of Angel or any insinuation that he planned for her to have the leading role in what was next on his agenda. His accomplice needed to believe that everything was going as planned and without deviation. However, it was clear that Jag had a few ideas of his own. In his mind, there was nothing wrong with having his cake and eating it too.

CHAPTER 13

▼

"Gem County Sheriff's Department, can I help you?"

"Hello, I am not really sure if I should be calling, but I am concerned about one of my co-workers, or friends rather. I think he could be missing."

"Can I get your name please?" the clerk cordially asked.

"My name is Ken Chaptner."

"Do you want to file a missing person's report, Mr. Chaptner?"

"I'm not sure. I can't be sure he is missing, per say, but he hasn't shown up for work in a while, and his wife claims that he ran off."

"You don't think that is the case?"

"Well, no, not really. It just doesn't sound like something he would do. She says he has done it in the past, but to me it just seems out of character for him. He is a pretty reliable guy. I don't want to jump the gun here, but I am a little worried."

"If you believe that foul play may have been involved, you should come in and speak to one of our officers immediately. The officer will be able to explain what constitutes a missing person's case and what steps can be taken," the clerk instructed.

"All right, I'll think about it. I may drop in later today or early tomorrow."

"Do you want me to see if someone is available to talk with you right now, Mr. Chaptner?"

"No, I don't want to overreact. I think I will try to contact him again and then go from there. I'll call back if I can't get this resolved."

"Well, have a good day, sir, and don't wait too long."

"Thank you," Ken cordially replied. "I won't." It was now up to him to decide where to go from there.

Ken's white Dodge four-by-four drove down the grassy patched road in hopes of discovering a rational explanation for his friend's unlikely departure. He was headed for Charlie's home and wondered if he might find him there alive and well. His instincts argued against the point.

A depressing shade of gray dressed the sky as he traveled down the muddy road. Leaves occasionally floated onto the windshield as Ken continued through the tree-lined path. It was still a little chilly from the spring rain, typical of Oregon weather, so he'd set the heater on low.

He approached the small and unimpressive home that appeared to belong to Charlie. He caught himself, distracted by its run-down exterior, and wondered why Charlie let it slip to near ruins when he made such decent money at work. Ken knew Charlie to be a proud man who always put his whole heart into everything that he did. It didn't make sense. The roof was in desperate need of repair, and the siding was cracked in several places. Weeds invaded the grass. Irritated that he was distracted by such trivial issues considering the current situation, he put the disrepair out of his mind and began his approach. He walked tall and strong. His long, white ponytail hung down his back and across his brick red and black flannel shirt; it swung with each step.

Knock, knock, knock.

A quiet pause followed.

Knock, knock, knock.

"Hello? Is anyone home? It's me, Ken, Ken Chaptner. Can I have a minute of your time?" He stood with a stone face, wondering if Mrs. Grapler was waiting quietly inside for his inevitable departure or, a more likely scenario, if she had simply stepped out. He closed the screen door and walked around to the side of the house.

"No vehicle in the driveway," he observed.

His weathered face boldly peered into one of the windows, but nothing seemed out of the ordinary. There were framed pictures hanging on the pure white walls; a colorful throw blanket was wadded up in the corner of the couch, and there was an overall stillness. He wasn't sure what he expected to find, but he felt that spying was the only available avenue at that point.

"I guess I will call again later," he thought to himself. "This is so strange. Charlie just takes off?"

He knew of the tension Charlie and his wife shared, and he hoped that it hadn't gotten so bad that Charlie had really just up and left. However, abandonment was a much better alternative to what his gut instincts were telling him.

"What now?" he pondered as he hoisted himself into the large cab of his pickup. He put the truck in gear. "Okay, think rationally. Don't jump to absurd conclusions. It's only been a few days. Maybe he just needed a bit of space from his wife. She *is* difficult; she *is* argumentative; and she *does* drive him crazy. Maybe he did take off. But why didn't he call me first?" Ken wondered.

He spent the remainder of his drive home thinking constructively about the situation.

"I guess I should call some of the guys from work, see if they've heard from him lately. I just don't understand why would he disappear and not tell me. He has always come to me, especially when he needed an escape from Roberta."

Ken began remembering the few times Charlie had shown up on his doorstep. He'd been seeking a nonintrusive friend and a couch to lay his head. Charlie wasn't the type to complain for hours about his problems, but it was known that his arrival at Ken's house was an escape from his own.

"He was always welcome at our house; he knew that. But why not this time? what was different about this time?" Ken wondered.

He had high hopes of finding Charlie at his own house talking to the missus about what had happened. He returned home hoping to walk through the front door to the sight of Charlie's enormous shoes resting by the closet and bed linens covering the sofa in anticipation of an overnight visitor.

Disappointment filled Ken's heart when he found his own beautiful wife sitting alone. She was reading *Country Homes* magazine while sipping hot apple cider. An extra blanket warmed her short legs.

"Hi, hon," he said.

"Hi," she said as she looked up and winked.

"Hey, have you by any chance heard from Charlie lately?"

"No, not lately. Why?" she asked leisurely.

"I'm worried about him. He hasn't been showing up for work. Roberta says he took off. Isn't that weird?"

Carla looked up with a perplexed expression. "Took off? Where did she say he went?"

Ken continued, "She said, quite defensively I might add, that he just left. She said she didn't know where he went, and she didn't know when he would be back. She went on to say that he does this all the time, disappears I mean. I'm not quite sure what to think of it all," Ken confessed.

"They probably had another one of their fights. I don't know why he stays with that woman," Carla said.

Ken removed his tan work boots and walked over to the black leather couch to sit next to his wife. She marked the page of her magazine and turned all her attention to her husband.

"Surely he's coming back. Let's give him another day or so. He knows we're always here for him. He'll show up here when the time is right for him."

She hoped her words comforted her husband.

"Why wouldn't he call, though? I just don't get it. Oh, and get this, Charlie has never mentioned us to Roberta. She said she didn't know who I was."

"That doesn't surprise me, sweetie. You know Charlie; he's a pretty private guy. The last thing he would want is for us to get caught in the middle of one of their squabbles. I think he considers us his safe haven. He wouldn't jeopardize that."

"That makes sense. You're probably right. You know, you're the cat's meow. I don't think I tell you that enough." Ken kissed his wife on the cheek and smiled, thankful that his marriage lacked the usual unhappiness.

"I think I'll call a few of the fellas just to see if anyone knows anything."

"Don't panic anybody, now. I'm sure he's just off sorting out his emotions."

Ken nodded in agreement, picked up the cordless phone, and began his search.

CHAPTER 14

▼

The BMW pulled into a gravel parking area behind the low-class motel at 7:40 PM. Night had already begun shadowing the day, exposing a brilliant orange glow from the sun that loomed on the horizon.

"It is a beautiful night, Dillon. The first of many for me," Jag said, as he raised his bottle of Jim Beam high into the air. "Here's to the future my man, to my forgotten days of yesterday. Anything you want to toast to D? No?" Jag asked his unconscious prisoner. "Well, let's see. What kind of toast is fitting for a man like you? Cheers to Dillon. Here is to the first day of the rest of your unhappy life. And here is to your sorrow never to be forgotten. Oh, oh, and I can't leave this part out. Listen up, D. Here is to your amazing wife, a woman soon to feel the touch of a real man." Jag smiled and pressed the bottle to his lips in search of one last swig of the good stuff. He knew that the five long drinks he had taken over the past few hours were more than enough for that evening's events. Turning up drunk was not an option.

His tattered jacket came off, as did his old, leather side-buckle boots. He reached into the polished backseat to get the important bag that not only transported his weapon, but also a long, black trench coat and a fancy hat. The coat felt soft around his bare neck and gave him the appearance of someone with style and charisma. "Cuz every girl's crazy 'bout a sharp-dressed man!" He sang one of his favorite ZZ Top songs to fit the occasion. Jag pushed Dillon's head forcefully into the dashboard. "Oh well, what's one more bump for old times sake, eh, D?" Jag said sarcastically. Roughly, he stripped Dillon of his designer sport coat and substituted it with a worn-out, paint-stained trench coat.

"A little help, D?" Jag said, irritated.

Dillon's designer shoes came off next, and on went the old side-buckle boots Jag had recently removed from his own feet. One last, very important item remained. Jag's old stocking hat came off his own head and was pulled harshly over Dillon's.

"We can't have you making your debut into society with all that blood in your hair, now can we?" Jag asked before placing a burgundy beret onto his own head. It was another item that had come straight from Dillon's closet. "What were ya thinking when ya bought this, D? It's definitely not the most masculine of hats."

There the two of them sat, looking completely different from the way they'd looked just moments before.

"Let's roll around front my man. I have a special guest waiting for ya!" Jag said.

The car backed up and drove around the motel to the front of his rented room. There were a few people scattered about, but it made no difference to Jag. The BMW may have stuck out like a sore thumb, but carrying a "drunk" man resembling a bum would seem all too familiar to any spectators. Jag got out of his new car, went around to the passenger side, and opened the door forcing Dillon's leg to collapse onto the cement. Jag then pulled Dillon's body out of the car, and it immediately smacked down onto the asphalt. With Dillon's body lying lifeless on the ground, Jag had found the perfect opportunity to dump a good portion of Jim Beam onto his hostage's shirt.

"Hey, can I get some help over here?" Jag yelled to a couple of guys having a smoke in the parking lot.

"Whatcha got?"

"My friend got wasted at a pub; nothing out of the ordinary. He's passed out, and I can't seem to pull him up. I don't want to have to drag him."

Jag remembered his plea for help earlier that night, a plea Dillon rudely ignored. He knew these guys wouldn't do the same. They may not have riches or so-called impressive lives, but they knew about the unwritten rule of sticking together. It was probably similar to the way Dillon supported his hoity-toity country club friends. A slender man with a thin comb-over sauntered up to the car.

"Drank too much huh? I've been there, the poor bastard. What room's he staying in?"

"Right there, 119," Jag responded.

Jag and the lanky stranger used their combined strength to lift Dillon off the pavement and up to the wretched door of room 119. His head hung forward, bouncing loosely with each step.

"Damn, smells like he bathed in whiskey."

"Yeah, he's a clumsy drunk. He was stumbling all around, liquor splashing out all over the place. I found him at the pub on Eighth Street passed out on the pool table. Bartender knows me; called me to pick him up."

Jag reached into the trench coat he was wearing and pulled the keys out of his faded blue jeans.

"Damn!" he thought, realizing he'd exposed his thrift-store clothes to the stranger.

"Yeah, got the call right in the middle of changing the oil in my wife's car. She is going to be pissed off if I don't get that finished tonight," he said quickly, hoping his quick thinking derailed any misconceptions as to why he had on torn jeans and a "Metallica Rocks" T-shirt under the distinguished coat. The stranger smiled and nodded. The door to room 119 flung open, and a haze of cigarette smoke slapped the men in the face. The two of them carried Dillon's body inside, plopping him facedown onto the bed. X was out of sight.

"Thanks, man. I'll take it from here. He'll just have to sleep it off," Jag said in an attempt to clear the room.

"What are you gonna give me for my troubles?" the man asked.

"Ah, well, how about the rest of the Beam? It's in the car," Jag replied. He couldn't believe he was being hassled for compensation.

"That'll work. That and a hundred bucks," the stranger said.

"I don't have a hundred bucks. Are you crazy?" Jag snapped.

"You pull up in here in a BMW, and you think I am dumb enough to believe you're broke. I ain't no idiot. Just give me my pay for a job well done, and there won't be no trouble for ya."

Jag was certain this dude was no challenge for him, and he was itching for some tension release.

"You want some of this?" Jag asked with conviction.

"You want some of *this*?" the man responded as he snapped open a switchblade.

Jag caged his anger for a moment and asked himself, "What would a weasel like Dillon do? How would it look if a rich kid with a silver spoon in his mouth starting whaling on some guy in a run-down part of town? The last thing I need is for the cops to show up. He sighed. I have to play the part. I can't have everything I worked for ruined over a measly hundred bucks."

He sucked up his pride and answered the stranger like a coward would, like his old self would.

"I don't want any trouble from you. I'll see what I have. Actually, there may be something in my ashtray. Go check it. Grab the liquor while you're at it. I'll look in my coat and meet you out there."

"You think I'm stupid or something?" the stranger asked.

"Dude, I'll be right out! I gotta take a wiz. I ain't goin' nowhere; my car's out there with you. What do you think I am going to do, hide out in this hole and pray that you go away? Get real! I'm sure there's some money out there. Just go check."

"Yeah, all right. But no money equals slashed tires and a good old-fashioned ass kicking," the stranger warned.

As soon as the man left the room, Jag sat on the bed and frantically searched Dillon's pants pockets for a wallet. It wasn't there.

"Did it fall out at the bank?" Jag wondered. "Did he accidentally leave it at work? I need that wallet. Shit! What the hell am I gonna do now? ... Stay calm, maybe there really is some money out in the car." Jag stepped outside to find the swindler going through a wallet, apparently one he found in the car.

"Give me that!" Jag yelled as he reached for the wallet. The extortionist pulled it back and opened the flap.

"You organize your money by dollar amount?" he asked in disgust before he started mocking Jag, "I don't have a hundred dollars. I just don't know if I have any money to give ya!"

An angry Jag grabbed the wallet and reached inside to pull out the money he'd apparently had all along. Jag snatched a crisp one-hundred-dollar bill from the wallet and thrust it at the man. "There, take it and be gone!" he said.

"Well, now I'm thinking it is going to cost you a bit more than I thought," the stranger said.

"Don't fuck with me!" Jag said with pure conviction as he grabbed the little man by the neck. "You got your hundred dollars, and I'm not in a mood to be pushed. I have had one hell of a night!" Jag couldn't be a total coward; it just wasn't in him. At least it wasn't in him anymore.

"Calm down, dude," the stranger said in a raspy voice. Jag released his grasp and the man started back stepping away from the car.

"Go see your shrink; you got issues!" the stranger shouted as he walked across the parking lot. The guy Jag had been so sure would help him out of pure human decency had ended up walking away with his money. Technically, it was Dillon's money, but Jag considered it his own now.

As soon as the unwelcome commotion ended, Jag stepped back into the room, closed the door, and secured the safety latch.

"You can come out now."

X silently walked into the room and approached the vulnerable body lying across the orange and brown bedspread. With an expression of repugnance, Jag's accomplice spit on Dillon in disgust before opening the nightstand drawer and pulling out one of the syringes. Jag rolled Dillon onto his back and pressed the hostage's arm flat against the bed exposing the biggest purple vein he could find. The silence was almost deafening to Jag, but he understood the impact Dillon had had on his partner's life. The years of built-up aggression, disappointment, and lack of respect had taken their toll on both of them. Jag remembered the first time he'd laid eyes upon Dillon just a few short months before. His emotions had been all mixed up. He felt sad, angry, confused, revengeful, and especially disgusted. The needle slowly punctured through Dillon's skin, penetrated the vein, and released the drug with an uninterrupted flow. With Dillon still lying motionless from the beating he'd endured earlier, the needle was extracted and placed in a tote bag that would soon depart with them. The second needle was an insurance plan for later.

CHAPTER 15

▼

Another evening of patient waiting ticked by. It was a ritual Lanie had grown accustomed to during the past six months of marriage. Tonight, however, would be different. She refused to sit around inspecting the ticking clock. Her patience snapped.

"Hello?"

"Hey, Rach, it's me. What do you have going for tonight?" Lanie asked enthusiastically.

"The usual, jetting off to England, dinner with a prince, dancing the night away to the philharmonic, waking up to tea and crumpets at Buckingham Palace. You know, the usual."

"Great! Then you're free?"

"Yep," Rachel replied.

"How would you like to go see a play, then grab a drink or two after?"

With her fingers crossed, Lanie hoped her best friend was up for a night on the town.

"Best offer I've had all night. I will have to call the prince though and let him know I won't be blessing him with my company tonight," she said.

Since Lanie and Dillon's wedding, it wasn't too often that Lanie and Rachel got together for a girls' night out. They had been friends for years, their friendship dating way back to their pigtail days.

"So what happened? He's working late again tonight, huh?" Rachel inquired.

"Working late every night is more the case, but let's not get into that. He's already dampened my night enough. Sorry, I haven't called in a while," Lanie apologized.

"Hey, I know how demanding married life can be. You don't have to apologize to me. Remember that little incident last year … you know, my divorce? Believe me, I was just as unavailable when I had a ball and chain wrapped around my livelihood."

She and Lanie laughed.

"Pick you up in thirty?" Lanie asked.

"Sounds great," Rachel replied.

A new excitement flushed through Lanie. She scribbled, "Got tired of waiting, don't wait up," on a piece of scratch paper and placed it on the refrigerator with a strawberry-shaped magnet. A semi-long, baby blue dress with a sheer overlay beautified her body. The spaghetti straps accentuated her toned arms and perky breasts, and the open back was tastefully revealing. Lanie had only owned the dress for about four hours, and it had been specifically chosen to prompt a double take. She reapplied her pink translucent lipstick and bolted out her front door. Being all dressed up and driving fast toward her best girlfriend's house brought back so many memories of their high school days. They had been carefree as they cruised the strip, waved at boys, and embraced life.

"Tonight is going to be a night to remember," she told herself.

Alternative music blared from the eight-speaker sound system as she pulled up to the modest, two-story house her friend had recently purchased to accentuate her new life as a single woman.

Honk! Honk!

Inevitably, the neighboring houses heard the blaring music as it pumped from the sound system in Lanie's slightly cluttered car. Rachel skipped down the steps of the porch, "Hey, babe!" she said. She wore a stunning red dress that, despite the ten pounds she had put on since her divorce, hugged her in all the right places. Her straight, black hair danced slightly against her shoulders and complimented the glow of her bronzed, Asian skin. Lanie smiled and gave a two-handed wave. Soon thereafter, they were off like the party girls they used to be.

"Remember when we used to drive the strip in my old, orange Fiat looking for Daven and Kurt? We thought they were so cool with their long, ratted hair and faded jean jackets."

Both girls smiled.

"Yeah, and that old van they drove around in with Twisted Sister blasting out their open windows, even in the dead of winter."

"Remember the mattress in the back they claimed was for camping? Like we were stupid enough to believe that."

"Yeah, too bad we *were* stupid enough to believe that."

Laughter exploded from their glistening lips. They were having a great time reminiscing about their past and the lives they had lived back then.

"Those were some of the best years of my life," Lanie said.

"Ya know, me too. Nothing but freedom and no responsibility."

After about twenty minutes, they found themselves in the parking lot of a decorative opera house where a long line of sophisticated-looking adults had assembled to enter the show. The women were dressed in high-end gowns that were complimented by matching purses that weren't big enough to carry anything more than a sample lipstick and a credit card or two. The theatergoers seemed to turn in unison as Rachel and Lanie drove up. They were no doubt wondering where the musical racket originated. Both girls smiled proudly and waved to the onlookers.

Lanie looked at Rachel, "How boring do they look? 'Hello, I am Miss Witherworth. I am rich, eat raw fish, and am extremely boring.'"

"And don't forget Mr. Arthur Decanter III over there," Lanie continued. "I'm an investment broker, drive a fast car, and have a small penis.'"

Gushing laughter shot out of them again as Rachel stomped her foot hard against the floorboard.

"Let's get out of here and have some fun like the good old days. Just 'cause we're supposed to be these grown-up, mature adults doesn't mean we can't spend one night letting loose. Does it?" Lanie asked.

"Hell no; let's blow this joint."

Lanie put it the car in drive, slammed on the gas, and attempted to peel out of the parking lot.

"What was that?" Rachel asked with a quirky smile.

"A peel out. Why?"

"That was the worst peel out in the history of peel outs."

They both smiled.

"Oh, I can peel out," Lanie humorously declared.

"Yeah? Prove it," Rachel innocently challenged.

"When you least expect it, Rach. When you least expect it."

Rachel knew Lanie never backed down from a challenge.

"Let's go there!" Rachel exclaimed, pointing as they almost blew past the small tavern. Lanie quickly whipped into the parking lot, hitting the curb in the process. Their misfit attire and natural beauty contributed to many stares as they strutted into the brick building with confidence. A total of eight men and one woman lounged at the long bar, each held a drink of some sort. Waylon Jennings played loudly from the jukebox, and the music drowned out the sound of peanut shells cracking beneath their high heels.

"I'll rack and you break?" Rachel suggested without a second thought.

"Hey, you know I can't break. I'll rack, *you* break," Lanie responded.

"All right, you win, but loser buys next round."

"Bring it on," Lanie replied with confidence. They ordered two whiskeys on the rocks, and Rachel set the cue ball in motion.

"Solids!" She shouted as she inhaled another enjoyable whiff of the smoke coming off a nearby Swisher Sweets cigar.

CHAPTER 16

▼

Dillon's dormant and naked body remained sprawled over on the motel comforter.

"Maybe he will break out in a rash from the polyester," Jag said with sarcasm.

"Well, Jorge, that was the old Dillon. Before you lies the new Dillon," X replied smugly. Jag took Dillon's designer suit into the bathroom and put it on.

"Out with the old and in with the new," Jag conceitedly said to himself while looking in the dingy mirror. He strutted out of the confined space and modeled his fancy new look.

"What do you think of these duds? You should see his closet. Dark sports jackets and pants, white dress shirts. His ties are the only things that ain't the same looking. Stuffy SOB."

"Stop yammering! Just shut up! I am glad you're having so much fun playing dress up, but can we get back to our crime here? You ain't stopped talking since we pumped him full of the drugs. Let's just do this."

"Ya know, I ain't got to talk to nobody for like three months. I've been doing what you say, when you say it; so excuse the hell out of me for wanting to have a conversation with someone other than the mirror," Jag shouted back.

"Okay, Jorge. I get it, but don't you forget who you're talking to. Don't disrespect me; I've had enough of that and won't stand for no more. Let's just get on with this."

Jag roughly pushed and pulled at Dillon's body until it was dressed in Jag's old, unimpressive clothing. Jag and his partner locked eyes.

"Scary, ain't it?" X asked.

Jag agreed, "You're telling me!"

At 8:20 that evening, the darkness loomed. All of Jag's belongings were packed away in an old duffel bag and placed in his partner's truck.

"Well, Jorge, we're one step closer."

Jorge cringed every time his partner called him Jorge. He didn't want to be known as that person anymore. He was different now—stronger, more clever—and hearing that name only made him ashamed of the cowardliness of his past. He sucked it up and pressed on with business, knowing that he would soon be on his way to a new life—a temporary life, but a hopeful one.

"Ya know, Jorge, you sure look different these days, especially in that suit. Don't forget where you come from. Don't get caught up in it all. Stick to the plan. Ya hear me? Jorge! Ya hear me?"

"Yeah, I hear ya. You're talking crazy. Everything is going to go just as planned," Jag responded.

"It had better; there is a lot riding on this."

Together they walked Dillon out to the truck, one on each side to support the limp and poisoned body. They hoisted him up into the tattered seat, buckled him in, and slammed the rickety door. Jag's partner looked around inconspicuously and found no one all that interested in what had just occurred. Jag returned to the door of room 119 to look inside one last time. As he shut the door, the same man who'd "helped" him earlier that night came around the corner and walked up sporting a peculiar look.

"Looks like he has alcohol poisoning or something. He won't stop puking. His probation officer isn't going to like this at all," Jag blurted out before the guy could say a word. "He never seems to learn. Maybe the stomach pumping approach will knock some sense into him."

"You sure like to talk a lot. What did you say your name was again?" the lanky man asked.

"I didn't," Jag replied.

Jag got into the BMW, his new car, feeling like a million bucks. Fully aware of the stranger's suspicious mind, Jag smirked at him and waved with confidence as he took a left out of the parking lot. It made it all that much more thrilling to know that someone was pondering his behavior, someone who knew nothing and could prove nothing

The truck followed Jag for a few blocks until both vehicles reached another darkened parking lot. It was home to the Dollar Store, a place Jag visited frequently during his stay in the low-income town. He knew many of the cashiers and occasionally roamed the aisles just to pass time. As soon as both vehicles came to a stop, Jag jumped out of his car and moved around to the back of the truck to begin removing the fake license plates. Exhaust fumes from the twenty-year-old vehicle gagged him as he thought about the upcoming events.

He handed the phony plates over to his cohort. "Take these. Keep them in a safe place. We might need them again."

The sounds of the city continued to carry on as if nothing was out of the ordinary. Jag took an unplanned moment and listened to the self-absorbed mentalities of the street. So much was going on, whether it was here in the Dollar Store parking area, over at the Burger King drive-through, or even down at the jailhouse. There were hundreds of thousands of lives being lived at this very moment, yet no one really knew or cared about them. To Jag, the next forty-eight hours would bring with them a life-changing experience, but to most everyone else in the world, the next two days would be a meaningless period of time. It was a strange and different thinking pattern for the simple man that he was, but since he had stepped out of his protected bubble of youth and into the sanctions of the real word, a different kind of knowledge was emerging from him. He was slowly gaining an outlook on life that books just didn't deliver.

"Jorge!"

His partner's holler yanked Jag from his train of thought.

"What?" Jag asked.

"What the hell happened to you? Where were ya just now?"

"Just thinking," Jag responded.

"Pull yourself together. It's time. Are ya ready?" X asked.

"Not really, but I'm as ready as I'll ever be. Let's just get it over with."

"You know I don't want to do this either, don't ya, Jorge?"

"I know, I know, just get on with it," he replied tensely.

The pair walked over to the BMW. Jag stood next to the car's driver-side door and took a long, hard, deep breath to prepare his mind. Before completely exhaling his breath, a fist came at him with what seemed like lightening speed. Horrific pain branded him as if a block of cement had been slammed against the left side of his face.

He yelled as he gritted his teeth and covered his face with the palms of his hands.

"Damn … take it easy! You don't got to go overboard!"

"It has to leave bruises, Jorge. We only get one shot at this. We ain't screwing up the one part we got complete control over!"

As Jag began raising his head back up, he saw a dull metal object hidden in his partner's fist. "What is that? What's in your hand?"

"I had to make sure you bruised. Sorry, Jorge, but I had to," X replied defensively.

"What is it? What are ya holding?"

X's fist opened, revealing a solid blunt object. "It's just that old piece of pipe you had."

"You could have warned me!"

Another two punches nailed Jag directly in the rib cage.

"Ooh!" Jag lost his breath and doubled over. He had taken some blows before, but this was worse than any underground fight he had ever experienced. Maybe it was because he couldn't fight back or maybe because the person delivering the punches was someone he had trusted for many, many years.

"I know that you're hurt and all, but just one more time. One more hit and we'll be done with it."

Jag didn't say a word. With much pain, he opened the car door and positioned himself in the driver's seat. X got in through the passenger side.

"Ready?"

"Go!"

His comrade threw a quick punch into the side of Jag's face. Jag's head abruptly slammed into the side window before his partner repeated the same act two more times. The third assault caused the window to shatter. Shards of glass and lacerations covered Jag's face, and blood spewed from his head. Without warning, the aggressive hand of his partner hurled Jag's face directly into the car's steering wheel. The sudden impact caused Jag to bite a chunk of skin out of his lower lip. Blood leaked into his mouth. Painful moans followed. X's job was complete.

Words of stern instruction and encouragement were exchanged before X and Dillon's lifeless body headed east. Blurred vision and a high-pitched ringing in his left ear kept Jag lingering alone in the parking lot for longer than he had planned. Finally, he was in control again. He took advantage of his alone time to go over the next step of the plan while he waited for his capacity to improve. His eyes blinked hard several times, and he shook his head hoping to clear his thoughts. His bearings were out of sorts and his confusion still very real. His head, eyes, ribs, and nose suffered severely as a result of the consensual beating he'd received. With sweaty palms, he shifted the car into drive, exited the parking lot, and turned onto the road. He looped around a side street to ensure his route was consistent with one that Dillon would typically take home from the bank. Wishing desperately that the agony would end, he finally found himself nearing Riverdale Drive where he would play out the next step of the inventive plan.

He took a deep breath, double-checked his seat belt, and pushed hard on the gas pedal. His speed neared fifty mph. As the car rounded the corner, fishtailing several times, Jag saw the big oak tree. It was closer … closer … closer than he remembered.

"Ahhh!"

Jag hammered the floor with the brake pedal. An expression of fright overcame his already damaged and pain-filled face, and the world began turning in slow motion. Broken glass sailed through the Beemer. The crunch of the car's metal frame dominated his screaming. Deep blackness followed.

The horn sounded and remained engaged. Jag's mind was silent, his body limp.

CHAPTER 17

▼

With three drinks warming her stomach, Lanie looked curiously at her watch.

"He's definitely home by now."

"Yeah, and you're not," her friend reminded her. He needs to realize you're not just going to hang around waiting for him all the time. This can be his wake-up call. Hey, the wild and crazy chick I used to know wouldn't let a guy bring her down," Rachel said with attitude.

"You are so right! Talk about a pathetic moment."

They clanked their glasses high in the air.

"This dress has got to go." Rachel said. "I could seriously go for some sweats and a tank right about now."

"You got that right. Hey, let's go back to your house, watch a chick flick, and order pizza," Lanie suggested.

"Sounds good to me."

They settled their tab, waved to the boys at the bar with smiles, and headed for the parking lot.

"Rachel, that blond guy sure seemed to be smitten with you, and you didn't even throw him a bone. You're ruthless."

"Yeah, well, men are on my list these days. They've been nothing but trouble lately. I had this blind date a couple of weeks ago …"

"Blind date? Really? You?" Lanie interrupted.

"Yeah, I know, talk about desperate. Anyway, I meet him at Loupe's for dinner. He was decent-looking, young, tall, blond, had a sense of humor. I was thinking, 'He seems like quite a catch. Did I luck out and get the last normal guy out there?' The check comes; he pays, another plus. We go out to his 'car,' and it turns out that he drives a polished new scooter."

"A scooter?"

"Yep, a scooter."

Lanie laughed.

"So, he wants me to get on the back and like, zoom off to the movies with him. I felt like a Wonder Twin or something, off to save the world. Needless to say, I agreed to get on. I was hoping that he was just charmingly quirky. So we took off. The scooter was barely able to reach forty mph. The faster we went, the louder this humming noise got; it was almost deafening. I swear, everyone we passed was secretly pointing and laughing at us. I felt like such a spectacle. So, the date continues, and he suggests we go see some shoot-'em-up, bang-bang flick. I agreed to go. You know I can appreciate a good cop flick now and then. We sit down, and despite the ringing in my ears, we talk until the movie starts. It turns out he is unemployed and lives with his parents."

"Well, did you at least let him get to second base for his efforts?" Lanie laughed.

"No! Not even after his smooth yawn-and-stretch maneuver."

"He didn't?"

"Oh, but he did," Rachel responded.

"Who in the world set you up with Mr. Dead-end Guy?"

"Trevor. He got an earful that night."

"That is awful," Lanie said, still laughing.

"Yeah, really funny. He won't stop calling me now. He thinks I'm great and apparently can't live without me, blah, blah, blah. I am going to have to switch playing fields one of these days, see how the other half lives."

Their next stop, the video store, took all of about five minutes. They picked out *When Harry Met Sally*, their all-time favorite chick flick, walked back out into the parking lot and there, parked next to the car, was a bright red scooter. After making eye contact with one another, their laughter exploded.

"No way!" Lanie voiced.

Rachel immediately hunkered down as she scanned the parking lot.

"It couldn't be. What are the odds?" she said during her visual search.

"Now you do look like a Wonder Twin. Where's your magical ring? If you find him, what are you going to turn into? Maybe water? An animal? Which Wonder Twin are you anyway?" Lanie couldn't help but crack herself up.

"Shut up. Let's just get out of here," Rachel laughed.

"All right, but you drive," Lanie said feeling the warmth of the whiskey. They jumped in the car and slammed both doors. The subtle aroma of artificial cherry still raged from a two-day-old air freshener. Rachel backed out of the space, put the car in gear, and squealed the tires as if Hannibal Lecter himself were tailing them.

"Now that was a peel out," Rachel declared with pure ego.

Flashes of blue and red lights could be seen up ahead, and Rachel gradually began slowing the car. They came to a complete stop behind a long line of cars, all of which were waiting patiently to get the signal to pass.

"I bet it has something to do with that corner up there. It's a nasty curve, I am surprised there aren't more accidents there," Rachel said.

"I wonder what happened?" Lanie replied. "I hope whoever's up there is all right."

Just as Lanie finished her sentence, sirens blazed passed them.

"Oh, I wonder who's inside. You know this is a pretty small community; we could very well know the person in that ambulance. It could be Sal from the hardware store, Ms. Rabon from the post office, or even one of our neighbors."

"Calm down, Lanie; it's probably someone from out of state. Everyone around here knows this road, just like they know about the speed trap on Sycamore Street. It's probably someone just driving through, no one either of us have even heard of before. You have a wild imagination sometimes," Rachel said.

Lanie switched the radio on to help pass the time as they moved up in the line about one or two feet every few minutes.

"Seems like they are slowly clearing the road. They wouldn't let people pass unless the cleanup was winding down."

"Plus, people are probably rubbernecking. That always slows everything down," Lanie countered.

The girls chatted as the car crept forward. The mood had calmed a bit; there was no laughing or storytelling, just simple conversation.

"Good, we are almost through. My stomach is yelling at me for some pizza. Hey, what kind do you feel like?" Rachel asked.

"That's a dumb question. Ham, pineapple, and peppers," Lanie responded.

"Of course. What was I thinking? The Lanie Lovers Plus Pizza. You might as well call now, we're almost to my house," Rachel said.

Lanie began dialing the phone. As they crept past the yellow and black police tape, the phone dropped from her petite hand.

Her voice exploded, "Pull over! Pull over!"

"What?"

"Pull the car over!"

Rachel finished passing the pile of wreckage and whipped a sharp right onto the gravel almost clipping a female police officer in the process. The door flung open and Lanie sprung out.

"Lanie! Where are you going?" Rachel yelled as her friend quickly ran toward the wreckage. Officer Paul Sherman stopped Lanie in her tracks, "Whoa, what are you doing? You can't go over there."

"That's my husband's car! Let me through! Let me through, damn it!" Her fists swung violently against the police officer.

"Ma'am ... MA'AM!" the officer shouted. "He's not in there; no one is in there." He wrapped his arms around Lanie's flailing limbs as he continued. "The person who was in the car was taken away by the ambulance to St. Charles Medical Center." Her spastic demeanor quieted.

"Is he all right? What happened?"

Dillon's once beautiful BMW hugged the targeted tree as if it had been manufactured out of pure rubber. Pieces of metal and daggers of glass masked the grass as deflated airbags hung lifeless within the compressed front seat area. Lanie stood staring at the destruction, weeping. The Jaws of Life rested against the mangled wreckage. With glassy eyes, Lanie fell to her knees.

"Hon, I'll take you to the hospital. Come on," Rachel said as she offered a hand to her friend. "I am sure everything is fine. He is safe at the hospital and getting medical attention."

Rachel slowly helped her friend to her feet and guided her back to the car.

"Buckle up. We will be there in no time, Lanie."

Rachel closed her friend's door and rapidly got in herself. The car made a sharp left toward the emergency room.

"He never made it home. I was all upset with him for working late and standing me up. How pathetic am I? I was all worried about being late for a play, a play that we had both already seen. He was out working hard. He was probably driving fast to get home to me, knowing I would be upset that he was late, and look what happened. This can't be happening!"

Lanie frantically blamed herself for the accident.

"Honey, this is in no way your fault. Come on now. Anything could have happened—a deer, an oncoming car. It could be anything. It doesn't matter how it happened, sweetie; we just need to focus on what happens from here. I am sure he is stable. That car of his is sturdy and safe. If I know Dillon, his seat belt was definitely on. Let's think positive. Dillon is a determined man; he is strong and capable. That will play a huge part in his state of health. You think he is going to let an accident keep him down?" Rachel continued on with her words of clarity and reason.

"You know you're right, Rach! Since when do I focus on negativity? I'm sure he is fine. I just need to pull myself together and be strong and optimistic. I will walk into that hospital with positive vibes and a smile. Dillon will expect that from me. He loves that about me. I just want to see him, see for myself that he is alive and well."

They quickly pulled into the emergency room parking lot. Rachel slammed her foot hard against the brake pedal, and both girls exited the car and ran hastily to the check-in desk.

"My husband was in an accident over on Riverdale Drive. He was brought here by ambulance about an hour ago. Name's Dillon Andresen. Can you tell me which room he's in?"

The clerk began checking the database.

"I don't see any patient by that name registered here. Are you sure he was brought to this hospital?"

"Yes! The officer told me Dillon was brought here to the St. Charles Medical Center!"

"Maybe he hasn't been officially checked in yet. Let me go ask the trauma nurses. Have a seat. I'll be right back."

The nurse walked off, and Lanie looked to her friend. "You have got to be kidding me!"

Lanie roughly stopped a resident in green scrubs and repeated her question.

"Yes, he was taken back to the operating room about fifty minutes ago," he said.

"Well, can you tell me what is wrong? How is he … is he going to be all right?" Lanie questioned frantically.

"I am not sure what his prognosis is at this time Mrs.… what was your last name?"

"Andresen, I'm his wife!"

"Well, Mrs. Andresen, he had several broken bones, injuries to his abdominal area, and blunt trauma to the head. He was unconscious when he arrived, but his heart rate was stable. As soon as the doctor comes out, I will give you as much information as I can. I will let you know if anything changes."

"I will be right here! Right in that chair," Lanie said with certitude as she pointed to an open seat.

"Please! If you find out anything, anything at all, I will be right here. I won't move!"

The helpful resident nodded with compassion, as the two close friends sat down side by side, holding hands to wait for news of Dillon's pending condition.

CHAPTER 18

The truck moved with the flow of traffic on U.S. 20, as Dillon remained unconscious. His head was slumped to the side across the strap of the seat belt, and the only apparent activity he was taking part in was a possible wild and vivid dream. X watched the man's eyes move rapidly under his closed lids and wondered if Dillon was recalling the past three hours. Heart quietly played on a classic rock station in the truck. Their destination was still about four hours away, but they were making great time. Amazed at the very sight of him, X couldn't help but have intrigue for the captured. It had been a long-overdue reunion, one that would surely shock Dillon when he finally awoke.

"Mhhh," came a moan from the passenger side of the truck as Dillon's eyes struggled to open.

"What the hell? That injection should have lasted at least another four hours," X thought. A surge of panic coursed through Jag's partner.

X pulled the truck over and frantically searched for that second syringe.

Dillon spoke roughly, "Where am I ... Who ... Who are you?"

"Quiet!" X instructed.

"The glove box," X remembered.

X tried to access the latch on the compartment, but Dillon's massive legs blocked access. Apparently, the perfect plan was proving to be not so perfect after all. Dillon continued to sit in a state of disarray.

"What are you gonna do now, tough guy?" X said, knowing Dillon had to be extremely weak from the drug.

"What do you mean? Who are you? What happened? My head is killing me." Dillon paused for a brief second before blinking hard, "Where are you taking me?"

"We are going to my place, far, far away from Bend. You won't be returning anytime soon, so don't get any bright ideas, Dillon." X said, while secretly griping the metal rod.

"Dillon? Is that my name? What is going on?" There was obvious panic and confusion in his voice.

"You don't know your name?"

"Well, no, but I assume it's Dillon. That's what you keep calling me anyway. I can't seem to remember anything about anything. What the hell is going on? Who are you? What am I doing here?" Dillon repeated his questions with confusion. He appeared to be upset and scared, and he didn't show any recollection of the evening's events.

"There ain't no way God would bless me with this. Dillon don't even know what happened," X thought. "Ah, this seems a little too easy. I could never be this lucky."

The kidnapper's face produced a smile, "What do you remember?"

Dillon sat quietly with squinted eyes trying to recall anything that seemed normal or familiar to him. His expression of deep thought turned to obvious fear as he said with worry, "Nothing! I remember nothing! I can't think of what day it is, what my last name is, who I am … nothing! What the hell happened to me? Help me!"

"Calm down, Dillon; just relax a minute."

"Relax? I don't know who you are. I don't even know who I am, and you want me to relax?"

X tried to quickly strategize the next move. "Stay calm," the kidnapper thought. "This can work out much better than we ever imagined. This is a huge blessing."

"Calm down, Dillon, I'm here to help ya. You can trust me, honestly. That's why I'm driving ya home, to nurse ya back to health. Just try and stay calm. Close your eyes, and take a deep breath. The doctor said your memory will return; the loss is just temporary."

Dillon had no choice but to trust what he was hearing. He was too vulnerable; he could no longer fight his urge to go back to sleep, and he finally gave in to his state. He rested quietly in the passenger seat of the truck, unaware that he was within an arm's reach of his biggest enemy.

As if holding the lead in a play, X could be anyone at this point. It was an amazing feeling, but there was only one person X desired to be. She wanted to be herself, Roberta Grapler, Dillon's biological mother. It had been more than twenty years since she had laid eyes on her son's face, and her initial love for him had slowly dwindled down to pure hatred and disappointment. He'd grown into a man she was ashamed of, one selfishly consumed with money and power. His greed had surely pushed him into illegal activities that included embezzlement and any other activity that would boost his bank account or status.

Roberta had been keeping an eye on Dillon from a distance for almost a year now, and she was unimpressed with what she'd seen. She had given him up for adoption when he was just a baby in an effort to give him a better life. She felt that she'd sacrificed her own happiness to grant him his, and all she'd received in return was a slap in the face. She was determined to take away his security and the pleasures in life that he so easily took for granted. It was her turn for an easy life, her turn to have enough money to live comfortably, and his turn to live with the abuse and poverty that she had endured all these years.

CHAPTER 19

▼

"Mama … Papa … Stop … Stop Yelling! Quit being so mean!" Jorge begged as tears streamed down his tender cheeks.

"Go back to your room, Jorgie. Mama needs to finish talking to Papa!" his mother had responded.

"No! I'm not going till you guys stop being bad!" Jorge said sternly from the midst of their ransacked living room.

His mother twirled around to face him. Red, glowing eyes and a strong, deep stare attacked him. Several moments passed as poor Jorgie remained frozen in a frightened standstill. The moments of time no longer ticked; it was just he and his mama glaring eye to eye. Unexpectedly, her head cocked mechanically to the side and her scary expression transposed into a loving one.

"Little Boy Blue, did you lose your shoe?" she said randomly with a tender tone and a sweet smile. In addition to her demeanor, her physical appearance had participated in the strange transformation. Her stringy, bleached hair was now light brown and pinned back neatly with purple butterfly barrettes. The skimpy cutoffs and elastic tube top had changed into a beautiful floral sundress. Jorge didn't know what to think about what he had just witnessed. He continued to stare in disbelief. All he knew was that the woman he loved was back. His mama was back. She approached her son and put her hand gently on his shoulder to comfort him. She dabbed his streams of tears with a rose-embellished hankie. Her manicured hands ran through his thick hair.

"Mama's here, Little Boy Blue. Mama's here."

Jorge believed that his strong little words must have made an impact. His mama and papa had stopped fighting, and he decided that he was to thank for it.

She and Jorgie embraced each other tightly, and he enjoyed the moments of reassurance that followed.

"Now run along to your room, Little Boy Blue. Mama will make you your favorite snack."

"Peanut butter toast and hot chocolate?" he asked.

"Yes, peanut butter toast and hot chocolate," she confirmed.

"Okay, Mama, I'll go read my books until it's ready."

She stood and turned away in a stiff and robotic manner. Her steps were slow and steady. Confusion crept back into Jorge's head as he watched his mother walk away from him and toward his papa. One inch at a time, her floral dress turned to red leather as if slowly colored with melted crayons. Her ratted out hair returned. His mama snapped a long leather whip as she strutted through the cluttered hallway.

"Mama?" Jorge's shaking voice cracked.

She turned and looked at him once again, "Little Boy Blue, don't make me kill you!" she shrieked as she lunged toward him. Her nails sharpened to daggers.

Little Jorge sprinted as fast as he could toward his room. Miles seemed to pass, but he fought hard to keep going. His mama was only inches away swiping at him and screaming, "You're mine, you little shit! I'm gonna shred you apart piece by piece!" He could smell her boozed breath and hear her high-heeled shoes stomping with every step. Only inches separated him from his crazy mama, but it appeared to be enough of a distance to slam his bedroom door between himself and her. He mustered every speck of strength he had in an attempt to push his chipped wooden dresser against the door. It wouldn't budge. Hysteria plagued him. He looked around for any kind of hope. Jorgie could hear his mama's pointed nails scrapping slowly down the unlocked door. He didn't know why she didn't enter, but he hoped her delay would buy him enough time to figure out an escape.

Remembering a scene from a horror movie, he propped his homework chair under the doorknob and hunkered down beside his bed, crying desperately for a sense of safety. His tightened chest tormented his breaths. The walls pushed inward, closer and closer. He just knew he would be squished flat if he didn't get out of his shrinking room. Frantically, he looked for a way out. Tears poured out of his desperate eyes as he searched for something heavy enough to hurl through his window. He needed a way out of the house, a house that had somehow become haunted. He grabbed for his wooden baseball bat with confidence and swung as hard as he could at the window. It cracked in several places, but did not break. The walls and ceiling were now only about three feet away from him. They seemed eager to squish his fragile little body. He quickly took another swing toward freedom. He heard the window break just as a glimpse of color caught his eye. There she was. His mother stood in the doorway with her arms stretched out to him.

"Don't go; don't leave me behind. I am the only one who can take care of you, Little Boy Blue. You need me just as I need you," she said.

Her bright red lipstick was smeared all over her mouth, and her leather dress was torn down one side.

"I can't stay here with Papa, Jorgie. I need you to protect me and love me and believe in me. Won't you do that for Mama, Jorgie? Won't you love me?" his mother said somberly.

"Stay away from me! Stay away! Who are you? You ain't my mama! Where's my mama? What did you do with her?" he screamed.

The zombie-looking woman began moving closer to him. He hurled his body out the broken window to keep her from reaching him. Jorge's small frame slammed hard against the ground. His little heart throbbed. His adrenaline pumped. He needed out. He needed to get far, far away.

"No! No!" he yelled. All the strength he could muster wasn't enough to move his paralyzed legs. He was so close to escaping the horror, but he knew he was just as close to being nabbed by the distorted woman claiming to be his mama. There she was, standing at the edge of the window looking down on him. His arms flailed about in an attempt to prevent the psychotic lady from reaching him.

"Stay away! Leave me alone! Please, don't hurt me!"

Her hand reached down and tried to grab his shaking body.

"Restrain him!" Dr. Campbell ordered sternly. "Restrain him."

"Doctor, his pulse is off the charts!"

Jag's unconscious body jerked vigorously in the emergency room at St. Charles Medical Center.

"Hold his body still. Somebody get his legs! Dillon, wake up! You're in the hospital. Dillon! Nurse ten cc's of Valium!"

Before the nurse had time to react, a loud scream startled her. "No!" Jag's eyes shot opened.

"Dillon, you're in a hospital. Try to relax; you're safe. We are here to help you."

Jag's struggle weakened, and his arm eventually lowered. The beeping of the heart monitor gradually slowed as he thought a moment about where he was and why he was there.

"It was only a dream," Jag reassured himself. But a very real and vivid feeling brewed inside him. It seemed as if a past reality had invaded his soul.

"That must have been quite a dream you were having. Do you know where you are?"

"Umm, the hospital I guess," Jag responded slowly.

It was all coming back to him now: the kidnapping, the accident, the plan, and Angel.

"Angel! Where was Angel?" he questioned silently.

"How are you feeling, Dillon?"

"Sleepy, and I have a hell of a headache. Doc, I can't see out of my left eye."

"It is all right, Dillon. Your eye is bandaged up. You'll be able to see once it heals," the doctor assured him.

"Well, what happened to me?" Jag asked, superficially.

"You were in a serious accident, do you remember what happened?"

Jag took a moment as he pretended to ponder the question, "Well, I think I remember being in a car, but then again maybe not; it's fuzzy. You know how you have a dream and then you wake up and remember having a dream, but you can't figure out what it was about? Like it's almost clear, but you can't quite explain it? That's how I feel. I remember something happening, but ain't sure what."

Jag felt like quite the actor as he continued his charade.

"Yes, you were in the car when your accident occurred. Your vehicle skidded off the road, and you hit a large tree while traveling fairly fast."

"Was my wife in the car? Is she all right? Where is she?" Jag said with pretend panic.

"Relax, Dillon; she's fine. She is in the waiting area right now. You were in the car alone; no one else was hurt."

"Oh, thank God!" Jag said faking relief.

The reality of his physical pain became more evident with each passing minute. Moving, talking, even breathing brought torment.

"What have I done to myself?" he thought with genuine concern.

"Doc, I'm in a lot of pain. Am I going to be okay?" Jag questioned.

He had come too far for the plan to fall to pieces this early on in the game.

"Yes, you are going to be fine, Dillon. You were very lucky. All in all, your injuries will heal, but it is going to take awhile for you to recuperate."

Jag exhaled.

"Do you know your full name?" the doctor asked.

"Um, it's Dillon ... Dillon Andresen."

"What year is it, Dillon?"

"2003," Jag replied.

"Good. Now I am going to recite a string of numbers to you and ask for you to say them back to me. 8649."

"8 … 64 … 9," Jag responded.

"Excellent!" the doctor said.

"If I can remember other stuff, why can't I remember the accident?" Jag asked.

"It is not uncommon for a person's memory to block out information that centers around a dreadful event. Typically, a person with an injury comparable to yours will regain their memory within twenty-four hours of their unconscious state. I don't think you have anything to worry about. You do have a concussion, but nothing detrimental to your brain function. I think the best medicine for you right now is rest," the doctor explained.

Jag knew his recollection of the accident, or any other fact he chose to forget, would not return that day or even that week. For now, it was all part of his strategy. He needed the leeway to be allowed some inconsistencies in the upcoming weeks. Jag had done his homework; he knew exactly what the doctor would say about Jag's so-called memory lapse. While continuing to fight the drowsing effects of the IV, he asked if his wife was going to be coming to his room.

"Wow, my wife," Jag thought pleasingly to himself.

"You will be able to see her shortly," the doctor replied.

"Has she seen me yet, doc? Has she been in here?"

"No, not yet. We just finished transferring you from the procedure room."

"Can I have a mirror? Can someone give me a mirror? I need to know what she's going to see when she comes in here," Jag claimed.

He brought his hand up toward his face to get a feel for what he was about to witness. Every touch seemed to reveal a bump, or cut, or a stitch.

"It isn't as bad as it looks," the nurse said as she handed him a small compact.

Jag slowly brought the mirror up. A horribly damaged reflection looked back at him.

"Wow! I look terrible. She won't even recognize me," he said aloud as he thought to himself, "I guess my trusted partner knew exactly how to handle this after all."

"Oh, it isn't that bad, I can still see your handsome face under there," the nurse said with a smile.

Jag smiled back, pleased that he looked as swollen and bruised as he did. He was even more confident that Lanie wouldn't recognize him as anyone other than Dillon.

"I'm real tired. Can I rest until Angel, or um … Lanie comes in?" He had discovered her real name quite some time ago thanks to his investigation. However, he felt that Angel was much more suitable for her. It was pure and special and known only by him. The hospital staff granted his request, and cleared the room. The last one to exit pushed the light switch down, "Sweet dreams."

Jag rolled over onto his side, closed his eyes, and waited for his new wife to enter. He knew it wouldn't be long. He just hoped and prayed that he could keep himself awake to be there for their first encounter. He wasn't thinking of money or the plan or how the real Dillon was doing with Roberta. Jag only thought about Angel coming into his hospital room and accepting him.

"Mrs. Andresen?" the doctor asked addressing both Lanie and Rachel. They both stood quickly.

"I'm Mrs. Andresen," Lanie said as she sharply extended her hand to initiate a handshake.

"Hello, I'm Dr. Feizer. I'm one of the physicians treating your husband."

"How is he? Is he going to make it? Is he all right?" she nervously asked.

"He is going to be fine. He had quite a bad accident. He is suffering from two broken ribs, a left eye injury, a broken nose, a broken arm, and a large laceration on the side of his head. He also has several superficial cuts and bruises. I am certain a severe case of whiplash will be setting in over the next few days."

Lanie continued to listen attentively.

"His wounds are not life threatening, but it is going to take quite a while for him to be his old self again. He is going to need lots of rest and TLC."

"Thank goodness; I was so worried. And believe me, doctor, I will take great care of him. You can be sure about that," Lanie assured him.

"I am sure you will, Mrs. Andresen."

"Oh please, call me Lanie," she requested.

"Okay, Lanie. There is one more thing. He seems to have blocked out all memory of the accident."

"Really?" Lanie questioned. "What does that mean? Is it some kind of amnesia?"

"No, I don't think so. It is just his way of dealing with the trauma. It is more of a mental defense mechanism," the doctor explained.

"Well, where do we go from here? Is this something we need to be worried about?" she asked.

"No, we did a full examination: MRI, CAT scan, PET scan, but didn't detect anything serious. His skull depression was not severe enough to cause any type of brain dysfunction, and there was no evidence to support brain swelling or hemorrhaging," he explained. "We will continue to observe him."

"Thank you so much, Doctor Feizer. When can I see him?" she asked.

"You can go on in now, he should be resting comfortably. He will be pretty groggy from the pain relievers, but you are more than welcome to sit with him."

Dr. Feizer shook her hand once again before disappearing through a set of double doors.

"Go on in, sweetie. If I know you, you will be sleeping here for the next few nights. I will catch a cab, but call me if you need anything. I mean it, a change of clothes, a shoulder to lean on ... whatever," Rachel said.

"Thanks, Rach. I will call you tomorrow."

They quickly hugged and said their good-byes.

Jag heard a faint shuffling in the hallway; the door began to open. He quickly shut his eyes. Lanie stood in the dimly lit doorway looking down at what appeared to be Dillon. She heard the beeping of the monitor and saw his injured body curled up in a white blanket. The door clicked behind her as she approached his motionless body.

"Oh, baby," she said softly.

She sat in the chair next to his railed bed and very gently rested her head on his shoulder while weeping quietly. Her hand rubbed across his side and she began praying aloud to thank God for saving his life.

"Lord, thank you so much for bringing him back to me. I don't know what I would have done without him. I know we don't speak to you very often, but I believe that you know we are good people. I would like to believe that you watched over him tonight and protected him. It could have been so much worse, God. The nurse told me it was practically a miracle that he was not hurt anymore than he was. She said he could have died. But of course you know that already; you know how close he came to death. He is such a good man, and I truly thank you for giving him a second chance at this crazy life. Thank you for loving him, and for loving me, and for letting us stick this world out together. Forgive me for the awful things I was thinking tonight, for trying to be revengeful. I know it was wrong. I was just so angry."

Tears raced down her soft cheeks, and she humbly closed her prayer.

"In Jesus's name, amen."

"I'll make it up to ya, Angel. I'll make your life better. You'll see ... you'll see," Jag silently promised her.

Her head raised up, and she moved the chair as close as she could to his bedside.

"Sweetie, you gave me quite a scare," she whispered. "I don't even want to think about what almost happened. I need you. I so need you."

Lanie had a lot to say to Dillon. She mostly wanted to ensure that he knew how she was feeling.

"You know, honey, I was angry at you tonight, angry that you were working late. I wasn't even home when you got into this awful accident. I was out with Rachel. Can you believe that? I wanted to punish you for taking me for granted, and I chose tonight of all nights to do it. I am so sorry for the bad things that I thought and the angry words I spoke about you."

Lanie hoped her husband could hear her every word, despite the stillness he maintained. Jag fought hard to stay conscious as he listened to his bride pouring out her heart. However, the IV drip sent him in and out of awareness. He needed to hear what she had to say; he wanted to know what she was feeling and how to behave when he showed himself to her. At this point she could only see the side of his bandaged face and the form of his camouflaged body.

"I went to see that play we were going to watch together, only I didn't make it there. Rachel and I went and played pool instead. I thought you would be home waiting for me, wondering where I was and when I would be getting home. You know, I thought it was odd that you didn't try to call me. That should have been my first clue that something was wrong. Why didn't I listen to my intuition? Why? I feel so bad for what happened to you. I assume you were rushing home from work to see me, knowing I was probably angry with you for being late. I am so sorry." Lanie paused for a breath. "I know what's important, Dillon. It doesn't matter that you work long hours or that I have to wait on you from time to time. Those things are just part of marriage, part of life. What matters is that we stay together and stay healthy."

Jag continued to think the thoughts he wished he could say aloud. "I am going to make you happy, Angel, you will see. Dillon will be a forgotten memory before too long. You are now married to a new man, a better man. One who will put you first." He knew it was only a matter of time before he could start his new life with Lanie, but for now the sedatives demanded that his mind stop thinking and he drifted into a hard sleep. He was sure that he would feel much better and stronger once he awoke. He assumed that it would be a perfect time to finally show his face to his new wife.

"Good night, sweet Angel. I will see you soon," Jag said silently before drifting off.

CHAPTER 20

▼

She pulled into the driveway, put the truck in park, and turned to look at the worthless man slumped over beside her. He looked so pathetic and she loved it.

"Dillon … Dillon … Dillon," she called repeatedly to wake him from his drugged state. "We're here. We're home," she said kindly, despite her deep hatred for him.

While still groggy and somewhat confused about the whole situation, Dillon managed to look out the window, "So, this is home?" His words were faint. The house was unimpressive; scattered weeds lived among the grass and a broken-down fence lined one side of the residence.

"I can't say that I remember any of this. I don't even have the slightest sense of familiarity," Dillon claimed.

"Don't worry, it'll come back to ya in time. The doc was sure about that."

The sound of his voice scratched at her tolerance. Though she wanted nothing more than to put a knife to his throat and cut it wide open slowly and painfully, she chose to resist for the good of the plan.

"You made a big mistake when you left me in the dust, a big mistake! You'll pay for your sins!" She thought silently.

"Come on inside, Dillon; let's get ya to bed. We can talk about everything in the morning and maybe, with God's blessing, you'll remember who I am, and who you are," Roberta said.

Pretending to be the warmhearted woman she wasn't, she got out of the truck and walked around to the passenger door to assist him. He was much larger than she was, but helping him hobble to the house was going to be a lot simpler than her original plan had been. They entered the house together, arm in arm, and she led him to the room that he would be living in until Jorge finished his part of the plan.

"This is where you will be staying. I think it's best if you get some sleep now."

Warm, stale air slapped Dillon across the face as he scanned the small room. A single bed, a handmade wooden nightstand, a chair, and a dresser stood on the brown worn-down carpet. White, naked walls bordered the dreary room.

"It feels like I have been sleeping for days. I don't want to rest. I want some questions answered. First and foremost, who are you?" Dillon asked impatiently.

Roberta reached into her pocket and pulled out a bottle of white pills.

"First things first. The doctor kept telling me how important these pills were." She handed him a strong dose and a glass of water. "Here ya go, drink up."

With a pounding headache and an extremely dry mouth, he welcomed the offering and eagerly swallowed the pills and the water.

"We'll talk tomorrow. I need to sleep. I did drive you all the way back here without stopping just to take care of ya," she said with a hint of animosity.

Dillon was a little taken back by her attitude.

Perplexed by her personality, he wondered if she was tired from the drive or if she was just an unpleasant and bitter woman. The answers to these and his other questions were all up in the air, at least for tonight. His attempt to rationalize the situation was pointless. It was clear she wasn't up for a discussion tonight, and in truth, he probably wasn't either.

"All right," Dillon replied. Confusion bounced around his head like a game of professional Ping-Pong. She left him sitting there on the edge of the bed, without another word. Every move he made caused his head to thump even harder. Surges of anguish trampled any hope for comfort. Little by little, he struggled to untie his shoes and remove them. Next, he removed his frayed jeans and faded T-shirt. Every movement was accompanied by a plea for a cease-fire. An eternity passed before he settled into the small uncomfortable bed, and his mind began to wander.

"She's not very affectionate. There was no hug, no kiss on the cheek, not even a 'How are you feeling?' We must not be close, or maybe we are, but we aren't comfortable showing emotions? Maybe she doesn't like me, or I don't like her? Why is she so cold to me?" he wondered.

His state of mind was cloudy, his energy level was at an all-time low, and his thoughts only invited anxiety and upset. The cold sheet was soothing against his hot skin, and it made him think about how good a cool washcloth would feel on his face.

"Ma'am?"

He tried to yell as loud as he could, despite the thunder and lightning storm thrashing within his head. No answer followed. He gave it another shot, "Ma'am?"

He waited again, but there was still no acknowledgment. The little white pills would have to be his saving grace, at least for tonight.

After waiting a good half an hour since hearing Dillon's final cry for help, Roberta felt confident that Dillon had finally been knocked out. Halfway to her bedroom, she briefly stopped at her prisoner's door to turn the skeleton key, securing him tightly inside.

"I ain't having any surprises tonight," she told herself. With satisfaction from the day, she slid into her bed before proudly saying, "That was easy as sin."

CHAPTER 21

▼

Another day passed without any word from Charlie, and Ken became more convinced that his friend wouldn't be returning to work, or returning at all for that matter. The question still consumed his thoughts, "What had happened to his best friend?"

Ken decided it was time to do something about the situation.

"Good morning, my name is Ken, Ken Chaptner, and I would like to talk to someone about a possible missing person," Ken said to the receptionist at police headquarters. She couldn't have been any more than twenty-five years old.

"Please sign in and have a seat. I will let an officer know you are here."

He took a seat and glanced through some informational pamphlets that were displayed on a side table as he waited nervously for assistance. A heavyset officer soon approached and offered his chubby hand in salutation. Ken stood up and reciprocated.

"Hello, Mr. Chaptner, I'm Officer Cox. I hear you would like to discuss a possible missing person," he said.

"Oh, call me Ken. And yes, I am concerned about one of my good friends," he replied as he followed the officer into one of several small cubicles. Each man took a seat around a nondescript metal desk.

"Go ahead and give me a quick rundown of the situation at hand, and then we can determine what the next step should be," Officer Cox instructed.

Ken educated the officer on the basic details of the matter, as well as his own suspicions. The short rundown turned into a drawn-out discussion that lasted well over thirty minutes, mostly due to Ken's talkative nature. Officer Cox took notes throughout the meeting and appeared engrossed in hearing what Ken had to say.

"Well, that is an interesting story. It certainly does seem a little odd," the officer confessed.

"So you feel a missing person's report is warranted, Officer Cox?"

"That is ultimately up to you, but I always preach the importance of instincts," Cox said.

"I am going to need you to put your story in writing. Be sure to include a full description of Charlie, and include any markings, scars, or tattoos he has. In the meantime, I'll get the additional paperwork you'll need to complete."

"Hey, Todd, I got an interesting one," Officer Cox said to his co-worker after stepping away from the desk.

"Something is actually going on in this boring old town. I have a possible missing person case, and it sounds pretty juicy. I'll give you one guess at whose name was brought up in association with it," he continued.

"No way. Old lady Grapler?"

"You guessed it," Cox replied.

"Is she missing?" Todd asked.

"Nope, it's her husband, Charlie. No one has seen him in more than three days. He hasn't shown up for work. Allegedly, Roberta is claiming that he just ran off."

"Interesting," Todd said.

"Yeah, tell me about it. I'll keep you posted."

Cox returned to his desk and handed Ken four forms that needed to be completed.

"Do you want some coffee while you're working on these?" Officer Cox asked.

Ken nodded and continued with his statement.

Two hours passed before Ken put his signature on the last required document.

"What now?" he asked.

"Well, the information you have provided us will be put into a completed package and sent up to investigations to begin the investigation process. They will contact Charlie's friends and family, visit his favorite restaurants, and ask questions anywhere else he is accustomed to frequenting. The investigation will go from there. It can be a slow process, but it's an effective one. They'll probably start with his wife," Officer Cox said.

"Will you keep me informed of any developments?" Ken asked. "I am very concerned about him. My instincts aren't leading me in a very good direction."

"I will keep you in the loop, Mr. Chaptner."

"Thank you for all of your assistance."

They shook hands and Ken departed the police station. His next stop was BT Construction, the place he and Charlie had spent many years working together. It was time to let his boss, as well as Charlie's co-workers, know about his suspicions.

CHAPTER 22

▼

Running … running … faster and faster.

"Stay away! Stay away!" Roberta screamed louder and louder and over and over. Something was hunting her, driving her through the woods, and calling to her.

"Keep running, Roberta. Keep running. I am right behind you," she heard the hunter say.

The terror felt all too familiar. It was as if she had been here before, passing the same whisking trees, and seeing the same frightening shadows lurking in the moonlit forest. Sweat dripped down her neck. She ran wildly dodging branches and black swooping crows.

"Where's your courage? Just a few short days ago you looked me in the eyes and shot me. Why don't you stop being a coward and look me in the eye again? You don't need your little gun. I'm already dead. Remember?"

Roberta was consumed by terror.

"Was Charlie out for revenge? Did his spirit return to punish me for what I done? Would God let such a bastard haunt me?" she wondered. Those and dozens of other questions traipsed through her distressed mind causing even more agony to invade her sanity.

"Why did you do it, Roberta? I loved you. I did everything for you. I worked long hours. I put up with your mood swings. I comforted you when you were at your worst, and all you ever did was criticize me, criticize and taunt me. I only wanted the best for you. I only wanted to save you," the loud voice sternly claimed.

"Get away from me! You didn't love me, you never did! You only loved your women and your drugs. Go back to hell where you belong!"

Despite the hours she spent running, she never managed to create any distance between her and her tracker. She was unable to escape his presence. Trying to block the sound of his voice, she put her hands tightly over her ears. It did nothing to drown out the noise; it only caused her pace to slow. She felt trapped, discouraged, and she just wanted to stop and give up. Running seemed pointless.

"Ooh!" she said as her eyes caught a glimpse of a shining light up ahead. Finally, she had a destination, a way out. Why the light was there or what it represented was beyond her comprehension, but it felt like her saving grace. Her loss of energy was replenished and her speed picked up remarkably. The light wasn't all that far away.

"Come on, Roberta. Move, move! Don't let him get you; don't let him catch you. It will be the end of you. Move, move!" Roberta convincingly told herself.

"You think that place over there is going to save you? You think the light has some magical power that can cast me away? This time, I'm not going to leave until I'm ready to leave," she heard Charlie's voice say. "Better get going. That light is fading from your existence."

She was unaware that her dead husband was driving her to the light, urging her to move toward it. It was no coincidence that his presence remained behind her at all times, pushing her, tricking her to move forward. She was so close. She only had about twenty feet left to cover. The light appeared to hang from the porch of a large, one-story building that appeared to be an office of some kind. Roberta was curious to know who or what was inside. It really didn't matter though; it was shelter from the wicked elements that surrounded her. She ran up the building's three steps, panting with exhaustion. Frantically, she grabbed the doorknob with her drenched palm.

"No!" she wailed as her fists hammered the locked door.

She began to weep uncontrollably. Her body gave up, and she slid down the door to surrender her soul. As she sat alone in the night, she took pause, noticing that the sounds of the night had extinguished themselves. The voice had ceased its torment, and the wind was now virtually obsolete. She smeared the tears away from her swollen eyes, took a deep breath, and raised her head.

"Ahhh!"

Charlie stood tall on the ground just below the first porch step. Blood spewed from the gaping bullet hole Roberta had left in his head. He was wearing the same startled and wide-eyed expression he'd worn the night she had pulled the trigger. She was trapped in a horribly vulnerable position. Quickly, she shot up and darted to her right, but her path was blocked. A wall had appeared. It was adorned with a framed photograph of her son. He wore a smile, and a baseball glove dressed his left hand. She darted to the left, but another roadblock greeted her. There stood a very large mirror reflecting the image of a gruesome, devilish being. The wicked fiend instilled a new level of fear, a level that only the depths of hell could create. Her legs gave out, the earth opened up, and her body plummeted far into the ground. She continued falling faster and faster.

Once again, she landed hysterically within the confines of her bedroom. Her conscience had beaten the hell out of her. A couple deep breaths flowed through her chest as she tried to calm herself. The description of the building stuck in her mind. It reminded her of somewhere familiar, but she couldn't place where. She quietly acknowledged that she must have some subconscious guilt about what she'd done. The nightmare was over, however, and the last thing she wanted to do was sit around analyzing it. She had never believed in all that mumbo-jumbo talk psychologists dished out about what dreams meant.

A deep growl prowled around in her stomach as she got up and covered her nightgown with her bedraggled robe. Flames danced under the gas burner, and two slices of white bread cooked in the toaster as she cracked four brown eggs into a plastic bowl. It took all of about ten minutes to prepare her meal and even less time to devour it. She placed her dishes in the sink and headed down the hall toward locked bedroom door. Slowly, and as silently as possible, she unlocked the door and entered Dillon's camouflaged cell.

"Well, Dillon, I see you're awake. What have you been doing in here?" She clutched the doorway as she awaited his response.

"Yes, I'm awake. I was just trying to remember anything I could about my past, but my mind is not cooperating."

"Well, ya can't force it; it'll just make it worse. The doc said it will come back when it's ready," she replied. She was laughing hysterically on the inside and loving his vulnerability. She prudently approached him carrying two more white pills.

"Here, take these."

Dillon gladly accepted and swallowed them.

"I smell something delicious, and I'm really hungry. Is breakfast ready?" Dillon asked anxiously.

Roberta hadn't even thought to make any food for her prisoner. The last thing she wanted to do was cater to him.

"Ah, almost," she said. "I'll bring it in as soon as it's ready."

With total control over every morsel that he would be eating, she actually looked forward to her new domestic role. "This ought to be fun," she mischievously thought as she headed off to the kitchen. If she *had* to cook for a man whom she felt deserved nothing more than a bowl of acid, she thought she would make the best of it.

"Let's see, what can I make for ya?" She poked around the kitchen, opened the freezer, and checked out the cupboards.

"Hmmm. Soup. Yeah, perfect. Every sicko needs soup."

Vegetable Beef soup splashed into a green plastic bowl. She topped it off with a nice big ball of phlegm that she had no trouble coughing up. She then grabbed the most important ingredient of all, Tabasco Sauce, as she chuckled.

"We can't have it bland, now can we. This is gonna be tasty!" she said to herself.

Ten or twelve splashes entered the bowl. With a little more consideration, she snatched the bottle again and dumped more, and more, and then even more into the oily broth.

"There, this'll grab him by the balls."

She returned to the bedroom and placed the hot soup on the old wooden crate that doubled as a nightstand.

"Here ya go. This'll hit the spot."

"Wow, it smells delicious, what kind of soup is that?" Dillon asked.

"It's your favorite, Vegetable Beef Delight," she replied.

Despite his apparent state of mind, Roberta still didn't trust Dillon a lick. For all she knew, he was playing her. He could be waiting for just the right moment to retaliate. Memory loss or not, she'd decided that he was still the same worthless and conniving person on the inside. She held the belief that some men were just born corrupt. She wondered why she was unlucky enough to have two bad seeds in her life. Like father, like son, she'd always said. Although pain stricken, Dillon propped himself up as best as he could. Roberta relocated to the foot of the bed and waited for the festivities to begin. His stomach grumbled as the spoon dipped into the seasoned soup. He blew on it slightly, placed it into his mouth, and swallowed his first taste of food in what seemed like days. Out of sheer hunger, he repeated the action before his taste buds were even allowed to savor the flavor. Just as the second swallow was going down, an uncontrollable cough exploded from his throat. His mouth shot open and broth gushed from it onto his bare chest. The intense spiciness closed off his throat.

"Water … water," he tried to say as his voice cut in and out.

He frantically fanned the inside of his mouth as he looked around for whatever drink he assumed his caregiver had brought for him. His eyes burned. There was no drink in sight. The soup spilled across the pillow and blanket in the process of the struggle.

"What's the matter, Dillon? What are ya trying to say? Oh my gosh, are ya all right?"

"Wa ... ter!" he tried to say again.

"Water? Oh, water. Okay, I'll be back, hang on."

She hurried out of the room to give the illusion that she was rushing to help him, but as soon as she was out of his sight, she turned her quick steps into a slow saunter. She twirled around and performed a little jig to herself as she slowly made her way into the kitchen.

"Dillon's on fire, ha ha ha. Dillon's on fire, ha ha ha," she repeated quietly as she continued to dance around. A good couple of minutes had passed. As she turned the faucet off, she heard a loud thump and then shuffling noises.

"What the hell is he up to now?" she wondered. She rushed in with the glass of water to see what was going on. His bed was empty.

"I knew it; he's up to no good. Dillon, where are you?"

She raced down the hall and found him kneeling down on the floor of the bathroom with a waterlogged face.

"What are you doing?" she asked angrily.

"What the hell did you do to me? What was in that soup?" he demanded. Tears soaked his face and his cheeks resembled a perfectly ripened Red Delicious apple.

"I'm sorry, Dillon, you always liked it that way. It's your favorite. You always said the hotter the better," she said innocently.

"The hotter the better? That wasn't hot; that was blistering. So you're telling me that I enjoy breathing fire. Maybe you got it wrong lady. Maybe ... just maybe I said something like, 'the more it burns away the flesh of my mouth and blisters the lining of my throat, the better I like it!' That could be the only feasible statement to support what I just swallowed!" he screamed sarcastically. His voice continued to fade in and out.

Her head tucked under as she made her words quiver, "I'm sorry, Dillon. I was trying to do good. I wanted to get it right for ya the first time. Usually ya tell me to keep adding more hot sauce 'cause it ain't hot enough. I just wanted to get it right the first time."

Dillon wasn't sure what to think. Did this woman really want to help him, or was she out to get him? And who was she? Who the hell was she? He had no other choice, at least for now, but to believe that what she was saying was the truth. She reached over and handed him the glass of water and he slowly took it from her. He put it up to his lips and then stopped in hesitation. He smelled it as inconspicuously as he could and pondered whether or not to consume it. His tongue seethed in pain. He desperately needed to soothe his anguish.

"Dillon, it's water!" Roberta walked over to him, grabbed the glass, and took a sip out of it to prove that it was as pure as Idaho water could be.

"See, I'm not here to hurt ya. We just had a misunderstanding. Now drink up. Please," she said with convincing sincerity.

He dumped the water down his burning throat.

"Let's get you back to bed now."

She approached him with caution, still knowing he could turn on her at any moment if he wanted. She hoped his memory would remain blank; it made things so much more fun. He got back into bed in the same irritated state that he had left it in.

"What are those pills you keep giving me?" Dillon questioned.

"They are to help with your pain. The doctor said they all need to be taken."

"What are they called?" He asked.

"Um, I can't remember the technical name. I'll get the bottle later and check it out for ya," she answered.

"Who are you?"

"My name is Roberta," she answered, knowing this inevitable question was going to have to be answered sooner or later. When it was all said and done, she wanted him to know exactly who she was anyway.

"Well, Roberta. Who are you to me?" he asked sternly.

She pretended to look upset as she said, "Dillon, it is just awful that you don't remember who I am. I'm the woman who took care of ya all these years, the woman who has loved ya through good times and bad. I'm … well … I'm your mama."

Dillon had suspected such an answer.

CHAPTER 23

▼

Knock, knock.

Ken entered his boss's eight-hundred-square-foot office to find the man working diligently on a new construction contract the company had recently been awarded. The office had recently been redesigned to appear much more modern with higher ceilings, hardwood floors, and large bay windows. The powerful smell of peppermint steamed off of his mug.

"Hey, Ken," Mr. Thorton said after he looked up from his black desk.

The company was a very successful yet humble business that employed approximately fifty individuals. Brent Thorton had put his heart and soul into his business, and he'd managed to build it from the ground up about fifteen years prior. He was a short little man, only reaching a height of about five foot two, but he was powerful nonetheless.

"Hey, Brent, it looks like you're up to your elbows in paperwork again," Ken replied.

They had a pretty relaxed relationship, as Mr. Thorton had with most of his employees. Ken, however, was considered one of his top collaborators and he often filled the role of site manager on high-profile projects. Mr. Thorton not only respected him as a strong and reliable worker, but also as a respectable man and friend.

"Yeah, which means you are going to be up to your elbows in work in a couple of weeks as well," Mr. Thorton said with a grin.

"Well, I have some disturbing news about one of your employees. It's Charlie."

"Grapler?"

"Yes."

"How is he? I haven't seen him lately. Didn't you say he had been ill?"

"I did, but there is actually more going on with him than I let on. I haven't actually spoken to him for a few days."

"I'm listening," Mr. Thorton said after removing his reading glasses.

"I just got back from the police station where I filed a missing person's report on him."

Mr. Thorton looked astonished as he continued to listen to Ken's words.

"No one has seen or heard from him in days, and I am worried that something terrible may have happened," Ken declared.

"Well, I'm confused. Why did you tell me he was ill if you thought something had happened to him?"

"Well, initially, I thought he was taking a few days off for the sake of his sanity. He's been having some trouble with his home life for quite a while. I guess I felt bad for him and wanted to cut him a break. I thought I'd let him have a day or two off to sort things out; at least I assumed that that was what he was doing. A day turned into two days, then three and, well, still no word from him."

"I assume you called Roberta?" Brent asked.

"I did. She claims that he ran off. She isn't at all worried and actually said he often disappears for days at a time. According to her, this is a normal habit for Charlie. It all seems fishy to me. Something is just not right about the whole situation."

"Well, you know Charlie a lot better than I do, so if you think something went down, it very well might have. What are you suggesting happened?" Mr. Thorton asked. He ran his hand through his thick, red hair, impatiently waiting for an answer.

"I don't know what I am saying, really, but one thing I do know is that if he was going to take off, he would have let me in on the secret. I hate to make accusations, but I think his wife has something to do with it, or at least she knows more than she is admitting to. I guess the police are going to have to take it from here."

"Wow, this is a lot to swallow," Mr. Thorton said. "I met Roberta a few times and she seemed like a pretty decent person to me, but I guess one can never know. Did you tell the police you suspected Roberta?"

"I expressed my concerns about her," Ken replied.

"Are they going to question her? Does she know you went to the police?" Mr. Thorton asked.

"I haven't told Roberta anything about it. The police said they would talk to everyone that was close to him. I'm not sure when, but pretty soon," Ken replied.

"The police are going to keep me posted."

Ken was surprised to hear such concern coming from his mentor. Mr. Thorton was usually a man of few words and one not all that genuinely interested in others.

"Well, keep me posted as well, Ken. And if there is anything I can do, just ask."

"Well, I would love to have a few days off to help with the search a little bit. Charlie is one of my best friends, and I just don't feel right about going on with my daily business knowing that he may be in trouble. I also want to go back to Charlie's house and talk with his wife, see if I can get any information from her."

"I'll give you a couple of days, but I'll need you to be available for the upcoming middle school contract. It is going to be a huge undertaking, and you are going to be supervising it. Sorry, but I still have a company to run. I am going to need your supervision on it," Mr. Thorton continued.

"All right," Ken said, not at all surprised at his boss's response. Mr. Thorton was a no-nonsense kind of a guy. Work controlled his life.

"Thanks for the time off," Ken added.

CHAPTER 24

▼

Mentally and physically exhausted from her husband's ordeal the prior evening, Lanie had been asleep for the better part of the day. While slumped over the side of the cushioned hospital chair, she remained by her husband's side unaware that he was now awake and watching her sleep. Jag felt a little bit stronger and was eager to finally see her face-to-face. There would be no more hiding in a dark hospital room or lying in a position that would keep his face out of plain sight. It was now just the two of them, from this day forward, regardless of the strict plan that was supposed to include leaving her behind.

As he watched her dream and patiently waited for their gaze to meet for the first time, his mind traveled far away. He thought about all the hard work he had put into the past few months to make this upcoming moment as believable as possible. The strict workout routine included back, biceps, abs, and running on day one. On day two he worked his legs, chest, triceps, abs, and went running. On day three he focused solely on running. On day four he rested. And on day five, he started over. He spent long hours reading each night. He studied topics such as banking and investing. He practiced Dillon's confident and well-postured walk, read newspapers to stay abreast of current events, and even practicing talking in a prestigious manner. He knew he was no distinguished business guru, but he believed he'd managed to polish himself up enough to play the part of one.

The movement of Lanie's arm interrupted his train of thought. Her quiet solitude was coming to an end as her eyes slowly emerged. It was time. Time to see just how convincing he really was. Her eyes kissed his stare.

"Good morning," he whispered.

Her hand breezed across his bandaged face.

"Good morning. I missed you," she replied with a smile.

Jag knew that all the physical and mental preparation he had completed was nothing without the simple gift of genetics that he had on his side. If all went as planned, Lanie would never know she was actually gazing at Jorge Grapler, son of Roberta and Charlie Grapler and identical twin brother to Dillon Andresen.

"How are you feeling, Dillon?" she asked.

He hated being called that ... Dillon. He would find a way to change it, but for now he would have to answer to it.

"I am all right. Kinda soa ..." He cleared his throat to cover up his misused pronunciation and began again. "Excuse me, I am quite sore, but I do feel better than I did previously," he said.

"How do people talk like that?" he asked himself.

"I was so worried about you, sweetie, I am so happy that you are okay. I just can't believe this happened. Do you need anything? Should I call in the doctor?" she asked, attentively.

"No, I just wanna ... want to be here with you. Just looking at you makes me feel better," he said. Jag reached out his hand as best he could, and Lanie smiled and placed her hand in it. Jag felt so many foreign emotions that the pain from the accident seemed to somehow dissipate.

"You look beautiful, Angel."

"Angel?" she asked curiously.

"Do you mind me calling you that? It just seems so fitting. I had this dream last night, and you were in it. I was sick and calling out to you, and instantly you appeared. A bright light wrapped around you and you glowed. I remember feeling better and warm inside. You reminded me of an angel. Do you like that nickname? Angel?"

"I love it!" she gushed. She was amazed by how loving and sweet he was being toward her. It wasn't unusual for her husband to be nice, but a whole new level of kindness was emerging.

"Boy, you sure are being extra, extra sweet, honey. You sure you're all right?" She asked with a chuckle. She took it a step farther and waved her hand in front of his face.

Jag wondered if he was being too obvious. He thought a moment, but figured he could really act any way he wanted. To her, he was Dillon.

"I guess when ya stare death in the eye it makes a person think about what's really important. My something is you," he replied, genuinely.

He was becoming concerned with his habit for slang, and wondered if she was noticing.

He wasn't sure why he was even worried about it; she would never find out. Jag was fully aware that Lanie had no knowledge that Dillon had a twin. Dillon had made it quite clear that neither Jag nor their biological mother had a place in his perfect, upper-class world.

"Oh, I will get you some water, hon, hold on just one second," she said. She departed the room for a brief moment and returned with a glass of water and Dr. Hernandez, another doctor who'd been assigned to Dillon's case.

"Well, how is the patient this evening?" Dr. Hernandez asked.

"I'm doing fine," he answered. "Although, I could use a toothbrush."

The doctor smiled, "Do you remember any of the accident?" he asked.

"No, not really. It's blurry. It's all right though; I'd rather forget it anyway. I don't even want to know what went on," he said in a serious tone. Lanie continued to sit while the men talked.

"When can I be discharged?" Jag asked as he took another sip of water.

"Well, you should be able to go home in two or three days," the doctor said.

"Two or three days?" Jag questioned with concern.

"Your body has been through quite an ordeal, Dillon. It is very important that you stay as immobile as possible to allow the healing process to successfully run its course. Also, your eye is going to need to be flushed and rewrapped about every six hours, and your vital signs have to remain at a consistent level for at least forty-two hours. Sorry, Dillon, but it is just not a feasible option to let you go home this soon after the accident," the doctor explained.

The happy couple looked discouragingly at one another.

"Well, at least you're on the road to recovery," Lanie said, optimistically, "And after all, we do have the rest of our lives to spend together," she reminded him. For Jag, this perfect moment confirmed his suspicions that the original plan was evolving into something bigger and remarkably better. In the end, he would not only have the revenge and fortune he originally came for, but he would also be granted the pleasure of Angel's company. He would make it work. He would have her and hold her from this day forward, until death parted them.

CHAPTER 25

▼

It had been nearly three days since Dillon arrived in Idaho and since he'd experienced his first encounter with Roberta. She remained as unpredictable as ever; she was nice one minute and cold the next. Dillon wasn't sure what to think of it all and made a decision to focus on the reasons behind it. He desperately wanted to know the history between them, and he knew it could only help to trigger a memory. He was almost scared to uncover his past, but he had to start somewhere, and for now, Roberta was all that he had to work with. His strength was gradually returning, and the throbbing pain in his head had nearly disappeared. The past few days of doing nothing but eating and sleeping must have been a contributing factor to his healing, just as Roberta had claimed they would be. The dismal space he'd lounged in for the past few days had worn out its welcome and the smell of sweat loitered within the stale bed. The overabundance of sleep punished his back, so it felt amazing to be upright and walking comfortably.

He decided to surprise Roberta with breakfast. "What better way to start off the day than with some croissants and jam?" he asked rhetorically. But to himself he thought, "Croissants and Jam? Where did that come from? I have had nothing but oatmeal and toast for breakfast since I got here."

He picked up the unattractive clothes he'd arrived in and dressed himself before heading to the kitchen.

"Boy, do I have poor taste in clothing."

From the looks of Roberta and the decor adorning what he had seen of the house, it was clear to him that money was a definite issue in his life. He thought about how much nicer it would be if he were recuperating in the confines of a mansion. He thought about waking each morning to a nice elderly lady serving him breakfast and running his bath, as opposed to Roberta the tyrant blasting through the door of his dingy room with a graceless presence. He desperately needed a shower, but he figured he'd make breakfast first. He didn't want to wake Roberta early and ruin the surprise. After all, he had to get on her good side and fast.

"What the?"

The door wouldn't budge. He turned the knob again and rattled the door, but nothing.

"Roberta?" he hollered. "Roberta, why is my door locked?" he yelled while banging on the upper portion of the door with his fist.

Luckily, Roberta had already been up for a good hour and heard the ruckus.

"Damn it. Why isn't he still knocked out?" she wondered. Her mind searched for a solution.

"Dillon?" she asked with a tone of confusion.

"Why is the door locked? What's going on here?" he asked nervously.

His suspicions of foul play soared. She rattled the door from the outside.

"Hang on a minute, Dillon," she said.

"Why is the door locked? Open this door!" he said angrily.

She struggled with the door, turning the knob back and forth again and again.

"Open it or I'm going to knock it down!" he shouted.

"Relax! It ain't locked; it's just stuck. It happens from time to time. Don't you dare knock down this door."

Again she wiggled the door, but this time in conjunction with turning the skeleton key which she then slid into her robe pocket.

"Stand back!" she yelled.

She pushed with force and turned the handle causing the door to fling open fast and hard.

"Dillon, relax. The door gets jammed sometimes. Don't be so paranoid!"

Dillon grabbed the door and looked at the outside of it believing he would find some kind of lock installed, but there was nothing. Again, he didn't know what to think. There always seemed to be a reason or excuse to curb his reservations about Roberta's intentions.

"You have to understand, I have no memory of anything. I don't know who you are, how our relationship is, what is normal or not normal. Until I figure that out, I'm probably going to be second-guessing just about everything that seems suspicious to me. You obviously don't understand how this is for me. One minute you're being helpful, and the next minute you treat me as if you can't stand the sight of me. It just isn't adding up. You see that lamp over there? I don't remember it. The truck you drove us here in? I don't remember that either. The house, these clothes, the view from the window, the type of toothpaste you have me using? All of it is completely new to me. I don't see how you expect me to just know things. How would I know that I enjoy tons of hot sauce in my soup or that I should expect my bedroom door to stick. I am learning it all again as if it was the first time. You need to cut me some slack, or we are going to continue having problems."

Dillon stormed out of the room, furious with frustration.

"Oh, shit," Roberta said to herself.

She annoyingly chased after him, realizing that she was going to have to start acting like a nurturing mother. She couldn't have him mistrusting her, even though she so enjoyed making him so miserable.

"Dillon?" She called out after him. "I get it, I'm sorry. You're right, I have been kinda cold to ya. There is good reason for it. You just don't know what it is 'cause you don't remember."

She had his attention.

"Go take a shower. I'll cook us something, and then we'll talk," Roberta said, calmly.

"That sounds productive," he shot back.

Roberta needed the time to think of some convincing story to tell to her deserter of a son. It had to be a good one and, more importantly, a believable one. Apparently, she wasn't doing such a great job with her hostage so far, so maybe a change of strategy was just the ticket.

Dillon emerged from his shower to the inviting smell of vanilla and maple syrup. His guard remained high, but he had nothing but time on his hands. He would just have to take what she said in stride. They sat down to eat. Roberta nonchalantly handed him two of the usual pills, poured him a steaming cup of coffee, and began telling the tale of all tales.

"Well, first off, your father was a total ass. I know it sounds awful, but it's mostly his fault you and I was on the outs in the first place." Roberta had to get that out of her system. Both of her sons needed to know the truth about their daddy, that he was good for absolutely nothing. Jorge already knew; now it was Dillon's turn.

"Your daddy used to hit me a lot, he drank like a fish, and was always hollering and carrying on about something. You two never got along. About a year ago, he started yelling at ya for staying out all night and showing up drunk when ya got home. He said you was a waste 'cause you hadn't been doing your chores or pitching in with money. You was hitting each other and cussing up a storm. It was your worst fight yet, and there was nothing I could do about it. That was the last day I ever saw ya. Well, until about three days ago when I picked ya up from the hospital."

Dillon continued to listen to her story.

"Ya know, me and you was close, real close. We always stuck together and was never apart. It was always me and you against him and the world. That is until ya left," Roberta proclaimed.

"So that's why you are upset with me? You believe I deserted you?" Dillon asked.

"Ya knew how bad things were here. Ya knew he abused me and that you was the only one who could protect me, and ya still left. Ya put yourself before me, your mama, and that is something that just ain't right. We always said we would stick it out together and someday take off in the middle of the night. We planned to go somewhere far, far away where he couldn't find us," she declared.

"Well, where is he now?" Dillon questioned before inhaling another bite of French toast.

"Don't know. About a week or so ago, he up and left. Don't know where he went and don't know if he's coming back." Roberta got up and started to clear the table of the dishes.

"Do you have any pictures of him? Or me? Maybe it will generate some memories for me," Dillon said.

"Maybe I will somehow remember the day I left—the day he and I got in that horrible fight," he continued. Roberta didn't see the harm in showing him pictures. She had plenty of them. Dillon was even in some. Well, it was actually Jorge, but Dillon wouldn't know the difference.

"Yeah, all right," she said. They walked across the hallway and into the sparse living room. She opened a small cabinet door under the coffee table and pulled out her collection of photos. The two of them sat together on the blue shag carpet.

"Why don't you have them in albums?" Dillon asked.

"Albums are like eight bucks each. Bags work just as good. What, bags aren't good enough for ya?" Roberta asked rudely.

"See, there you go again, getting defensive on me. It was just a question," he said irritated.

"Sorry, Dillon. I'm trying. It's hard for me to have to keep justifying why I do or don't do things. You ain't the only one affected by this memory thing."

Roberta's new and improved strategy was simple. From that moment on, she was going to pretend that Dillon was Jorge. Every time words needed to be spoken, she would speak as if Jorge were the listener. She assumed it would make it a lot easier on the both herself and Dillon. He pulled out one picture at a time and asked her who each and every person was.

"There you are mowing the lawn. Ya must have been about sixteen. Here ya are reading a book for school."

"Who's that in the background?" Dillon asked.

"That's Charlie, your father."

Dillon held the picture closer to his face.

"He's a big guy," Dillon proclaimed.

"Yeah, I know. I guess you can see why I was so scared of him. There was no way I was able to fight back. That's why I needed ya. Well that, and 'cause I loved ya," she said.

"That's me on my birthday cutting the cake," Roberta said. "I remember I got an iron that year."

"An iron? Is that what you wanted for your birthday?"

"Well, it was better than what I got the year before—a broken nose—but not as good as what I got the year after."

"Which was?" Dillon asked, wondering why she hadn't finished her sentence.

"Oh, Charlie left for a few days. It was the best present ever," she said.

As they continued reminiscing through the different pictures, Dillon noticed something odd.

"How come we are never in a picture together?"

"Because I took your picture, and you took mine."

"Well, how come I don't have any pictures with friends? You know, playing baseball, having birthday parties, or being in school plays, things like that?"

"I hate to have to tell ya this, but you didn't really have any friends, Dillon. After about the third grade, I pulled you outta school 'cause you were picked on so much."

"I was? Why?" he asked.

"Kids are just mean. They called you names and beat you up. It was awful heartbreaking. You used to come home crying, begging me to not make you go back. So, I homeschooled ya."

"Really? I was homeschooled?" He'd noticed how uneducated Roberta sounded, and he wondered how in the world she'd been able to teach him the required subjects of high school.

"So, you taught me all of the subjects? Reading, math, history? All of it?" he asked.

"Well, I did the best I could. We didn't have any money for the actual official teaching stuff, so we took trips to the library a lot. You would check out one learning book and one fun book. So actually, you kind of taught yourself."

"What was my father doing through all of this? Did he try to teach me anything?"

"He was always gone working or getting into trouble. He would disappear most nights, but that was a good thing. When he took off, we got to have fun, play games, and goof off. Just the two of us."

"Did I graduate from high school?" Dillon asked with skepticism.

"Well, not according to the state, but you were just as smart as those other kids," she explained.

Dillon was not at all happy to hear what his mother was telling him. He was realizing that his life was apparently a disaster. He had no friends, no education, no money, an abusive and absent father and, apparently, no special childhood memories. If what she was saying was true, maybe it was better that he didn't remember any details from his past. He wasn't even sure if he wanted to know anymore.

"Was I a happy child?" he asked.

"Sure ya were. At least you were when your dad wasn't around. We got to do lots of great stuff, like draw, play cards, watch TV, make up stories, write poems, stuff like that," she said. The stories of her son's past were all true, right down to the last detail. The only deviation was that they all happened to her sweet son, Jorge, her honorable son, the one that deserved happier times than he'd received growing up. Roberta knew how different Jorge's past had been from Dillon's, but it satisfied her to know that Dillon at least thought he was the unfortunate one. He may never have experienced hardship, but he was sure going to believe that he had. It was almost as good as the real thing.

All the reminiscing made her miss Jorgie and how they used to spend time together, but for now she was just going to have to deal with an unsuitable stand-in. When it was all said and done, Dillon would know what real hardship was, and she would be laughing all the way to the bank, literally.

"I am getting pretty tired," Dillon said. "Do you mind if I take a short nap?" he asked.

Roberta wondered why he'd been so wide awake that morning. The pills should have put him to sleep an hour or so ago.

"No problem. I have work to do anyway."

Dillon excused himself and made a trip to the bathroom on his way to his room. He pulled the little white pills out of his pocket and flushed them down the toilet. It was the second time since the previous night that he'd disposed of his medicine. He was still unaware of what the pills actually were. All he knew was that without them he felt much stronger and much more alert. He climbed into the bed and spent the next hour analyzing what he'd just been told about his past.

CHAPTER 26

▼

Lanie and Jag pulled into the driveway after a long day at the hospital. The knowledge that Jag's new life was about to begin practically knocked him off his feet.

"Home at last!" Lanie shouted with her hands thrown into the air.

Jag just smiled. He was barely able to comprehend that he was entering this home, *his home,* with this woman, *his woman,* on his arm. The sight of the tan couch, the expensive electronics, even the ugly art warmed him. He owned it all now. He knew that he had to start working on the inside investigation into Dillon's criminal dealings, but he was content to put it off for a few days while his body regained strength. Lanie dropped his bag of medications on the table in the entryway and helped Jag to the light orange recliner.

"I can't believe I am actually here," Jag confessed.

"I know what you mean. That hospital started to feel like our second home. We were only away a few days, but it felt more like months. I'm exhausted," she said. Jag agreed. His body and mind had been through quite an ordeal.

"Do you want to take a nap with me?" Jag nervously asked. "I'm sure your … our bed will be a nice change," Jag added.

He needed to lie down, but at the same time, he didn't want to miss even a moment with her. After all, she was now *his* wife. He waited apprehensively for her answer, wondering if his daydream of them lying together would soon become a reality.

"You know, that sounds perfect," she said. "I could use some good sleep."

Jag just knew that Lanie liked the new Dillon. The Dillon who was never going to take her for granted again. The one who had a new attitude toward life and toward her.

"You know, sweetie, you have handled this remarkably well. I am really proud of you for concentrating on getting better instead of worrying about the hundreds of work issues that are piling up. You're amazing," she said.

As they slowly made their way up the stairs, Jag responded, "I had my priorities all mixed up. I know what is important now. I guess we got the accident to thank for me wising up."

The slang was getting easier to control, but he still found himself making the occasional slipups. She hadn't seemed to notice.

She pulled the covers back, sat him down on the bed, and leaned over to untie his shoes. He sat there silently, not knowing what to say to her. She pulled the shoes off of his feet and did the same with his socks. Next, she began unbuttoning his green, short-sleeved shirt, being careful to not cause any more pain to his battered body. One button at a time, her fingers moved down the line. The idea of sex briefly distracted him from his injuries. Once she reached the last button, she removed his shirt one arm at a time. Soon, he was wearing nothing more than a pair of fancy black slacks. His black leather belt slid out of the loop before his zipper came down. Anxiety floored him, despite her innocent intentions. She slid his trousers off of his legs.

"Do you want your pajamas?" she asked.

"Uh, no," he responded, nervously, worried that at any moment she could notice an inconsistency between him and her real husband, Dillon.

She propped him against the goose down pillows and pulled the plush covers over his battered and almost naked body. Her delicious lips were inches from his own lips. Her breasts were just in his line of sight. Jag prayed that his expression didn't reveal the sexual thoughts surging through his imagination.

"Chill out! Act natural. Act like a normal husband would," he instructed himself. He briefly closed his eyes and breathed deep. She placed a quick peck against his lips.

"I am going to take a quick shower," she said.

Her shirt came off, along with the rest of her clothes. Jag's eyes widened; he didn't know what to do. Look, turn away, close his eyes; it was a brand-new situation to him. He had never even considered these types of moments when he was imagining his stay there. His daydreams flowed so nicely, he never expected to feel nervous or uncomfortable in the reality of it all. He watched her beautiful, naked body as she strolled across the soft carpet before disappearing into the bathroom. She did this as if it was a totally natural and normal act. Again he resorted to deep breaths. He again ordered himself to relax. "I am Dillon. I have seen her naked hundreds of times. It is nothing new. Just act natural."

Shortly after, she came back into the room smelling of scented soap, pears maybe. Black cotton panties and a light green camisole covered her body, and into the bed she climbed. She reached over and clicked off the gold-trimmed lamp.

"You look so pretty," Jag said to her sweetly. His desires brewed from deep inside.

Over the past few days, she had proven to be just as remarkable as he had assumed she would be. He could feel her soft, warm skin against him under the covers. It was a torturous feeling, to say the least. Her body moved even closer to his, and she delicately leaned over and kissed him again; this time on his cheek.

"Sleep well, honey. If you need anything, just let me know," she whispered.

Her hand ran softly, yet carefully, through his hair avoiding the bandaged area. She settled in on her side, placed her hand on his chest, and crossed her foot over his. Somehow she managed to hold him close, without hurting one ounce of his wounded body. "So, this is what marriage feels like," he thought, as he closed his eyes.

A delicious smell filled the air as he awoke from his perfect nap. Lanie was no longer beside him, but she surely hadn't gone far. He painstakingly pulled himself out of bed and made his way down the stairs to see her angelic face. A short, silky, black robe outfitted her and exposed her long and lean legs.

"Hi, Angel," he said watching her stir a pot full of something. The smell of garlic enticed Jag's appetite.

"Hey there, hon; you're awake. How are you feeling?" She went over and locked her lips to his once again. It was almost inconceivable that he could feel passion emulating off of her with each and every show of affection she offered him. Jag was still in complete awe by the way they were together. Not in his wildest dreams did he ever think he could feel so much goodness in this life. He had always defined life as a hardship made up of constant difficulties and disappointments. He had no idea what life could really be like. There was no way he was letting this end—not today, not tomorrow, and certainly not three months from now.

"I am feeling perfect," he replied, "just perfect." He walked over to the black and chrome refrigerator and removed a bottle of apple juice.

"I just can't get over how attentive and complimentary you have been since the accident. I just love it. I feel like we are falling in love all over again, sweetie. I love you," Lanie said.

She wrapped her arms loosely around his shoulders to spare him from any additional pain, and he did his best to reciprocate to the utmost of his ability.

"Do you want me to run you a bath?" she asked.

He assumed that he didn't smell all that pleasant considering his baths over the past few days had consisted of a bucket of water and a sponge.

"A bath sounds great, but I'll take care of it. You seem to have your hands full down here," he replied before inching his way up the stairs.

Not even ten minutes had passed before he noticed her standing casually at the entrance of the bathroom.

"I figured you could probably use some help," she said, as she pinned her hair up into a loose bun.

She was right. He could use the help, but he was still uneasy about obliging her. He was nervous about being her husband and wasn't all that comfortable with her seeing him naked. He wasn't ashamed or embarrassed of his body, but still paranoid that she would notice some difference between him and Dillon. Maybe a mole or a freckle would be out of place. Unbeknownst to Jag, Dillon could have acquired a scar. There were numerous things that could be inconsistent between the twins, and Jag just wasn't prepared for any surprises. Hesitantly, he accepted her offer. It would have looked suspicious otherwise. The event went off without a hitch, despite how badly he desired her. He dressed in Dillon's hunter green flannel night pants and a white T-shirt before heading downstairs. Lanie dished up the chicken and pasta that she had made, and the two of them sat on the couch to enjoy it.

"Hey, do you want to watch this movie?" he asked.

When Harry Met Sally was on the coffee table, still rented from the night of the accident.

"Since when does a movie like that spark your interest? You always said it was a chick flick. You hate chick flicks. You've always said that they're unrealistic."

"Well, I've been wrong about lots of stuff," he said trying to cover his tracks.

"Oh, this is just getting better and better," Lanie thought to herself.

They put the movie in the DVD player and carried on with their meal. To Jag, this was the best first date he had ever had.

CHAPTER 27

▼

Sunday ticked away at the pace of a snail's crawl, leaving Roberta infuriated. Jorgie had failed her miserably by not calling on the agreed upon date and the cameras he had installed revealed nothing but static on her twelve-inch monitor disguised as her bedroom television set. Worry crept into her thoughts as she dialed the hospital in Bend to check on Jorge's well-being. Her worry mutated into paranoia after discovering he had been released days earlier. Dozens of scenarios raced through her head: he was too sick, his new so-called wife would not leave his side, or maybe Jorge had just decided to leave her out of the loop. At this point, stewing was about all she could do. She had her own assignment with Dillon to worry about.

Things were better than could have been expected. She played the role of a loving mother, while he reciprocated as the attentive son. Her guard lowered as each day passed. She no longer felt threatened by him, and she planned to continue with her optimism until he gave her a reason not to. They ate together, talked together, cleaned house together; it was just like her good son was back in her life. She actually felt loved and appreciated, and most importantly, she felt needed. Dillon, however, refused to slide into his new role so easily. Sure, he played the game in her company and often gave her the benefit of the doubt, but he still took everything she said with a grain of salt. He had some concerns of his own. He questioned the differences in their dialects. He found it odd that his speech was very articulate, yet hers was not. Their television preferences also set an alarm off in his mind. She watched talk shows and game shows, and he seemed to be more interested in the news or documentaries. According to Roberta, they used to spend hours planted in front of the small, eighteen-inch television screen. So naturally, Dillon assumed they watched the same types of shows. Dillon's intuition screamed with suspicion.

With no milk, eggs, or meat lining the fridge, Roberta knew she needed to get to the grocery store. "Dillon?" she yelled.

He got up from the living room to see what she wanted. Two little pills went from her hand to his. He put them in his mouth to give her the illusion that he'd swallowed them. He went to the bathroom, flushed them as usual, and returned to the living room. After about forty minutes, she approached him with news of her departure.

"I gotta get to the store for groceries," she said. "I'd ask ya to go, but I'm sure you're getting tired."

He snatched a hold of his opportunity to finally be alone.

"You are right about that. I can barely keep my eyes open," he lied.

He stretched out on the light blue, flowered couch and pulled the knitted blanket over his strong body.

"Don't ya think you'd be better off in your own bed?" she asked.

The last thing she wanted to do was leave him unattended in the living room.

"Oh, no. I think I will be just fine out here. This couch is sure comfortable. Besides, I'm so tired, I would just rather not have to get up."

She knew she couldn't insist. After all, she had managed to curb his original feelings of distrust toward her, and the last thing she needed was for him to start questioning her motives again. Feeling as if she had no other choice but to leave him there, she hesitantly agreed and departed in the truck. On her way down the unpaved street she detoured to Sam's humble wood cabin. A few squirrels scampered up a big oak tree as Roberta parked. Sam peered out of the front window.

"Shoot!" Begrudgingly, Sam opened the door.

"Hey, Sam, how ya doing?" Roberta asked.

"Fine. Just fine," Sam replied.

"I haven't heard from ya in a while. Is something wrong?"

"No, I'm just focusing on my book. I have been getting some great ideas, and if I take a break I'm afraid I will lose my train of thought," Sam said. She was using the book as an excuse to stay far, far away from Roberta.

"Well, if ya work too hard, you're gonna burn yourself out ya know. I sort of have a favor to ask of ya. It'll give ya a little break from all that writing."

Sam hesitated, "I am not feeling so well today, Roberta. I have a pretty bad headache."

"Sam, this is real important. Just listen for a sec," Roberta demanded.

"What is it?" Sam asked.

"Well, remember how I told ya I have a son?"

Being new to the area within the past three months, Sam had not met Jorge, but she had heard of him.

"Yes," she replied.

"Well, he was in an awful accident, and I got a call from this hospital. To make a long story short, he's at the house," Roberta explained. "He's on painkillers and he's sleeping, but I was wondering if you could stay with him while I go to the store? You won't have to do nothing. Just be there in case he wakes up."

Sam wanted nothing to do with her murderous neighbor, justified or not, but she knew Roberta wouldn't leave until she got the answer that she wanted, a yes.

"How long are you going to be gone?"

"Just an hour or so, Sam. It's just a little while."

"Okay, I'll go over there. Does he know I'm coming?"

"No. Like I said, he's sleeping."

She handed over the key to the house and said thanks before abruptly turning to leave.

"Oh, and by the way, he has amnesia," Roberta blurted out on her way back to the truck.

Sam cringed at the thought of being sucked into more of Roberta's drama.

Meanwhile, Dillon was up and around looking for anything that could either confirm or deny his doubts about how he fit into the life Roberta had described. His mother's room was the most obvious place to start. He was both surprised and repulsed when he uncovered an assortment of sexual paraphernalia in her nightstand. He quickly slammed the drawer, hoping to shake from his head the visual of her various battery-operated devices. He moved on to the closet somewhat leery of what he might find. The sound of a vehicle pulling up into the driveway quickly diverted his attention away from his snooping and onto the fact that his mother was back.

"What the? How is she back so soon? It's only been like fifteen minutes?" he thought as he scurried out into the hallway.

He dove onto the couch and nervously covered himself up. A broken spring jabbed him in the rib cage and the throw pillow smelled of stale cigarettes. His eyelids slammed shut. The sound of the lock turning broke the intentional silence. The door opened, then clicked closed. Pretending to be awakened by the noise, he peeled his eyes open.

"Who are you?" Dillon asked, startled.

"What are you doing in my house?"

"Don't be scared. Your mom asked me to look in on you in case you needed anything. You must be Jorge."

"Jorge? No, my name is Dillon. Who's Jorge?" Dillon asked.

"Oh, I'm sorry, Dillon. I must have remembered wrong. It has been a while since Roberta mentioned you. My name is Sam. I live a few miles down the road."

"Short for Samantha I take it?"

"Yes, short for Samantha. Never liked the name, but what can a girl do," she responded with a shrug.

"I have to say, your pictures don't do you justice," she said, innocently.

He wore a plain dark T-shirt with a small hole near the neckline and a pair of blue sweats that were on the verge of being too tight. Despite his attire, Sam was drawn to Dillon's masculine way. He had fresh stubble growing across his chin line and a mouth that presented a perfect smile. His chin was slightly squared, but not so much that it drew attention.

Dillon raised up off of the couch thrilled to see a new face. "So how long have you known Roberta, or should I say, my mother?" he asked.

"Not long, just a few months or so. I'm actually new to town; I moved here from the big city to get away from the busyness of it all," she replied.

"So, what do you do now that you're away from the big city?"

"Well, I work part-time for the newspaper, but I'm actually writing a novel. I had hoped this small city would magically give me a sense of creativity or inspiration or something," she said.

"So, has it?" he asked.

"Well, it's surely given me something, but it isn't either of those things. I guess you could say I have gained futile knowledge." They both smiled.

Dillon was grateful to finally have someone he could talk with, especially someone that was so intriguing. She was simple, yet stunning with a silvery streak dancing through her wavy brown hair. And although he would never propose to ask, he believed her to be at least fifteen years his senior.

"Do you want some tea or coffee?" Dillon asked.

"Yes, I'd love some. But wait, aren't I supposed to be taking care of you?" she asked.

"No, I'm fine. For the first time in a long time, I feel just fine."

His charm and whit impressed her. Roberta always had nice things to say about her son, but Sam had no idea she would enjoy his company to such an extent. The two of them sat in the kitchen making small talk for the next hour or so.

"So, you have no memory of your past?"

Their conversation played out as if they had known each other for years.

"No, not a thing. I'll tell you something though. I feel completely out of place here. I am not sure why, but I do," he responded.

"Well, if it makes you feel any better, you do seem quite different than Roberta. That was clear within the first two minutes of our conversation," Sam confessed.

"So it isn't just me then?" Dillon rhetorically asked.

"I am thinking that maybe it has something to do with that year that I was gone. Roberta said that after I left, she didn't hear from me the entire time. Apparently, I was just found on the curb of the hospital. No one seems to know how I got there or who left me there. It is all some big mystery. I guess my whole life is just one big mystery," he said matter of fact. "Hey, this entire situation sounds book worthy. There's no need for you to have to think up anymore story lines; you've got me now. Mystery man, small town … throw in some drama here and there and you've got yourself a place on the Best Seller's List."

They both had a good laugh as Dillon poured the two of them a second cup of tea. "If you only knew that the drama had already been thrown in," Sam thought with guilt. "If you only knew that your murdered father was buried just out back. All the story line we need is right here under our noses, and you just don't realize it."

Sam wasn't sure if she would ever forget that night.

"Sam? Sam?" Dillon repeated.

"Oh, sorry."

"Where were you just now?"

"I was lost in thought I guess," she replied.

"Are you all right?"

They both heard the loud sound of the old truck pulling up alongside the house.

"Well, looks like she's home. I guess my babysitting job is over," Sam said with a smile.

Roberta walked in and saw the two of them drinking tea.

"Well, I guess ya met. You seem to be having a good old time," Roberta snapped in a brash tone. Dillon had no place charming her best friend!

"So what have you two been gabbing about?"

"We were just getting to know each other," Dillon said.

CHAPTER 28

▼

"Troubled waters rise no more
For my stormy life has closed its door
The key has locked it, at least for today
If all goes as planned, it will be cast away

My yesterdays and tomorrows differ as night and day
Contradictions lie between the two in many shades of gray
Life can be simple and free and even great
It's not always a struggle when I need to liberate

For yesterday I lived with love, but also sadness too
A love for my family, but a sadness for something new
My tomorrows will still have love, more than I ever thought
But along with it I will have the freedoms that I always sought

It is not just about the money or the sound of my Angel's voice
But also about the ability to make my own choice
No longer a puppet following a lead
Now my inner voice can forever be freed

I lay in this bed eager for health
Waiting to heal and ..."

Jag jumped roughly, closing the notepad to his most recent works of poetry. Angel stood by the bedside.

"What are you doing?" her expression reflected curiosity.

"Nothing, uh ... just doodling," he answered.

"Doodling? Since when do you doodle? Oh, that's right, you do a lot of things now that you never used to. Newfound perspectives or something. Right?" she asked grinning.

"That's right, newfound perspectives. I got kind of bored just lying here, so I thought I would keep myself busy. I am feeling a lot better though. Most of my aches and pains don't seem to be around anymore."

"Well, that's great. So I guess you got along all right while I was out?"

"Yep, just doing the same thing I've been doing for the past few days. Resting, resting and, you guessed it, more resting. I am about all rested out."

"Do you want to play a board game or something?" she asked. "It'll help pass the time."

Jag had spent the past few days sticking close to Angel. He'd watched her dress and watched her move. A board game was not what he had in mind. He wanted their first time to be special, but he didn't want to wait any longer. His urges gnawed at him.

"If you want to play a game, it's fine with me," he said unenthusiastically.

"Well, I just don't want you to be bored in here. It's up to you."

Jag dug deep down within himself and nervously reached out, putting his hand on her thigh. He then looked up at her with telling eyes. His nerves shifted into high gear, but his desires outweighed his apprehension. She smiled, reached over, and extended a kiss to him.

"Honey, you are hurt. Making love would be painful. Just think about your ribs."

"I don't want to think about me; that's all I've been able to think about lately. I am ready to think about us."

Although his heart was thumping and his hands were embarrassingly wet and clammy, his best efforts went toward speaking confidently, the way a husband would to his wife, however that was.

After slowly pulling her shirt over her head, she made eye contact and continued with the unveiling of her body. It wasn't until she slipped into bed that her eyes left his gaze. Her fingers softy grazed across his body. Their lips met, and then it happened; they shared their first real kiss. Jag was amazed at how natural it felt, but just like with everything, he worried in the back of his mind that she would notice a difference. There was no pulling back or any sort of body language to lead Jag to believe that Angel suspected anything out of the ordinary, so he did his best to put his worries at bay and enjoy the incredible moments of the here and now. Her soft hair dangled around his face as she whispered into his ear, "Tell me if you feel any pain." She continued her seduction without pause and it wasn't long before Jag knew what it was really like to be the husband and the lover of such a remarkable woman. The entire situation was surreal, as if he was dreaming. Had the plan really come together so easily? Was he actually in the arms of the woman he had been secretly watching for so long? Was he actually playing the role of loving husband? It was true; it was all true and now he laid freely in her arms with no inhibitions or worries of discovery. After all, he was Dillon now. Their bodies meshed rhythmically together as his hands explored her body for the first time. With open eyes he watched her sensual expressions and paid close attention to what her body hinted to him. He had never been with such a beautiful and special woman before, and he relished in every moment of their sexual encounter, hoping she felt the same satisfaction he felt.

When the magic was over, she rested beside his healing body as he stroked her arm without the accompaniment of conversation. The silence made him a little nervous, and over and over the question surged through his mind, "What is going through her head?" Beyond that, guilt brewed. Guilt from knowing that the one woman he was crazy for had just been intimate with a man she barely knew. He wondered if he somehow had cheapened her, even though he was much better for her than Dillon ever was. It was an idea he didn't want to deal with, at least not now. All that mattered was that in the end the two of them would stand tall in victory, while Dillon paid for his lack of loyalty. Slight snoring began whistling from her perfect little nose.

With slow movements, he inched his way out of bed. His stomach hadn't seen the likes of a real meal in quite some time, and he was craving something of substance. There would be no more pasta or soup and salads for him. Before scanning the inside of the refrigerator, he noticed a roughly scribbled note affixed to the outside of it, "Got tired of waiting, don't wait up." A shiver attacked him remembering that night.

"You brought this on yourself, Dillon," he told himself.

The cupboards had little to work with, unless he took into account tuna fish, vegetables, and soy products.

"Nasty," he blurted out.

"I'll just order out," he decided. "I can do that now. I got money and there ain't no one around to tell me I can't."

Two giant bacon cheeseburgers were soon on their way to the house accompanied by fries and milkshakes. Jag sluggishly walked around the house wondering what he could do to pass the time.

"The study," he decided.

Once again he found himself by the big leather chair, remembering how he had been there only days before. Now, he could take as long as he needed, finger through papers, unlock the desk … whatever. He was Dillon now. Angel would never think twice about seeing him in there. He gently sat into the familiar leather recliner and took another look at the map that hung on the wall. He was determined to find out the story behind the coordinated pushpins.

"It's got to be big," he thought. "Mother said he was in deep with something bad."

He tapped his fingers against the desk. Feelings of empowerment teased him. Somehow, he managed to have it all: the house, the wife, the money, and the happiness. The question was what would he do with it all, and how would it all end for him.

"The camera!" he remembered after noticing the lampshade. It reminded him of the call he was supposed to have made to Roberta days before, but didn't. He wasn't sure exactly what day it was, but he was certain Sunday had come and gone. He backed away.

"Shit! Mother is going to be pissed."

He thought it over in his head. "Calling her now would be stupid. Angel is just upstairs, the delivery boy is probably on his way, and besides, what would I tell her."

He had no pertinent information to give, which would surely upset her. A little bit of reality was going to need to be incorporated into his dreamland status if he was ever going to make any progress. He determined that the next time Angel left to run errands, he would tackle his search-and-destroy mission. Once any ounce of information was gathered, then and only then, would he call his mother. He did wonder how his mother and Dillon were getting along; he hoped his long-lost brother had caused trouble and was lying dead somewhere undetected.

"It would make everything so much easier," he thought.

Even though he knew his mama didn't have it in her to do such a thing, he still fantasized about it. However, for now, he was going to enjoy his last night of taking it easy. He waited for the meals to arrive; sure that Angel would be thrilled to have dinner waiting for her when she awoke.

CHAPTER 29

▼

Dillon answered the door and was surprised to find two men standing on the other side. An overpowering fragrance of musk emerged.

"Can I help you?" Dillon asked.

He had no idea who they could possibly be, but then again he had no idea who anyone was except Roberta and his new friend Sam. The two men looked shocked to see him.

"Good morning, my name is Detective Chase and this is my partner Detective Whitaker. Who might you be?"

"If you are looking for Roberta, she's in the shower. She'll be out shortly," Dillon said as he noticed their civilian clothing. One wore a plain brown, short-sleeved shirt with faded jeans and the other dressed to impress with pressed slacks and a jacket.

"Do you mind if we come on in and wait for her?" Chase asked.

"Well, yes, I do mind. What is it that you want?" Dillon asked, curiously.

"We are investigating the disappearance of Charlie Grapler. Do you know him?" They asked.

"Well, that is a long story. I guess you can say I know him. He is my father."

"Your father? You must be Jorge?"

That was the second time Dillon had been mistaken for this Jorge character. He had to play this smart and figure out what was going on.

"What would make you think I'm Jorge?" he asked.

"Stop playing games here. We just want to ask a few questions," Chase said with a condescending undertone.

"I'm not playing games. What makes you think I'm this Jorge person?"

"Well, if you're claiming to be Charlie's son, why wouldn't I think you were Jorge?" Chase replied, rudely. The detectives exchanged a peculiar glance.

Dillon heard the bathroom door opening. He immediately cut their chat short.

"Well, sounds like Roberta is out of the shower. Wait outside, and I'll tell her that you're here," Dillon said hastily before closing the front door.

He bolted down the hall and informed Roberta about the presence of the detectives. She threw her hands straight up into the air. "What did you tell them? Did you talk to them?"

"Relax, I told them you were in the shower and to wait outside until you had finished."

Dillon's jitters bounced around under his calm demeanor. He didn't want to divulge any information that would cause Roberta to become defensive. If he was going to try and fit the pieces of his life together, it was best that he did it alone. Playing the dumb, naive one was the smartest way to go with her. She stormed toward her front door. He followed suit.

"What do ya think you're doing? I can take care of these yahoos; I don't need no help. Go to your room or something!"

"Excuse me?" Dillon snapped. "I am a grown man. You can't send me to my room."

Roberta turned to him in anger, "This ain't none of your damn business. These guys have been hassling me for years. It's always something they 'suspect' I's doing or they 'assume' I have info on. I've had it with them. This ain't gonna be pretty. Just leave me be."

Dillon was surprised to hear how angry she had gotten, not only about the presence of the detectives, but also about her demand for privacy. To avoid an even bigger scene, he pretended to oblige her and waited down the hall with hopes of eavesdropping on the conversation. Roberta opened the front door and shifted gears.

"Well, good morning officers. What brings ya to my neck of the woods?" she asked with a smile and a pleasant tone. She wore a lime green sweat suit and had her hair swaddled up inside a blue towel.

"We were wondering if you have any information about the whereabouts of your husband, Charlie?"

"Well, I can't say that I do. He up and left a week or two ago," she said without emotion. "Ain't sure where he went. He don't tell me stuff like that. Ain't called or nothing."

"Is that his white truck out there?" Detective Chase asked.

"Yes," Roberta simply said.

"Do you have a second vehicle, Mrs. Grapler?" Detective Chase continued.

"No."

Her short and unrevealing responses irritated the hell out of Detective Chase. "How did he leave without his vehicle?"

"He must have gotten a ride."

"Do you remember someone coming here to pick him up?" Detective Chase questioned.

"No," she said.

"Don't you find that odd, Mrs. Grapler? Don't you find the entire thing odd?" Detective Whitaker chimed in.

"Well, no. It's just what he does. He's done it before and he'll do it again."

"Do you mind if we come in? It's a bit chilly out here," Whitaker firmly asked, as if no wasn't an option.

"Well, I don't know what else to tell ya. He was here one day and gone the next. That's it. That's all I know," she said. Her voice remained cordial.

"I would like to get some more details about the last time you saw your husband. Can we please just come in for a few minutes?" Detective Chase asked, while repeating his partner's earlier request. She didn't want to seem uncooperative or suspicious, so she allowed the detectives to enter her home.

"All right, but there is really nothing to worry about. He'll turn up. He always does."

Detective Chase got out his pen, flipped his notepad open, and started with his interrogation.

"You said he had disappeared before. When exactly?"

"Well, I don't know exact dates. I don't think twice about it no more. I just go on with life as usual."

"A rough estimate is fine, Mrs. Grapler."

Her heart raced. Panic ricocheted through her every thought.

"Do you mind telling me who told you he was 'so-called' missing?" she asked with a growing unpleasantness.

"It was one of his co-workers."

"Let me guess, Ken?" she interrupted.

"Yes, Ken," the detective answered.

"He called here. I told him the same thing I's telling you. Take it or leave it." Her voice had become rude.

"So, once again, can you give me an estimated date on the last time Charlie disappeared on you?" Detective Chase repeated.

"Last winter," she said.

"How long was he away for?"

"I don't really remember, maybe a couple of weeks or so."

"Did you contact the police about it?"

"No, not officially. Like I said before, it's just what he does. If I called ya every time Charlie got restless, you guys would have a file thicker than the Bible."

"Did you ever ask him where it was that he went?"

"Nope," she said.

"Why not?" Detective Chase asked.

"Didn't care," she said.

She decided the less she said the better.

"What day did you last see your husband?"

"I don't know the exact day. I don't see him much anyway, even when he's home."

"Well, a Friday … a Saturday …?"

She sighed deeply and calmly answered, "I guess it was on a weekend. I do remember that much. That Monday morning I didn't have to fix no breakfast 'cause he wasn't around. He always made me fix him breakfast. So yeah, I guess it was … she looked at a calendar that the detective had conveniently handed her … the weekend before last."

"So, the weekend of May 10 and 11. Now we're getting somewhere. Do you remember seeing him on Friday, May 9? Did you make breakfast for him that day before he went to work?"

"Maybe. You guys are making more of this than ya should. I don't know if I made him breakfast. I ain't really sure of anything, except that on Monday morning he wasn't around."

"Were you two having marital problems, Mrs. Grapler?"

"That's none of your damn business. Do you and your wife have problems in the sack, Detective Chase?"

"Excuse me?" he asked, rudely.

"I figure if you wanna pry into my private life, I'd do the same. So, are you disappointing the missus?"

"You know, we can either do this here or at the station, Mrs. Grapler. It's your choice."

"You know my husband has made a fool outta me already. Why are you wanting to do the same? Just leave me be. If I hear from him, I'll let ya know."

"I just have a few more questions. It will be easier all around if you just cooperate," Detective Chase said.

"What else do you wanna know?" she asked shortly.

"What were you doing that weekend? The weekend of May 10."

"Errands, I guess. I don't go out much unless I'm doin' errands."

"Were you with anyone that weekend?"

"Well, maybe. If I was, it was just Sam."

"Sam who?" the detective asked.

"Sam's my friend; she comes over sometimes."

"Can you give me a last name?"

"Oh, don't go harassing her. She don't know nothing neither," she snapped.

"We're done," she insisted. "I got things to tend to. I'm tired of feeling like I'm on trial here. I ain't done nothing, so be glad I said what I did and just go away. Oh, and if you try contacting me again, I won't talk to ya. From now on I only talk to Officer O'Mally. He knows how Charlie is, what he's like. He'll believe me."

The detectives found her statement quite odd, and they had every intention of following up with Officer O'Mally once they returned to the station.

"Well, we appreciate your time and we'll be in touch if we hear anything," Detective Chase said.

They knew they would be back, not only to talk to Roberta, but also to talk to her son, Jorge. Detective Chase took a moment to record some notes into his notepad, "Check Charlie's work attendance, ... talk to O'Mally, ... who is Sam? ... talk to Jorge, ... Charlie and Roberta's possible marital issues, ... check local hangouts, ... talk to Ken again."

The front door slammed and Roberta stormed into the kitchen, noticing the shadow of Dillon as she blazed by the hallway. She stopped, turned, and headed straight for his bedroom door.

"I thought I told ya this ain't no business of yours! What gives you the right to listen to my private conversation?"

Roberta's temper was at an all-time high from the questioning, and her rational train of thought was on a derailment. Screaming at Dillon wasn't the smartest move on her part. It was only going to lead to an inevitable argument and would undoubtedly make her look suspicious about the entire Charlie situation.

"Do you think scolding me is going to help matters? Apparently, you are my mother and I am your son, which would make Charlie my father. So, that alone makes it my business! I live in this house too, and whether you like it or not, I am a part of whatever is going on between these four walls. So that is what gives me the right!" Dillon responded with conviction.

"You ain't even been around! You don't know shit about this family! Don't you dare think you can step in now and be all interested in my life? You weren't there for me! You haven't been there for me for a while! This is my problem, not yours, and certainly not ours!"

Her fury for Dillon escalated to a record-setting height. All she could think about was how he had ignored her for so many years. How dare he pry into her affairs now, after all these years of not wanting to be a part of her life.

"Here's one for you, a question you could consider my business. Who the hell is Jorge, and why do people keep addressing me as such?"

Roberta's hateful tongue froze. She wondered whom he had been talking to, who could have possibly said that name? Then it hit her, *Sam!* Dillon stared into Roberta's unsure eyes, waiting for an answer to his shocking question. Her eyes darted in several directions while her body remained statue still.

"You want to answer my question … MOM?" he asked smugly.

She fought for composure and eventually claimed, "That's your middle name."

He stood there without reaction. She had an answer for everything. Frustration brewed inside of his body, begging for a release. "I'm going for a walk!" he said, as he turned to put on his Velcro running shoes.

"A walk? Where?" she asked hastily.

"Just around. There is enough land around this place to put in a few good miles. I've been cooped up in this place for way too long for my sanity to remain intact."

Roberta knew she couldn't stop him; he was far too determined. Offering him a little white pill was certainly out of the question. He was a smart guy and would surely put two and two together, realizing, of course, that she used them as a tool to keep him tired and at close range. Instead of speaking one more word, she calmly removed herself from his room and sat down at the yellow, aluminum kitchen table with a beer and a cigarette. He took that as his queue to leave and disappeared into the woods. She knew he would be back. He was trapped just as she had been when Charlie ran the show. Dillon had no car, no memory, no friends, no money, and no idea what the truth really was. He would be back. She banked on it.

CHAPTER 30

▼

Jag heard the sound of a car door slamming. He assumed the delivery boy had arrived and sure enough, a young man sporting baggy khakis and a backward baseball hat approached. He carried a large, white, grease-stained sack in one hand and a double drink holder in the other. Jag opened the door and greeted the awkward teenager.

"That'll be $14.09, please."

Jag paid the pimply faced boy with a crisp twenty-dollar bill and sent him on his way.

"Angel?" he whispered softly. He rubbed her arm gently.

He could imagine himself living the rest of his life in this very moment. Her eyes slowly opened. She shot him a grin.

"Hey, honey. How long have I been asleep?"

"Just a couple of hours, I guess. I ordered us some food, are you hungry?" She rolled over, looked at the clock, and saw that it was almost dinnertime.

"Sure. Come to think of it, I didn't even eat lunch today."

She put her robe and slippers on and headed downstairs with her faux husband.

"Burgers and fries?" she questioned.

"Yep, smells good don't it?"

"Well, yes, but it is just not what I expected."

Not knowing why she was so surprised, he threw out his usual cover-up line.

"You know me, living life to the fullest these days. Do you not feel like burgers?" he asked nervously. He still had no clue as to why eating burgers was such a big deal.

"Well, I love them, but have never actually seen you eat one."

"That was the old Dillon, remember?" he replied.

He wondered how long he could use that excuse before it got old.

"Well, let's dig in," she said. Jag's mouth watered over the heavy aroma of pickles and mustard. He popped a fry into his mouth before folding the burger's wrapper halfway down the speckled bun. Cheese dripped onto his hand as he brought the burger up to his mouth.

"Stop! Dillon, what are you trying to do, put yourself back in the hospital?"

"What?"

"What do you mean, what? There's cheese on that."

He lowered his sandwich and looked at her, hoping she would say something else to divulge the reason why cheese was such a strange thing to have on a cheeseburger.

"You're allergic to cheese," she said, confused. "Dillon, don't you remember that you are allergic to cheese?" she said with worry.

"Damn restaurant!" he sternly said. "I didn't ask for cheese. In fact I specifically told them not to put cheese on mine. I guess they messed the order up or something," he quickly replied.

She didn't say anything after that and began eating her fatty meal.

"Damn it!" he thought.

After scrapping the cheese off his burger, he followed suit and ate his meal without another word.

He was busy having a conversation with himself, "Think before you act, don't assume anything, and don't suggest things unless it is something you are absolutely sure seems normal. You're slipping up on your talking too. You suggested watching a chick flick; you ordered food you're allergic to; what's next? Are ya gonna tell her your real name?"

Scolding himself silently would hopefully make him think twice about his upcoming choices. He needed to remember what was at stake and how crucial his role was in the big scheme of things. His level of comfort within his new life was going to do him in if he was not careful.

He finished up his meal by giving himself some advice. "Be a follower in things, not a leader, Jag. Don't suggest things, don't initiate things, just go with the flow and let her run the show!"

"I don't know what has gotten into him, Rachel. It's like he's a totally different person," Lanie said as she swiveled from side to side on her leather-cushioned bar stool.

"Well, sure I like it, but it is a little bit eerie too. The man who hates romantic movies, despises junk food, and is a workaholic is now interested in watching *When Harry Met Sally*, eating fast food, and could care less about returning to work."

"No."

"No."

"Well I guess that could be true."

"I know. You're right, but it's like I have to get to know my husband all over again. At first I loved his new attitude, but now I miss how passionate he was about work and that he used to organize his closet by color. I even miss how he combed his hair exactly one hundred times before bed each night. Yes, but the quirks are, or were, part of who he was."

"I suppose, but what defined him seems to no longer exist."

"I know, I know. You're right, he has turned into the perfect attentive and romantic guy, but that is not who I fell in love with."

"Yes, I suppose I could talk to him about it, he has just been through so much and I don't want to squash his enthusiasm for his new and so-called improved self."

Jag heard his Angel laughing as he listened attentively to her one-way phone conversation.

"Yeah, okay."

"It's just that I love what he has become also. I love the new Dillon, I really do. Sometimes I wish I could just take parts of the old Dillon and parts of the new Dillon and create a much more balanced version. It seems to be one side of the extreme to the other with him."

"No, I think I am just going to be patient and see how it all plays out. After all, he has been through a lot. Who am I to tell him not to reevaluate his life? He is who he is."

"Oh, Rachel, you're hysterical. I'll keep you posted."

"Take care. Talk to you later."

"You too. Bye now."

Angel hung up the black cordless telephone and went on with her business. Two hours had passed and Angel and Jag still remained separated within the house. Each was doing their own thing, and neither one approached the other. Angel quietly read a romance novel on the cushioned chair in the living room, and Jag rested upstairs in their bed. He occupied himself with his poetry and thought about what his next move should be, considering Angel's apparent disappointment in who he was. His heart felt a little bit broken as he poured therapeutic words onto the pages of his notebook.

Within a few hours, after nothing more than a quick kiss good night, the two of them were closing their eyes in preparation for a solid night's sleep. Jag couldn't leave it like this; it wasn't how it was supposed to be.

"Angel?"

"Are you ever going to call me by my real name, Dillon?" she snapped.

He laid there in shock. "I thought you liked it when I called you Angel?"

"I do. I'm sorry, honey; I am just tired and frustrated. I just wish things were the way they used to be. I love you dearly, but you are such a different person these days, it's hard to adapt to everything."

"Well, that is what I wanted to talk to ya about. I have been keeping a secret from you since the accident, and I think it is about time I let you in on it," Jag said, nervously. Angel switched the bedside lamp on and turned to him curiously. "I'm listening."

CHAPTER 31

▼

Dillon found himself in the midst of some beautiful evergreens as he continued to walk off his latest stint of rage. Living with Roberta had proven to be difficult, and he suspected that it was why he had walked out on her just a year or so before. If living with her then was anything similar to living with her now, she most likely drove him away. The enormous task of searching for his memory or some speck of his past exhausted his existence. There were so many unanswered questions and so many emotions he didn't understand. He hated feeling like a stranger in his own skin.

He let out a frustrated scream, "Ahhh!"

He let its echo linger for a bit before he belted out a second scream.

"Ahhh!"

Disturbing nothing but nature, his outbursts released his pent-up irritations. For the first time in days, he was able to let loose and take a moment to actually react to what ailed him. While sitting on a large, semi-round rock, he took a moment to enjoy the small amount of tranquility he allotted himself. The panoramic view calmed his outrage. Dozens of different colored wildflowers grew below the large hill he rested upon, and a soft breeze blew the delicate branches and leaves within the forest. He felt free. Free from the suspicion that he was trapped in a life that he didn't belong in, free from the feeling that he lived under a microscope every minute of every day, and, most importantly, free from the control of another. His renewed spirit reminded him that any day now his memory would return, bringing with it an understanding of his ambiguous life. A few hours of serenity passed before the clouds began blanketing the declining sun. He stood up and stretched tall while inhaling the scent of pine and cherry blossoms. A small, wooded structure quite a ways below the hill caught his roaming eye.

"Why not?" he thought. After all, he had nothing better to do than go back to the place he had just escaped from. Climbing down the side of the uneven hill proved slightly difficult for him and his low-top shoes, but he hoped the journey would be worthwhile. He used his hands as guides as he climbed over knocked-down trees, and he stepped carefully through pitted terrain. A snake crossed his path; it didn't seem to faze him. A small, rustic cabin stood nestled within the tall timbers of the forest. He was told that his mother and father owned all the surrounding land, which, technically, would make the little cabin his property. The window offered an invitation and revealed a small, cozy interior. At first glimpse, the cabin appeared to contain nothing more than a large, wooden desk, a small kitchen area, and a living room decorated with a thick couch, a rocking chair, and a couple lamps.

"Who could live here?" he wondered.

He thought of the name Jorge. Maybe Jorge wasn't his middle name at all, but instead, the name of someone Roberta didn't want him to know about.

"Could this Jorge person live here?" Dillon wondered.

Ideas rattled around in Dillon's head as he went through his thought process.

"Roberta claims to live alone; Charlie's disappeared … Charlie! Of course, Charlie. That makes perfect sense. Charlie couldn't stand living around her either. He is probably hiding out here, doing his own thing."

Dillon felt much more confident about this latter theory. Maybe he was finally making some progress with his disaster of a life. He wondered if his missing father was behind the closed bedroom door within the cabin. Enthusiastically, he rapped on the door. Not only could this mean he would meet his father for what would seem like the first time, but it could also solve the apparent investigation. More importantly, he would be one step closer to learning more about himself and his mysterious life. Again he knocked, only this time he knocked harder and longer. The result was the same. No one answered, nor was there the slightest indication that anyone was home. With a turn of the doorknob, the door clicked open.

Soon Dillon stood in the middle of the living space. He found himself moving toward the closed door. Even though he was technically on his own property, he felt as if he was invading someone's space. Slowly, he pushed the closed door open and peeked in the room. His eyes scanned from the double bed, to the dresser, and finally to a small, open closet. The bedroom was tidy and clean, with a hunter green throw rug resting in front of the four-post bed. A brown and red flannel shirt hung on the closet door handle above a pair of brown, leather work boots. Dillon stood there in silence, convinced that he had solved the mystery of where Charlie Grapler was, and had been hiding for quite sometime. Still remaining was the intriguing question as to why he was hiding. Dillon couldn't resist an urge to poke around. Unfortunately, the more he snooped, the more he began to second-guess the belief that his father was alive and well. Dillon remembered Roberta and the officers declaring May 10 as the weekend Charlie was last seen. Interestingly enough, the daily desk calendar reflected a date of May 8. The leather work boots he initially didn't give much notice to were quite interesting upon reexamination. Dried mud clung to the outer edges of the soles and sprinkled the floor around the boots. However, Dillon hadn't seen rain since he'd arrived at Roberta's. The closer he looked, the more he began to feel that Charlie had intended to return to the cabin, but for some reason hadn't. There was a full gallon of milk in the refrigerator with an expiration date of May 12; one day before Dillon arrived in Emmett, Idaho. In addition, old coffee sat in the coffee craft beneath dry coffee grounds and there was a sink full of cool, standing water. Dillon's rational side kicked in as he tried to curb his imagination. For all he knew, Charlie wasn't even the one who lived here. For all he knew, it was a hideaway for Roberta. Maybe Roberta was having an affair, and that was why Charlie left. Then again, he thought, maybe Charlie and Roberta were renting the cabin out to someone. And maybe that someone was out buying groceries or taking a walk, in which case, he was trespassing.

Dillon was driving himself crazy. His entire life seemed to consist of unknowns, guesses, and questions. The sun was waving good-bye for the day, forcing Dillon to end his investigation, at least for the night. As he turned to leave, his hip bumped into the side of the desk, triggering a thick blue notebook to smack against the floor.

His conscience debated on whether or not to open it. He fingered to a random page and began to read.

> "... I am tormented as to what my next move should be. The tables are slowly turning and the love I once felt has begun its transformation into a blurred collage of anger and resentment. Why me? Why me and why her? There are no rational explanations, no sense of clarity or understanding. All that seems to remain is the notion of faith and truth and the belief in their combination bringing fourth a triumphant ending."

Chills shot through his spine as he read those few sentences over and over again. "Who on earth could have written such profound words?" Dillon wondered. He turned to the last page, then turned the book over, and finally flipped back to the first page of the book. He searched for ownership, something that would clue him in to who had written the sad and desperate words. It would also answer the nagging question of who lived in the authentic log cabin on the middle of Roberta's property. His heart skipped a beat when he saw the following scripted on page one of the journal.

Charlie
Jan. 1, 2003, another year gone

CHAPTER 32

▼

"I'm listening," Lanie repeated as she and her imitation husband propped themselves up on their bed.

"Do you remember earlier today when I ordered us food from that hamburger joint?"

"Uh ... yeah. Why?"

"Well, the restaurant didn't slip up with the order. I actually did order a cheeseburger. In fact, I requested extra cheese."

Lanie looked puzzled.

"What are you talking about? The something you had to tell me is that you ordered a cheeseburger? I don't get it, what does that have to do with anything."

"And do you remember when I wanted to watch *When Harry Met Sally?*"

"Yes, I remember," she answered, still wondering where her husband was going with this. "And?"

"Well, I didn't know I didn't like that particular movie, and I had no idea that I was allergic to cheese."

"What are you saying, Dillon?" she paused. "Spit it out. What are you getting at?"

"I ... I can't remember a lot of stuff about me and about my life. There, I said it. Ever since the accident, I can't remember a lot of stuff, and that is why I've been acting so strangely."

"Why on earth would you hide the fact that you can't remember things? Do you remember anything? Do you remember me? You remember me, right, honey?"

"Yes, of course I remember you. You're my wife." Saying those words never got old for Jag. The only thing he loved more than saying them was hearing them being said.

"So, why have you been pretending? Why not let me, and the doctors for that matter, help you with this?" Lanie asked.

"Well, I was lying in that hospital bed listen as you prayed for me, and I knew your voice. I did. I recognized it. I knew it was a familiar voice, a loving voice, but I couldn't think of your name and that alone broke my heart. It broke my heart to know that there you were pouring your heart out, weeping and praying for me, and I couldn't even remember what to call you. I pretended to be asleep because I didn't know what else to do. Don't get me wrong, somehow I knew you were my wife, my friend … it was just the name that I couldn't come up with. I called you Angel, remember?"

"Is that why you called me that? Because you couldn't remember my actual name?"

"Well, yes, but what I said was true. I did have a dream as I fell in and out of sleep. You were there with a ray of light over you, just like an angel."

Jag was getting so good at covering his tracks that he was actually beginning to impress himself. He wasn't proud about lying to Lanie, but he had to. The lying was necessary for the good of the plan. He knew she would never find out about it and therefore, to him, it was justified and warranted. Maybe Jag was a force to be reckoned with, and maybe, just maybe, he had a little bit of his father in him after all. Now that was a thought he knew his mama could never hear him say. His mama prided herself on being not just the primary, but the *only* influence in Jag's life. She used to always say, "Don't ever turn out like your daddy. He's a liar and a cheat with nothing to offer but a hidden agenda."

Jag often thought about those two little sentences his mama used to sum up his father. It seemed that these days, Jag fit that description to a tee. He, in fact, was a liar and a cheat with a huge hidden agenda.

"Have you found that your memory has improved since the accident, or has it stayed the same?" Lanie asked.

"I guess it has mostly stayed the same," Jag replied.

"I am going to call Dr. Hernandez first thing tomorrow. This is important, Dillon. You could have something really wrong with you. My goodness."

Jag knew that all he could do was agree, and then hopefully he and Lanie would be able to get back to where they were before she started disliking him.

"You're right, Angel. I probably do need to talk to the doc. What do you say we go to sleep now?" Jag asked ready to put an end to the day's drama.

"All right. Good night, honey."

She leaned over and nuzzled his neck before clicking the lamp off.

Morning came quick and the couple's sleep was disturbed by a ringing telephone at around 8:00 AM.

"Hello?" Lanie said in a groggy tone.

"Hello?" she repeated, but still no one responded.

Before she had a chance to say it one last time, she heard a click. She threw her head back down onto the pillow.

"No one there?" Jag asked.

"Nope."

"Do you want some coffee?"

"Absolutely," she responded.

As Jag wandered down the stairs he wondered about the phone call they'd just received. Maybe his mama was trying to contact him. He scooped the coffee into the maker and sat there thinking of his next move while it brewed. He carried the two cups of strong coffee up the stairs and decided that today was going to have to be the first day he took this job seriously and got down to business. The unknown caller caused a slight paranoia in him, and the last thing he wanted or needed was to make his partner angry. She could blow this wide open. As soon as they both settled back into the bed, Jag blurted, "I don't remember the combination to the desk drawer in the study."

"Huh?" Lanie said.

"The drawer. I sat in the study yesterday waiting on our food delivery and I found myself staring at the locked drawer with a total blank as to what the combination was or what was even inside. I want to look through my stuff to help me remember, but I can't even get to it."

"Oh yeah, that reminds me," Lanie said as she picked up the phone and called Dr. Hernandez's office to schedule the first available appointment.

"All right, we will see you tomorrow then, 10:00 AM sharp."

She set the phone back down and said, "Napa."

"Napa? You want to go to Napa?"

"No, that is the combination to the safe. The numbers that correspond to the letters N-A-P-A on the phone's keypad. Do you remember when we went to Napa Valley last year?"

"No, I don't think so."

"Well, you were robbed. You were hit over the head with a lead pipe and the crook took your wallet. Since you'd been robbed in Napa, you thought it would be a fitting password, one you wouldn't forget. You were so pleased with the irony of it."

Jag didn't have much to say in return so he simply took another sip of his coffee.

"Well, I am going to jump in the shower. I have to go into work for a few hours. Duty calls," Lanie said as she sprung out of bed.

Only about an hour passed before the natural beauty grabbed her purse and gave him his usual good-bye peck. She always seemed to take his breath away. She waved and smiled from the car's window, and he happily reciprocated.

He quickly dialed the phone, feeling nervous, and then suddenly hung it up. His chest contracted as he took a deep breath and dialed again, slower this time as he tried to think of what he was going to say. He was quite a few days late and he knew how his mama worried about him. In addition, she wasn't shy about letting him have it when the moment struck her. Jag hated when she was mad. He knew she only scolded him out of love, but she had a way of making him feel completely guilt stricken when he disappointed her.

"Yeah?" The voice said.

"Mama? It's me."

"Jorgie?"

"Yep, it's me, Mama. How is everything?"

"What the hell took you so long? You was supposed to have called me forever ago. You're obviously okay, so what have ya been doing all this time?"

"I've been recuperating. I was pretty banged up you know. Doctors said it was a miracle I survived at all. I hit that tree a lot harder than I meant to. My whole life flashed before my eyes."

"I was worried, Jorge. I was beginning to wonder if you'd double-crossed me."

"Double-crossed you? Why would I do that? I need you, Mama. You know that."

"Then why you got those cameras in the house shut off?" Roberta accused.

"What do you mean?" Jag answered.

"I ain't seeing nothing but static on the camera screen over here." Roberta said.

"I don't know, Mama, honestly. I didn't turn them off." Jag replied. "I'll check my remote control. Maybe I have to turn something on first for you to get a picture."

"Then all is still as planned?"

"Yes, Mama, all is as planned," Jag responded.

"So, what is going on with Dillon? Is he there? Has he hurt you at all? Is he still locked up?" Jag asked.

"He can't remember nothing. He don't even know who he is. He just hangs out here assuming he is who I tell him he is. I told him he was my son, and he believes it. Don't worry, I don't treat him like a son, I pretend though. He knows his name; that's about all. I called him by it before I was wise to him losing his memory. The only reason I can stand him in my house is 'cause he looks almost just like you, and I just pretend it's you looking back at me. We got into it yesterday. He's so damn rude, don't respect his elders. You can tell he wasn't raised good. He took off in the woods after throwing a tantrum. He's back now in his room, or in your room, I mean." She continued to talk quietly with an eye on the kitchen entryway, just in case Dillon made an appearance.

"So, Jorge, what have you got for me? You have to have tons of dirt on him by now. Whacha got?"

"I have the key to unlock all his dirty little secrets. That's what I have. Today is going to be a fruitful day for us."

"Fruitful. What kinda word is that? Fruitful. You'd better not come back to this house talking like no rich snob. I'll tell ya that right now!"

"It's part of my act. I am getting good at it too, Mama. I have to sound like Dillon; after all, I'm living with his wife."

"How's that going, you and her?"

"Fine, I guess. It's just a job to me. Could take her or leave her."

"I'm glad to hear that. She's nothing but trouble, I'm sure. Keep your head in the game."

"I know, Mama. I can't talk long. I have to go check out the study before she gets back."

"The sooner you get the dirt and the money, the sooner we can be done. I'm counting on ya now, Jorge. I'm doing my part; be sure you do yours."

"I know, I am taking care of it and will call ya on Monday or Tuesday. It'll depend on Ang … on Dillon's wife."

"Next time you call you better have more than a bunch of snobby words. We ain't got a lot of time. I love you, baby, make me proud," she continued.

"Love you too, Mama. Talk to you soon. Hey, what's going on with Papa?"

"Uh, he's gone. Hasn't called or nothing, which is what I expect from him, so let's not talk about it."

"Okay, Mama. I'll drop it. Talk to you later."

Jag entered the study to get down to business. He sat in the leather chair and entered the numbers 6-2-7-2 into the lock on the desk drawer. He pushed the knob to the right and pulled the heavy wooden drawer open. The first label that caught his eye read, "Exports." Jag knew this drawer held the key that would eventually unlock his future and close the door on Dillon's.

CHAPTER 33

▼

"You wanted to see me?" Officer Tate O'Mally asked as he approached Detective Chase's spotless cubicle.

"Hey, do you know of a woman named Roberta Grapler?" he asked as he traced his uniform with a lint brush.

"Sure, who doesn't. Why?" O'Mally asked.

"Well, I am in the process of investigating the disappearance of her husband, Charlie. Roberta claims he just ran off. She says he always takes off and that you would back her up on that statement. Do you know anything about it?"

"Yeah, he has been known to leave from time to time; she used to call and talk my ear off about it. I'm not quite sure who gave her the number to my direct line way back in the day, and she never would say. It's been quite a while since I heard from her though, thank God," O'Mally said.

"I don't understand," Detective Chase responded. "There are no reports on file, no evidence that she ever contacted the police department."

"That is because there isn't any documentation; it doesn't exist," O'Mally responded with some hesitation. "The first time she called was over a year or so ago. She refused to give her name. I remember that pretty clearly because it was my first no-name caller. I was still pretty wet behind the ears at that point, and I remember being intrigued by the call." O'Mally took a seat in a metal chair next to Chase's desk and crossed his thin legs.

She was in a panic and said she was worried about the whereabouts of her husband. At that point, I had no idea who I was talking to. I tried my best to provide as much police guidance as I could. She wanted to know the proper procedure to report a missing person and what all it involved. In the end, she chose neither to make the report, nor to disclose who she was. She said she wasn't one hundred percent sure her husband was actually 'missing,'" O'Mally continued while making quotation marks with his fingers.

"She said she feared a possible affair. Once she found out how public a missing person's investigation could get, she told me to pretend like she had never called. She said that if she changed her mind, she would call back. She went on to say that she couldn't bear the humiliation of learning her husband was cheating, and knowing the whole town of Emmett would be in on the secret. So, basically I had no name and no concrete information. She called again about seven or eight days after that and told me that her husband had returned smelling of perfume and whiskey. She was furious and went on and on about how relieved she was that she hadn't filed that report. She called her husband a few choice words; she was basically venting. I don't think I was able to squeeze in more than a dozen or so words during the entire conversation. I assumed that would be the last time I would hear from her. But sure enough, the same thing happened about four months later. She called again and made the same claim. She said that he'd disappeared and she wasn't sure if he was in trouble or if he was cheating again. She claimed their marriage was so much better, and she said she couldn't imagine that he would cheat again. Sure enough, a week or two later she called again to confirm he'd been out fooling around."

"How did you come to find out it was Roberta Grapler?" Detective Chase asked.

"One of the times she called she revealed her name after I promised never to tell anyone about how her husband cheats and runs out on her for other women. She told me that I was a great listener and that she had no one else to turn to. She also said she felt she could trust me. I'm not sure why; it was all pretty ambiguous. I know all about her personal problems and her life, but I couldn't tell you what she looks like. I've never seen the woman. I've only spoken with her on the telephone," O'Mally said.

"When is the last time she called you?"

"Well, it was quite a while ago. Actually, late December, now that I think about it. I remember her saying something about starting the New Year off right because he had left town again."

Detective Chase took note of it all and jotted down "December."

"Well, thanks O'Mally I am sure we will be picking your brain again on this case. Oh, and be prepared to meet with her. She says she will only speak with you. The rest of us are 'pond scum.' At least I believe that was the term she used. I wasn't sure if she was referring to us as the male gender, or to us as the police department. Apparently, you are the exception in either case." Detective Chase smacked O'Mally on the upper back with his palm and offered a goodhearted smile.

O'Mally nodded politely, and went back to his corner desk to tackle some paperwork.

Whitaker plopped into the passenger-side seat of their unmarked Pontiac, while Chase took the wheel as usual. He activated his blinker and carefully pulled into traffic.

"I swear my grandma drives more aggressive than you," Whitaker blurted. "Your driving makes me nuts." Whitaker shook his head from side to side. He sported a loose, green, button-up shirt than hung untucked over a dark pair of jeans. Brown socks and loafers dressed his feet.

Detective Chase glanced over to his good friend and partner, "Slow and easy is what got me Beverly," he cleverly retorted about his wife before turning the radio to a classic rock station.

They arrived at BT Construction at precisely 10:00 AM and passed through a small portion of the five-acre lumberyard to get to the main office.

"Thank you for meeting with us on such short notice, Mr. Thorton."

"Sure, this whole thing seems pretty serious. If there is anything I can do to help, I will oblige," Mr. Thorton responded. "Have a seat, Officers."

Chase unbuttoned his gray sports jacket before taking a seat in one of the cushioned, red chairs. "First of all, we will need Charlie's attendance records for the past five years as well as his performance appraisals."

"Sure," Thorton responded confidently. "I will have to get with Darie on that; it shouldn't be a problem."

"How well do you know Charlie?"

"Not so much on a personal level if that is what you are asking. I mean we socialized at our company Christmas parties and BBQs, but it was always casual conversation. He was a strong worker, and he had a lot of friends here. I can't say that I have had any problems with him."

"Did he miss a lot of work?"

"Not to my knowledge, but then again, I am not usually informed of those kinds of issues. My site managers deal with the attendance and production levels at each job site. I am big on delegation; without it I wouldn't be where I am today."

"Who was Charlie's manager the week before and after Saturday, May 10?" Chase asked.

"It was Ken Chaptner; he was acting site manager for the project they were working on. Charlie almost always works with Ken. They work well together. Ken is probably the guy you should be interviewing. He knows Charlie better than probably anyone else does."

"Did Ken outrank Charlie, so to speak?" Chase asked.

"Well, yeah, I guess you could say that. Ken has a lot more responsibility because he puts himself out there and takes chances. Ken wants to be involved in anything high profile. He loves the challenge of supervising and coordinating, and he thrives under the high pressure of the job. Charlie is the opposite. He enjoys working behind the scenes and putting in a good, hard day's work. He is happy just driving a forklift or working on a high-rise. Ken says Charlie is an extremely competent worker and that he'd be a successful leader, but Charlie refuses to go that route. The oppositeness about them is probably what makes them such a great team," Mr. Thorton said.

"Is Ken available?" Detective Chase inquired.

"Actually, he's not. He requested a few days off to help search for Charlie. He said he wanted to talk with Roberta and remain available for any assistance the police may need."

"Do you know anything about Charlie's personal life? How his marriage was? Whether he was happy at home?"

"I can't say that I do. Like I said, I didn't know him all that well on a personal level. You really need to contact Ken."

"If at all possible, we could really use those employee records on Charlie by the end of the day. Can you work that out, Mr. Thorton?"

"I am sure Darie can get that information together for you. I will have her call you as soon as she has it together. It'll probably be a couple hours or so," Mr. Thorton answered.

"Well, thank you for your time; please contact us if you have anymore information."

Detectives Chase and Whitaker continued their investigation. They stopped at local restaurants and hotels, hoping someone, somewhere knew something of importance. An all-points bulletin advertised throughout Oregon and the local news stations included the case in their broadcasts. The investigation proceeded with full force while the two women who held all the answers sat quietly in their respective homes. One sat thriving from her smug feelings of satisfaction. The other wanted desperately to right her wrong.

CHAPTER 34

▼

His digital clock turned to 10:16 PM, as Dillon lay in his bed waiting for the hall light to diminish to darkness. He could see the light shining under the door to his room. It was a clear indication that Roberta was still awake. The journal taunted his curiosity; he had to know the rest of the story. Every ounce of his perceptivity told him that the key to unlocking his past was written in the pages he held in his hands at that very moment. It was vital to keep his discovery a secret. He still didn't trust Roberta, and he believed that the only unbiased words were those written on the pages of his father's journal. It neared midnight before the stream of light beneath his door vanished and the welcomed state of darkness roared.

"Today marks a new day, a new beginning. I know that isn't true, not for me, but the ideality of it soothes my thoughts. These four walls have proven to cage my sanity, allow it to still exist, even amongst the chaos of life. I had another fight with Roberta, just minutes before opening this journal to a new page. I can't reason with the woman. I say up and she says down. I say yes, she says no. The ability to communicate, to just get along has grown to be nearly impossible. I feel as if I am no longer welcome in my own house. A place I have lived in for more than twenty years is slipping further out of my reach with each passing day. Losing all that makes a house a home is perhaps the worst of it all. When I look in her eyes I see a stranger. I can't find the woman I fell in love with so many years ago. I can't find the compatibility that used to house our love. I don't think she will ever see me the way she used to, and in a way I hope that burden rings true. I am exhausted. My biggest concern is Jorge. What effect this will have on him. I fear he hates me. I fear that woman has turned him against me and that he doesn't know any better than to follow her lead. A boy needs his father; Jorge needs me.

I seem to always be one step behind though. The next few months could make or break my chances with him. He deserves to know the truth, to understand my explanation. How could he not know already? How could he not know? I suppose he is her pawn in this game of cat and mouse. Tomorrow I will fix this. I have to."

There was that name again—Jorge. Dillon crept out of bed and quietly turned the knob on his bedroom door. The house appeared to be undisturbed, and there was no evidence that his mother was up or even awake for that matter. He sat himself down on the floor by the cabinet that held all the pictures and memorabilia he and Roberta had looked through a few days back. He remembered spotting a couple of books that Roberta didn't offer to let him to look through. He prayed that something useful garnished their pages. Dillon quickly reached for a light blue book that was covered in satin and had old-fashioned gold spirals woven through the bindings.

"A baby book," Dillon thought.

Slowly, but eagerly, Dillon opened the book's front cover, and revealed the introductory page. "Jorge Alvin Grapler, born to Charlie and Roberta Grapler on this day, February 11, 1979."

A small picture of a little baby swaddled in a mint green blanket accompanied the announcement. The book fell out of Dillon's hands. The pit of his stomach tightened. Panic overcame his confused mind. If he wasn't Dillon Jorge Grapler, then who was he? Was his name even Dillon? Who was Jorge? The differences between himself and Roberta traipsed back into his thoughts. Why were he and Roberta so different? Why were there no commonalties? He remembered how cold she was to him in the beginning and how cold she occasionally still was. The soup incident, the cabin, the journal, Charlie, the little white pills, the police ... there were too many topics splashing around in his head for there to be a sense of understanding for any one of them.

"Where do I go from here?" he thought in a panic. "Where do I go from here?"

There was only one person he felt he could turn to; there was only one person he knew besides Roberta, and that was Sam. For some reason he trusted her. He wasn't sure how their brief interaction constituted or justified a level of trust, but it was there regardless. After all, choices and options were few and far between. With everything back in its place, except the light blue book, Dillon closed the cabinet door and returned to his bed. Frantically, he opened his father's ... or Charlie's journal, to where he had left off.

"I returned from work today to find Roberta frantically tearing my shirts out of my dresser drawer and scattering them all over the bedroom floor. She had found a small velvet box with a silver chain inside. There was a small but beautiful teardrop-shaped emerald dangling from the chain. I could barely make out what she was saying. There was no reasoning with her. I told her over and over again that it was a gift for her, a gesture of love. She wouldn't accept it. She didn't believe me. She swore it was for one of my 'whores' as she refers to the imaginary mistresses she's convinced I have. She screamed so loudly, I don't even know if she actually heard my words of explanation. My capacity for tolerance is shrinking right along with her sense of rationalization. I had to raise my voice louder and louder to be heard over her screeching. Jorge was in his room, as usual. He surely heard the destructive words exchanged between us. So, here I am, back in my serenity. Back where the only sounds heard are those from the crickets and the birds. I sit here wondering what my son is thinking of me. Roberta is poisoning his mind with ideas that I am a bad man and an even worse father.

I called Dr. Bombay today. She welcomed my request to meet with her. I am counting on her for my salvation, and for the salvation of Roberta and Jorge."

CHAPTER 35

▼

Jag pulled a thick stack of documents from Dillon's desk and leaned back in the leather chair to try to make heads or tails of it. There were several columns starting with an exhausting list of countries, all recorded vertically and in alphabetical order. Then horizontally, the titles "date of withdrawal," "amount of withdrawal," "routing number," "account number," "dollar amount," and "point of contact." "You're going down, Dillon," Jag said to himself. He continued his research and pulled out any piece of information that he deemed important: bank statements, investment portfolios, bonds, and the names and numbers of Dillon's so-called business associates. It really wasn't all that important for Jag to understand all points of interest in the crimes Dillon had committed, just so long as the evidence made it to the police station one way or the other. Accompanying the documents was an envelope marked "private." It contained a passport, a driver's license, and a credit card, all bearing the name Danny Wellington.

While storing the documents in an inconspicuous place, he heard the sound of Lanie's Lexus as she pulled into the driveway—his driveway. Excitement surged through his body. He had gathered enough evidence against his brother, at least for today, and Lanie would be his reward. She popped her head in the door and smiled as she held up a large brown bag.

"I stopped by that little Greek restaurant you like so well. Let's see …," she said as she poked around in the bag, clearly toying with him.

"We have favas, your favorite. And, of course, we can't have favas without vassilopita."

She stood there holding the bread up and waiting for a response. He wasn't sure what all that Greek talk translated to, but he knew enough to know that he was hungry.

"Great! I'm famished," he said as he slowly got up from the leather chair and walked over to the map he had wondered about so many times.

"What do all of these pushpins represent?" he asked.

"Oh, they represent the countries we have provided aid to. You don't remember the details of the humanitarian work you're involved in?"

"Not really. I feel a familiar vibe from just being in this office; I just can't remember specifics," Jag said, deceitfully.

"Were you able to recall any memories from the files you went through?"

"Well, not really, at least not to the extent I wanted to," he said.

"So, international aid. What is that all about?" Jag asked, knowing she was probably just as clueless to the truth as he was.

"It is so bizarre that you are a stranger to our life. I guess I now understand why you aren't in a hurry to get back to your life. I was worried you had lost your ambition, but in actuality you have just lost your memory of having ambition. Dang, I wish you would have been able to get in with the doctor today. It worries me waiting even another second."

By this time, Jag knew any differences Lanie may have noticed between the old and the new Dillon were obsolete. He could feel one hundred percent confident in her belief that he was who he said he was. After all, without knowledge of Dillon even having a twin, she would never even think to suspect.

"Angel, I think I want to go to the doctor by myself tomorrow. I have been relying on you for so long now. I think it's finally my turn to carry some of the burden of my healing process."

"I want to go with you, Dillon. It's important for me to hear what the doctor has to say. I want to know what I can do to help you regain your memory," she said.

"I will fill you in. It's embarrassing enough as it is. I feel inadequate, like I'm no longer the man of the house. I need to feel competent again, and this is the best place I know to start. Just let me do this on my own. I need to do this on my own," Jag pleaded. "I am sure you have things to do tomorrow anyway," he continued.

"Just the same old stuff, more research. It doesn't *have* to be done tomorrow, but I suppose it can be if you don't want me to be with you."

"It's not that I don't want to be with you, it's just that I don't want you to keep putting your life on hold for me. It's not right."

Lanie gave up the battle of words and agreed to let him do this on his own. However, she would have loved to be there.

Jag soon discovered that their gourmet meal was nothing more than soup and bread, and although it was a much simpler meal than its name implied, his taste buds thanked him. He and Lanie spent their time together talking about the international aid relief work the couple was involved in. Lanie explained her roll: researching needy countries, deciding what they most desperately needed, determining quantities, and then assembling informative presentations. Jag learned that Dillon supposedly coordinated funding, arranged for shipments of the humanitarian aid, and handled the logistics involved in the exporting of goods.

"Do you ever go to the shipping docks and check the supplies going out, or supervise the packaging, or even just do random inspections?" Jag asked.

"No, we have people that do that. Actually, you are one of them. Why?"

"I am just trying to get the process straight in my head. This is a lot to take in. It helps me to visualize the process. Maybe sometime you can take me to one of the shipping ports or warehouses?"

"Sure, hon. Why don't we see what the doctor has to say first. We don't want to overload you with information. He may recommend hypnosis techniques that will help recapture your memories. Hey, that could be a possibility, hypnosis. I wonder if Dr. Hernandez is going to consider that?" Lanie thought aloud as Jag concentrated on the next day's events.

"Let the embezzlement begin," he thought to himself.

CHAPTER 36

▼

Charlie Grapler's personnel file didn't impress detectives Whitaker and Chase. His history didn't show anything out of the ordinary. He'd taken a day or two off here and there, but nothing habitual. His evaluations were outstanding; he received regular raises; and the days Roberta claimed Charlie had gone AWOL didn't necessarily coincide with the days he'd missed work. Their next stop was Ken's house.

Ken had spent his time off conducting his own form of investigation. It seemed as if no one knew anything. Charlie was last seen at work, climbing into his truck to go home for the day. He stopped for gas at the local Chevron and then went on his way. That was the only known trail. Only a few short miles separated the Chevron station and Charlie's home, and the chances of something bad happening to him during that short drive bordered slim to none. No one had seen anything, there were no accidents reported, and no out-of-the-ordinary commotion was detected. Ken concluded that between Charlie's arrival home on Friday evening and the time he was due back at work on Monday morning he'd gotten into some trouble at the home front.

As Ken pondered his thoughts on the matter, he eagerly awaited a visit from the two detectives assigned to the case. He hoped they would have some information to share that would help shed some light on the disappearance of his good friend. Shortly after a feast of spicy ribs and garlic-mashed potatoes, Ken and Carla each grabbed a beer and sat down on their small front porch to wait for the detectives. The full moon beamed like a spotlight. They covered themselves with a light throw blanket as their one beer turned into two. Eventually, an unmarked police car pulled up their gravel drive. The couple stood as the officers approached. "Evening, detectives," Ken said.

"Evening," Detective Whitaker replied as Detective Chase bowed his head in salutation.

They entered the house and sat at the dinner table. Carla served the detectives lemonade.

"So, for the record Ken, you don't remember Charlie ever before leaving Roberta for several days, or even weeks, at a time?" Detective Whitaker clarified.

"That is correct. He would stay with us on occasion when he and Roberta fought. He never really spoke about the root of the arguments, but would basically say 'she was at it again' and that he wanted company. I never really pried. Sometimes he would share more than other times. I kept the ball in his court in terms of that."

"What is the maximum time Charlie ever stayed consecutively?" Detective Chase asked.

"I would say two days maximum, but it was usually only one," Carla answered.

"What do you think 'she was at it again' meant?" Detective Chase continued.

"Just that she was yelling a lot. She was always upset with him about something."

"Do you think Charlie would ever hit Roberta out of frustration?" Whitaker asked.

"No way. Charlie doesn't have it in him. He is considered a gentle giant in my book," Ken quickly stated.

"You guys were pretty close then?" Whitaker asked.

"Yes, we have been for years," Ken noted.

"Do you think you know him better than anyone?" Detective Whitaker inquired.

"There is no doubt in my mind," Ken replied.

"Why do you think it is that Charlie never told you the specific details of their arguments?" Detective Whitaker asked, as he readied to write something in his notebook.

"Well, he was a private person. He didn't like to burden others with his troubles. He felt it was his responsibility to handle situations on his own," Ken replied with conviction.

"Then do you think it is possible that he could have been physical with Roberta?" Detective Chase intervened.

"Why are you two so interested in this topic? We're supposed to be trying to find him, not looking for a reason to crucify him if we do," Ken said in a raised tone.

"We *are* trying to find him, but despite our efforts, no one seems to know anything. There have been no sightings, no leads, and nothing from the public. I am just trying to establish if there was a motive for Roberta to commit a crime. I'm trying to piece the scenario together in my head," Detective Whitaker said. "Roberta's accusation that Charlie apparently takes off frequently, even though we have no evidence to support it, does not seem reason enough for Roberta to attempt foul play."

"I think it would have been out of character for Charlie to abuse Roberta, but like I said, he was a private person. I guess you can interpret that statement anyway that you want to, but I have never seen a violent side to Charlie in all of the years that I have known him," Ken proclaimed.

"Apparently, Roberta told one of our officers, Officer O'Mally, that Charlie was abusive and that he drank a lot," Detective Chase claimed.

"He would have a drink or two with me now and then, but a drunk? I haven't seen it. He's no alcoholic. He is a reliable and hard worker and is always on time. Those traits don't describe a man with a monkey on his back," Ken responded, emphatically.

"I am just telling you what she said. She claims she is quite the victim," Detective Chase added.

"When I see proof, and only when I see proof, I will believe it. Until then, Charlie is still the same old Charlie I have known and respected for years. He is considered part of my family, and I find it extremely difficult to take the word of Roberta when it contradicts everything I believe."

"What do you know about Jorge, their son?" Detective Whitaker asked.

"Well, not a lot. Charlie loved him, but never seemed to be able to relate to him all that well. I am not sure why. I am sure it has something to do with his wife," Ken replied.

"How well do you know Roberta?" Detective Chase inquired.

"Well, I don't really, not all that much. I just know what Charlie has told me. I did talk to her a couple of weeks ago when I was concerned about Charlie not coming to work. She was extremely defensive about the whole situation, not at all poised or pleasant. She seems pretty callous," Ken said.

"So, you only talked to her the one time. Everything else you know about her, and about them as a couple, is based on Charlie's words," Detective Chase clarified.

"Well, yes, but I have known him for years. I know his character," Ken replied.

"I am not trying to discredit him, Ken. I just need all the facts to be put into perspective so I can conduct this investigation as fairly as possible. My instincts are on the same page as yours, but I still need to think rationally," Detective Chase persisted.

Ken understood where the detective was coming from, but he'd grown tired of the entire conversation. They obviously didn't know anymore than he did.

The detectives pulled out Charlie's attendance records and went over them as closely as possible. A couple of the days Roberta claimed that Charlie had gone missing were possibly spent at Ken's house. Ken didn't remember exact dates, but knew it was around New Year's. Ken clearly remembered inviting Charlie to a New Year's Eve party, which the man had passed on. The detectives were able to determine that Charlie had attended work regularly even if he hadn't spent the night with Roberta.

"It's possible that Charlie was having an affair," Detective Whitaker pointed out.

"It seems as though you are just trying to create a motive, and you're smearing Charlie's good name in the process. Charlie abusing Roberta? Sleeping around on her? Being an alcoholic? All of those ideas are completely ridiculous!" Ken exclaimed.

"Ken, try to look at this objectively. The only way I can get to the bottom of this is to believe everyone and take it all with a grain of salt," Detective Whitaker defended.

"I am finished for tonight, Detectives," Ken plainly said. He wanted to talk to Roberta himself.

The next morning, detectives Chase and Whitaker planned another trip to Roberta's house. They wanted to talk with both her and Jorge. Officer O'Mally would be accompanying them this time in hopes of lowering the woman's defensive walls just a bit. Their investigation was slowly burning out. In reality it had never even been lit. Charlie had been gone for more than two weeks and no one had heard from him. A grown man just doesn't disappear, unless he didn't want to be found. That didn't seem logical in this case. Something was off. Either Charlie escaped from Roberta or Roberta escaped from Charlie. Detective Whitaker closed his notepad.

CHAPTER 37

▼

It was around 8:30 AM when Sam heard a knock at her door. She peeked out from behind her curtains.

"Dillon? Hi there … uh, come on in."

Roberta was the only person who ever stopped by since Sam had arrived in Emmett, so seeing Dillon standing at her door evoked a smile. However, her level of alertness remained high, and she wondered what he could possibly want. Dillon walked in and Sam quickly became mortified as she watched him looking around her house. A half-empty pizza box covered her coffee table, crumpled-up paper littered the carpeted living area, and several crushed beer cans gave her usually clean home an overall messy appearance. Staleness thickened the air.

"You all right, Sam?" he asked, concerned.

She led him into her kitchen and they sat at the small dinner table.

"Oh, gosh. I apologize for the mess, I usually keep my house clean and comfortable. I have just been up for what seems like days working on my novel. I got myself on a roll and haven't been able to stop."

She sported a navy blue robe with the letter "S" embroidered on the lapel. A loosely crafted bun held her greasy brown hair. With embarrassment she pulled her robe closed a little tighter. "Once you conquer writer's block, you can't take your time for granted. You must write, write, write, until the writer's block inevitably returns again."

Lies flew from her lips too easily these days. Charlie's murder was the real reason disarray had plagued her life. Her partly written novel had sat untouched since she saw the first newscast on the disappearance of Charlie Grapler. She had irrationally, and somewhat unintentionally, locked herself inside her house hoping to somehow make it all go away. It all needed to vanish, just as Charlie had.

"Well, I hate to bother you then, but can you spare a few moments? It's really important," Dillon asked, humbly. She couldn't help but notice his biceps bulging from beneath his muscle shirt. She secretly caught a whiff of his sweet cologne, and it reminded her of a chocolate dessert dazzled with berries. She didn't dare ask him what it was.

"Do you know my dad?"

Sam needed a distraction, not a reminder, and she felt like an idiot for not expecting this topic to come up. After all, this was Charlie's son. The last thing she wanted to do was talk about the one person she was trying so hard to forget.

"I don't really know him. I've spoken with him a few times in passing, but I've never had an engrossing conversation with him," she responded.

"Have you ever witnessed any interactions between him and Roberta?"

"Well …" she paused, "I guess I haven't. Roberta never really talks to him when I'm there. I guess that isn't all that strange though. She does hate the man after all," Sam said.

"Has Roberta ever mentioned if my dad ever hits her?"

"Yes, all the time. She says he's abusive in many different ways. She said that he yells and screams at her, calls her bad names, and hits her. She says he drinks a lot, too. According to your mother, your father is an all-around imbecile."

"Have you actually witnessed any of this, or have you just heard it from Roberta?"

"I heard it from Roberta. She showed me a couple of bruises though, and she's given me detailed descriptions of how he gave them to her. I remember one time he sliced her arm pretty deep in order to keep her from going into town. Why are you wanting to know all of this now, Dillon?" she asked curiously.

"He's hitting too close to home," Sam thought. "Does he know something? Is he suspicious of me? What has Roberta told him?" she wondered.

Several questions raced through Sam's mind. She remained hysterical on the inside, while managing to appear calm and cool on the outside. Dillon didn't answer her question, but instead continued on with his own.

"When we first met, you called me Jorge. Why? Do you know a Jorge? Does Roberta know a Jorge?"

"I am not really sure why I called you Jorge. I honestly thought that was your name. I'm pretty sure that's how Roberta referred to you during our conversations, but I must have gotten it wrong."

"What did she used to say about me?" Dillon asked.

"All good things; she always raved about how amazing you were. She said it was you two against the world."

"Did she ever say anything bad?" Dillon continued.

"Not that I can remember, no."

Dillon just sat quiet for a moment.

Sam didn't say anything to him; she waited patiently, appreciating the silence. She tapped her feet in an attempt to maintain her game face. She prayed to God that she appeared normal. She watched him place what appeared to be a baby book onto her table. She looked puzzled. "What is it?" she asked.

"Open it up, just to the first page, and tell me what you see," Dillon said.

Sam turned the cover back. "Is it yours?" she asked just as she noticed the name.

"I don't get it. Jorge Alvin Grapler? Is that you?"

"No, I don't think it is. I don't know. I am confused. I hoped you could shed some light on it. You are the only one I know here, so I am hoping I can trust you to try and help me make sense of this. Something is off, way off," Dillon said.

"I don't quite know what I can do to help," Sam replied.

"You could talk with her. Not as if you suspect wrongdoing, but as a friend just making conversation," Dillon suggested.

"Well, Roberta isn't the easiest woman to talk to unless it is a topic she chooses. I hate to say this, but I am not all that fond of her these days. It's not that I don't like your mother, Dillon, it's just that she has turned out to be a woman I wouldn't normally socialize with."

"Well, I have to agree with you there. I may not remember who I am or how I got here, but the one thing I do know is that I am nothing like her."

Sam teetered on her decision to commit to helping Dillon. She was already in over her head, and she didn't need this added headache. But then again, maybe this could help resolve her guilt-stricken conscience. In addition, Sam felt that she needed to know the truth about Charlie. Had she helped Roberta in vain, or was it all for the good of the cause? Was Roberta the victim or the victimizer?

As Sam contemplated her decision, Dillon continued to speak.

"There is a cabin out in the woods behind our house that my dad apparently used to spend time in. I discovered it yesterday when I was out clearing my head."

"Roberta never mentioned anything about a cabin," Sam said.

"I found his journal, and to me it sounds like Roberta was the hateful one, not Charlie." Sam reached for her squared, black-rimmed glasses and turned to the page Dillon had marked for her.

"My eyes cry silently tonight for there are no more tears within me to shed. I confronted Roberta about her ridiculous and crude behavior, and she responded with hateful words and a harsh slap. To her, my intentions are those of a man seeking to collaborate with Satan himself. She is blind to my wanting the best for her, blind to the concept of dealing with the bad before you can benefit from the good. I am going to stay at Ken's tonight to get away from her and this place. I need to lay my head in a place that is filled with happiness and the warmth of a relationship that is real and consistent. While my wife has caused our relationship to regress into an engulfed hell, Ken's marriage has blossomed and grown, moving forward each day. The positive energy of their house seems to soothe my thoughts of aggression. One day, I hope to be happy again. One day, I will not have to deal with Roberta. I hate myself for saying that, but I also fear the alternative."

Sam lifted her head slightly, although not high enough to make eye contact with Dillon. Unable to speak, she was revolted by what was going through her mind at warp speed: the grave, the body, the thick pool of human waste, the stench of death, and Roberta's facial expression as she coolly stood at her husband's feet on the day of his demise. Sam thought about the splattered blood on the doorframe in the kitchen, the feel of Charlie's dead body in her hands, the gun laying on the counter, and all of the stories Roberta had told about Charlie and how he mistreated her regularly. The worst, however, was Charlie's expanded stare as he lay there damaged beyond repair. The memories played in her mind over and over, faster and faster. Sam pushed herself away from the table and darted toward the hallway. The bathroom door slammed behind her, and she began heaving into the toilet. Vomit exploded from her three or four times. Dry heaving followed. The memories of her actions haunted her.

"Sam?" Dillon called and waited for a response. "Sam? Are you all right in there?"

She managed to respond, "Yes, I'm fine. I've been a little under the weather lately. I just have a touch of the flu," she hollered convincingly through the door. "I'll be out in a minute." She brushed her teeth twice, hoping to disguise the odor of regurgitated food.

When she returned, she apologized, took a deep breath, and closed the journal.

Dillon put his hand on hers. "Sam, I need you. I need a friend to help me. I have so much going on right now, I just want to break down and run. I don't know who I am or even what my name is. My mother tells me that my father is horrible, but this journal tells me that my father is the exact opposite of horrible. Meanwhile, he is missing and the police are trying to find him. It's just too much for one man to take. For some reason, I trust you and feel connected to you. I can't do this alone; I can't figure it all out without help. Will you help me, Sam?"

She couldn't disappoint him the way she had disappointed herself. She would fix this; she had to. Before it was all over, she hoped to learn that her good deed was in fact just that, a good deed.

"I will help you, Dillon. I don't know what exactly I can do, but we can figure this out together."

"Who's Jorge?" she thought quietly to herself. "And where have I heard that name?"

CHAPTER 38

─────────── ▼ ───────────

"Dillon Andresen?"

Jag's fake name was finally called after a thirty-minute wait in the busy reception area. A large woman dressed in all white escorted Dillon into the examining room, where he was sure he would wait another thirty minutes before he was able to see his doctor face-to-face. Jag didn't even want to be there, but he had to continue to play the part of the wounded husband. Arousing suspicion in Lanie was not an option. Soon, she would be with him living it up somewhere far away, just the two of them, for the rest of their lives. Well, the two of them and Mama, he remembered.

The nurse took his vitals and asked the usual questions: "Are you taking any medications? Do you have any allergies? How much do you weigh?"

Another fifteen minutes passed before Dr. Hernandez knocked once and entered the small, sterile room.

"Well, hello there, Dillon. How have you been? Have you completed all of your postoperative appointments?"

"Yes doc. I'm feeling much better. I just recently got that annoying cast off and my Angel has been taking great care of me."

Dr. Hernandez took a quick look at Jag's injuries and nodded his head in approval.

"It looks like you are close to being back to your old self, except for your memory, I hear. Mrs. Andresen said you don't remember a lot of your life's particulars?"

"Nope, I just don't recall facts that are vital to my life. Take work for example. I can't remember my position at the bank. I don't remember my boss's name or even how to do my job," Jag answered.

"Does your job seem to be the center of your memory loss or are there other aspects of your life you can't connect with?" The doctor asked.

"It is a lot of different things."

"Do you get headaches?"

He didn't know how to correctly answer that question.

"Occasionally," he said.

"Can you remember recent information about topics that occurred after your accident?"

"Yes, all the things I have experienced since I was discharged from the hospital have stuck with me," Jag responded.

"I am pretty sure it is not a physical issue we are dealing with here, but rather a psychological one. I am, however, going to order another series of tests to back up that assumption before I make any definitive decisions. Once the tests are conclusive, I will most likely refer you to a psychologist who specializes in the effects of posttraumatic stress."

It irritated Jag that waiting to be seen took about five times longer than the actual appointment itself. After all, he had places to go and money to steal. He was relieved that the appointment was finally over. Next stop, Plantains Bank Plus, Dillon's one and only, his mistress.

Jag parked the rented Mercedes in the exact location where the kidnapping had taken place all those weeks ago. The plan that began playing out in the very spot he now stood seemed to be unfolding like clockwork. Dillon now lived many, many miles away, while Jag was content to stay right here and live out his new life. The tables had turned just the way Jag and his mama had anticipated. He was now assuming his brother's identity, living in his house, sleeping with his lovely bride, and about to withdraw a lot of his so-called, hard-earned money. With a grin of satisfaction, Jag sauntered into the double doors with confidence and a bit of arrogance. As he entered the building a few people waved and he cordially smiled in return before they all returned their eyes to their individual tasks. A slight bustling of papers whispered into his ears as he continued his walk. Everyone appeared busy and Jag was glad for the lack of attention. He figured Dillon must have been one major ass for his co-workers to be so unconcerned about his well-being. His eyes roamed the room. His pulse accelerated. Jag continued his approach to the withdrawal window.

A short, chubby man dressed in a blue pin-striped suit stopped him short of the window and shook his hand. Jag couldn't help but notice that the man's extremely thin hair was wrapped more than once around his balding head.

"Glad to see you up and around, Dillon. We need you around here, when are you coming back?"

Jag had no idea who the loud-spoken man even was, but he replied as if he did.

"Oh, I'm not quite sure. I am still having some medical concerns, but thanks for asking."

"Come on Dillon; my pocketbook needs you. You manage to work the numbers like no one can. The shareholders are getting antsy. Come on back to my office."

The short, overbearing man escorted Jag to a rather large office with glass for walls. It gave the impression that he didn't quite trust those who worked for him. The nameplate on his desk read Cart Henry.

"What kind of a name is that," Jag thought to himself.

"I really don't have a lot of time," Jag said, as they sat down around the oak desk.

"Are you aware that your convalescent leave is up in less than three weeks?" Mr. Henry asked.

"Yes, I'm aware of that. I'm doing all I can to get better, truly. Upon my return, I want to be the asset I always was, and I will be. Just be patient Mr. Henry."

"Mr. Henry?" Cart looked taken aback.

"Lanie stopped by yesterday afternoon and told me about your memory problem. I am concerned to say the least, Dillon. You have been out of commission for too long, and I need to know if you are going to be able to get back in the saddle again. I am very sorry about your condition. Really, I am. But you know, or at least you used to know, the importance of consistency and reliability in our business. People need to trust where their money is, and trust who is investing it. In many cases, you are the one people call upon for assurance and advice."

Jag grew tired of all this business talk; he just wanted to withdraw the money and be done with it already. Clearly Cart and Dillon were both all about business and nothing else.

"I assure you Mr. Henry, I will be back to my old self again in a couple of weeks. I'll be back before my convalescent leave runs out, I promise," Jag pledged.

"All right, I will hold you to that," Cart responded.

Cart Henry was pretty high up on the food chain at Plantains Bank Plus. He played the role of leader to many, but to Dillon he was also a strong and invaluable mentor. They had a fabulous cutthroat relationship in the business world, and they shared similar tactics and values. Their motto was, "Money makes the world go round, and without it you're just standing still."

"So, why did you come here if not to indulge in witty banter?" Cart asked.

"Actually, I was hoping to withdraw some money from my account."

"Oh?" Mr. Henry asked as he raised his eyebrows.

"Yes, I have come across some property I want to invest in," Jag responded with fake enthusiasm.

"Really, where is it?"

"I hate to cut you short, but Lanie is waiting on me, and I just have this last errand to take care of before I can get home to her."

"You really are sick, putting your personal life before business. Take two and call me when your head is on straight," Cart kidded.

They both chuckled as if this fat man was somehow clever. It made Jag sick, but he played the game.

"This is a surprise for Lanie, so it is just between us," Jag said, as he finally managed to walk away. He marched directly to the teller's window. The agent's dimples stood at attention.

"Can you give me my checking and savings balances please, Sonya?" Jag said with a smile, noticing her nameplate.

Her smile dropped. "Oh, all right, Dillon. I guess we will get right down to business. No problem."

Jag assumed he offended her by his lack of small chat. She and Dillon must have been good friends. Or maybe more. Jag wondered.

After a few moments, she slid a piece of paper across the counter to him. Jag practically lost his balance when he saw the amounts she had written down. He discreetly regained his composure as sweat beaded up in his palms. It was just like the night he and Lanie had made love for the first time. He was in deep and had to remain strong and confident. This job his mama had sent him on was going to make him the man he'd always wanted to be.

"I have a couple of transactions I need to have taken care of. First, I would like to withdraw seventy-five thousand dollars from my savings account. There is this great house I am going to be investing in, and I gotta jump while the market is hot."

Jag had no idea if the market was anything, but he had heard the term so many times it just sounded appropriate.

"Do you want me to just wire the money into the seller's account for you?" Sonya asked.

"Nah, it's chump change. I'll just hand carry it. I'll make more of an impression that way. We'll leave the wiring for the big bucks," Jag said hoping he'd come across the way he wanted to—nonchalant and overly cocky. It was surely the way Dillon would have handled it.

"It may take a few moments for us to get that much money counted and packaged for you," she said. She walked over and conveyed the instructions to a stumpy-looking co-worker, and returned shortly thereafter.

"What is your second request, Dillon?"

"I would like to change my online personal identification number. I like to do it every quarter or so," he said casually, "but the problem is that I can't remember the old one, and I can't remember the answers to the secret questions I set up with the account. This accident has just done a number on me."

After about twenty minutes, his banking transactions were complete, and he was on his way back to the car. He felt like he was about ready to explode from excitement and nervousness. He was accompanied by the bank's security guard, an older woman who seemed to have aged well before her time.

"Thank you, ma'am," he said respectfully.

She was obviously no strong arm, and he surely didn't want to be around if the place ever got robbed. She nodded and said he was welcome before she walked away.

He did it! He'd pulled it off. He not only had seventy-five thousand dollars of Dillon's cash, but also an all-access ticket to Dillon's accounts. It wouldn't be long now. All he needed was time and that incriminating evidence that would close the deal.

"Yes!" he screamed, as he turned sharp out of the parking lot and onto the very street he had driven so many times before. Jag's hands clutched the leather steering wheel as he wove in and out of the light traffic. Empowerment surged within him as Def Leopard screamed from his eight-speaker sound system. With his window lowered, he belted out every word of "Pour Some Sugar On Me." No longer would he be the pathetic son his father had been embarrassed of or the scared little boy his mama had enjoyed feeling sorry for. He was officially Jag, a boy who'd transformed himself into a man that they could all feel proud of. He was now a man with money, a man with stature, a man with the world in the palm of his hands, and most importantly, a man with Angel by his side forevermore.

CHAPTER 39

▼

When Detective Chase and Detective Whitaker showed up at Roberta's home, she really had no choice but to let them in. The only reason she allowed it was because they'd promised her that Officer O'Mally would accompany them. Sure enough, the slender young officer entered behind the detectives. O'Mally was about five foot nine inches tall with stick-straight black hair. Charm and innocence dripped from his expression, just like it did from her son Jorge's. A freshly-pressed uniform complimented his healthy physique. Roberta smiled at him and instructed each of them to have a seat on the sofa.

"Did ya tell them about all the times we talked? All those times I told ya Charlie had left? Nobody wants to believe me. You're the only person who knows. Did you tell them?" Roberta asked Officer O'Mally.

"I did, Mrs. Grapler. I told them everything I could remember," O'Mally said.

The detectives continued their questioning and heard a lot of the same statements as before. They felt as though they just kept running into the same brick wall. There was no concrete proof to back up any of what Roberta claimed, but there was also no proof to discredit it. She left no trail either way.

"We are going to need to speak with your son now, Mrs. Grapler. It is Jorge, right?"

She wasn't going to even address it. She was furious with herself for even mentioning the name Dillon all those days before.

"It ain't a good idea to talk with my son. He ain't been doing good lately, ain't been feeling well. With that and his father missing, well, you can understand, can't ya?"

"Your son is sick? What is the matter with him?" Detective Whitaker asked.

"I may as well just fill ya in 'cause I know you ain't gonna leave without prying in our business anyway! He disappeared a little over a year ago. He and Charlie had a pretty big fight about responsibilities and stuff like that. Anyway, they got into it, and Jorge split. A couple of weeks ago, I got a call from him. He was all confused acting. Didn't know who he was. For some reason our phone number was scratched on a piece of paper inside his wallet and so he called it. I picked him up and he has been here ever since. But he don't remember nothing prior to me picking him up," Roberta said with concern.

"Why haven't you mentioned this before?" Detective Whitaker asked angrily.

"It ain't got nothing to do with nothing."

"Jorge just happens to call you within the same time period that Charlie turns up missing. He can't remember anything, and you don't think there could be a connection? Come on now, even you ain't that ...," he stopped his sentence before speaking the obvious.

"Like I said before, Charlie ain't missing! He left, just like he always does, just like he will continue to do when he gets back. It's just how he is. Damn it, you guys got rocks in your heads or something? I can't make myself no clearer!"

"Why don't you have Jorge come on out so we can speak with him?" Detective Whitaker insisted.

"My son ain't here! He's finally coming to terms with everything and you guys are just gonna make it worse," she argued. "Back off!"

"We are going to have to talk to him one way or the other, so either let us know when he'll be back, or we can summon him to the station. It's your choice."

"You ain't scaring me! Why are you letting them talk to me this way, O'Mally? I thought you was on my side. I thought you was the one I could count on to stand up for me. You do believe me, right O'Mally? You believe I'm innocent and so is my son, right?"

O'Mally just stood there, possibly tongue-tied.

"Right?" she repeated.

"I believe you, Mrs. Grapler. I believe you."

It just seemed like the right thing to say. Her angry eyes softened. She smiled and offered O'Mally some lemonade. She returned with an ice-cold beverage for the officer, and glared rudely at the two detectives as she handed O'Mally the glass. O'Mally thanked her and kindly asked if she would allow him to interview her son.

She thought about it, "All right, Officer O'Mally. I trust ya, just you though, no one else! I mean it. He ain't been doing well and I won't allow you two," she said pointing directly to Chase and Whitaker, "to hurt him or trick him or whatever y'all may do. I can make this really easy for ya or really difficult, so it's O'Mally or the runaround!"

The detectives had had their fill of the crazy bat for the day, and they were ready to just get out of there as quickly as they could.

"Fine Mrs. Grapler, O'Mally can do the questioning. Name the time and place and we will accommodate you and your son."

"Fine, you can just come over the day after tomorrow at around 10:00 AM. He'll be here to tell O'Mally exactly what I've told ya!"

Chase smoothed out his brown slacks and his tailored dress shirt as he headed for the front door. "Thank you for your time, Mrs. Grapler," he said.

CHAPTER 40

▼

Sam looked at herself in the oval mirror as she placed the baseball cap on her head. She realized that she could no longer be proud of the person she saw staring back at her. With a desperate need for redemption, she sternly grabbed her keys and left to meet Dillon by the big rock a mile inside his property. Today, they would start their own investigation into who Charlie really was, and whether or not Roberta's depiction of him was true or make-believe. Sam desperately needed to know the truth. Dillon was already leaning against the smooth rock as she approached.

"Thanks for coming, Sam. It means a lot."

"No problem," she replied as she removed her jacket and the two began their hike to Charlie's cabin. Her stomach ached from guilt as she pressed on silently. She wondered if he noticed her behavior, but she definitely didn't want him to ask her about it.

Dillon opened the door for Sam. "This is the place. I think this is the place he refers to as his place of serenity. The place he feels safe and at peace." He pulled a chair out for her at the desk.

"I read another entry from his journal last night. I think you will find it interesting," Dillon said as he handed her the book.

"Well, the day I had been looking forward to finally arrived. Dr. Bombay agreed to help. I thought I would be jumping for joy, having a celebration. But instead I feel a sense of guilt. It is like Roberta is in my head telling me how I need to feel, what I need to do. I almost feel that she has the ability to erase my own sense of logic and replace it with her brainwashing words. We have been together for so many years, what will it be like with her out of the picture? How will Jorge react to it all? I think he is too vulnerable to handle it. I think I will give it more time ... a month or two, maybe, and see how I can connect with him between now and then. I am his father after all. Surely a part of him is filled with logic and a sense of compassion, even when it comes to me. Maybe I can bring him here, to my safe haven ... no, bad idea."

"So, what do you think?" Dillon asked.

Slowly, Sam closed the journal.

"I think we need to find Dr. Bombay. Surely, he or she can shed some light on this. Just play the part of Roberta's scared son, and let the doctor do the talking. In my experience, when you want to know something, it's best to not say much at all and let the other person spill."

"There is no way. Doctor-patient confidentiality will keep the doctor from revealing information," Dillon said.

"What about if we tell the doctor about Charlie's disappearance? In some cases, breaching the confidence is allowed, and actually expected, in order to protect someone who could be in danger," Sam replied.

"If a doctor does breach, they chance losing their license if they're wrong. It's all very iffy. I think our best bet is to talk with Ken, the co-worker he mentioned."

They began their walk through the cabin. A comfortable temperature maintained a coziness within its walls.

"See Sam, there is coffee in the coffeemaker, a full gallon of milk in the fridge, and a sink full of water. This does not look like the home of someone who would just take off. He had every intention of returning. I think something unfortunate has happened."

Disgust captured her already upset stomach. She wanted to tell him about the murder, but she knew that it would only split her off from the investigation, and she felt that she needed to be a part of it. She knew she could help him with his search, more so than others. She had connections. After all, up until just a few months back she had been a big-time reporter. She could still get phone records and information not meant for public viewing; she could even tap into her sources. If she could do nothing else for Dillon, she at least wanted to help him find the answers he sought.

The quiet little cabin contained a gold mine of information. There were scrapbooks of articles about Charlie's many construction jobs, pictures from work picnics, and certificates of achievement. Charlie's friend Ken graced many of the photos, only proving how close they were. They often posed together in front of forklifts and newly constructed buildings. Finally, Dillon felt like he was getting to know his father. He sensed a warmness about him. His eyes seemed honest and compassionate and his smile genuine. Dillon detected an obvious physical resemblance between himself and his father, and surprisingly, it touched his heart. He felt at home in the comfortable cabin and wished he could stay there instead of in the house with Roberta. Although happy that they were finding so much information, all references to a son only referred to a boy named Jorge. It didn't make sense, not to Dillon and not to Sam. They had spent most of their day exploring the well-maintained cabin, and they eventually agreed that it was time to return to their respective homes. Roberta could suspect nothing. Sam departed with a large to-do list weighing on her shoulders. It was time for her to deliver, and she had every intention of doing so.

When they arrived at the rock, Dillon rested on it. "Thanks for all your help, Sam. You are a true friend. I really feel like we are going to figure this out, just the two of us. It is all going to fall into place."

Sam stood there with a half smile. A constant feeling of betrayal cursed her well-intended heart. Dillon leaned in slowly and gently put his lips onto hers. Her plump lips briefly reciprocated before she pulled away. Their eyes met. He admired her, but said nothing.

"I have to get back now. I'll see ya in a few days," she blurted out.

She turned and ran toward her own safe haven. He watched her leaving, hoping she would look back, but she never did. As soon as her tall figure had disappeared, he started home himself.

"Where have you been?" Roberta asked rudely. She had on a skintight tube top, her green bra straps showing, and a pair of cutoff jean shorts. Her exposed thighs were freckled with small spider veins and a good dose of cellulite.

"I was just out walking like I always am. I can't stay in the house twenty-four, seven. Why do you ask?" he asked inquisitively.

"I was just getting a little worried about ya, son. We've got a lot of land you ain't familiar with, and most of it is overgrown. I don't want ya getting lost or hurt or something."

"Oh, I'll be fine. I'm sure I have been out there hundreds of times. It will come back to me sooner or later," he said with a devilish grin. He removed his red fleece pullover as he exited the kitchen.

CHAPTER 41

▼

With the entire house to himself, Jag had found a perfect opportunity to call his mama. All of his hard work would surely impress her, especially the thousands of dollars he'd already secured. After one and a half rings there was an unexpected voice at the other end of the line.

"Hello?"

Jag froze. He was unable to speak. He was furious that Dillon had answered the phone and apparently had free reign over the house, as if it were his own house. Jag slammed the phone into its holder.

Roberta entered the kitchen and noticed the bewildered look on Dillon's face. She was certain she knew who'd been on the other end of the line.

"Hmmm, wrong number I guess. They didn't say a word, just hung up," Dillon said.

"Probably one of your dad's buddies, there ain't a polite one in the bunch," Roberta said without skipping a beat.

Dillon looked at his mother and shrugged before exiting the kitchen. She quickly dialed Jorge's number in hopes that he would answer. He did.

"What, Dillon just hangs out as if he owns the place?" Jorge quipped.

A sense of betrayal filled Jorge. He was irritated that he'd been so easily replaced.

"Don't talk to me that way boy! You know the deal. He ain't got no memory," she whispered as she maintained alert eyes. "He thinks he lives here and that he's lived here all his life. What did you think I was gonna do, tie him up to a tree like a dog? Use your brain Jorgie. For once, use your brain."

Jag thought about what she was saying, and although he felt that her rude comment was uncalled for, he agreed with her logic.

"I know, Mama. You're right, it wouldn't make sense to treat him bad if he doesn't know anything."

"So, ya got news for your dear old mama?"

"I do. I have news and seventy-five thousand dollars."

"That's my boy. I knew you could do it. I knew you would be able to pull it off. You and me against the world, remember Jorge? You and me against the world."

"I remember Mama; I remember. I won't let you down. Not only did I get seventy-five thousand dollars, but I also got his PIN number and information about his stocks and bonds. I still have to figure out how to turn all that into money though. I remember what ya said. 'Cash only.' It all has to be untraceable."

"Yep, that part is very important. Just in case."

"Oh, Mama, I checked the remote control, I shut the cameras off and then turned it back on again. As far as I know the camera should be working."

"Oh, I got to hang up now, Mama. Lanie just pulled into the drive. I love ya, Mama."

"Love you too; bye now."

Roberta hung up the phone. She turned to find Dillon standing in the middle of the kitchen watching her. She jumped a bit, "Damn, you startled me. What's ya sneaking up on me for?"

"Who was that?" Dillon asked with true curiosity.

"Uh ... oh, just Sam. I called her to see how she's doing."

"Oh. So how is she doing?"

"Pretty good, I suppose. She's still writing some book."

On the outside, Dillon appeared casual, but on the inside he knew his mother was lying to him. Either that or Sam was playing him like a fiddle. However, for some reason, the latter just didn't seem plausible.

"I'm home," Lanie yelled. "Did you miss me?"

"Hi Angel, how was your day?"

"Good, I guess. Went to the library, stopped by the office for a bit, and then hit the yoga scene. How did your doctor's appointment go? I want to hear everything that happened, everything the doctor said."

"Well, he didn't really say anything new. I am apparently blocking out certain things, likely to give myself a mental break from the stress of life. He is going to run some more tests. If all is normal, which he is pretty sure it is, he wants me to see a shrink. I'm guessing that's to find out why I'm remembering some things and not others."

"So that's great. The doctor must believe your memory loss is all psychological."

With a smile she wrapped her arms around Jag's body.

"I have to go jump clean."

Jag knew that was her way of saying that she was going to take a shower, so he eagerly followed her up the stairs. Moments later their bodies were pressed together as the water danced around them. Their lips grazed one another's several times before beginning their long kiss. Her fingernails traveled aggressively along his strong biceps and down his back. Jag's craving intensified. His desires begged for more. Her body language insisted on taking it slow, and Jag cooperated despite his overwhelming urge to seize the moment. He decided to let her remain in control, at least for the remainder of their shower.

CHAPTER 42

$\blacktriangledown$

"… and I'll have the special, minus the mushrooms," O'Mally said as he closed his menu. "So, Roberta's son was just about as helpful as she was," he told detectives Whitaker and Chase. "They're both telling the same story. It turns out he did indeed contact his mother from a pay phone near a hospital in Bend, Oregon, exactly as Mrs. Grapler claimed. But then again, he's just going off of what his mother has told him. He doesn't actually remember. So, I did a little checking of my own. There is no record of him actually being treated at that hospital or at any of the neighboring ones. I did checks within a one-hundred-mile radius of where Roberta claims to have picked Jorge up, and there is no proof he ever set foot in that town. No police records, no telephone number registered to his name, not even a library card to speak of. Whatever he was doing during the past year remains a mystery," O'Mally said in frustration. "I also talked to Samantha Barker. She's the lady Mrs. Grapler claims she 'may have been with' the weekend Charlie disappeared. Samantha confirmed that she was with Roberta for a short while that Saturday. She dropped by the house to visit, they chatted a bit, and then she left. She said she didn't see or hear Charlie, and she didn't notice anything strange or unusual," O'Mally continued. "Sam was calm, nonchalant even. I didn't get the impression that she was covering anything up. She also said that she'd never actually witnessed any abuse between Roberta and Charlie, verbal or otherwise, but she'd heard stories of his bad-boy lifestyle. There's not much else to tell. It is the same old story, just told in a different day. Have you guys come up with any new leads?" He asked the detectives.

"Nope, the trail is as cold as a two-bit whore asking for payment," Whitaker responded.

They all laughed.

"The lieutenant is going to be spitting fire, but we can't just pull evidence out of our asses," O'Mally pointed out. "If you ask me, Charlie probably just up and left like Mrs. Grapler said. That scenario just makes the most sense. Charlie is what, six foot four, six foot five? Roberta is much smaller."

"I wouldn't be so sure that she's innocent. There is no telling what that nut job could do; I don't think she is right in the head," Chase said.

"Nobody thinks she is right in the head," Whitaker agreed loudly.

Again, they laughed in unison.

"Without a warrant and without a witness, our balls are in the palm of her hand. Unless we find someone who saw something, knows something, heard something, or can produce something, we have nothing. Hey, for all we know, her mental state is fine and she's really a victimized wife. It's doubtful, but one never knows," Chase added.

"Somebody tell me how I got sucked into this case? I was happy just walking the beat, handing out tickets, and meeting my quota each month," O'Mally said with a laugh. "I am going to need a few more Benjamins if I am going to be doing all you guys' work for you."

"You just continue being Old Lady Grapler's bitch like the good little officer you are, and let us detectives take care of the real police work," Whitaker chided.

"I could say the same thing about you two and the lieutenant, " O'Mally responded in a cocky tone. "Enjoy briefing him tomorrow on all of your clever detective work, and take your spankings like the good little girls you are."

O'Mally threw a twenty-dollar bill on the table and swaggered out smugly.

CHAPTER 43

━━━━━━━━━━━ ▼ ━━━━━━━━━━━

The moon shone bright and full as Roberta looked up with blurred vision. There were no sounds from nature; there was no movement of any kind. The trees didn't rustle, the wind didn't blow, and the crickets kept to themselves. It was a familiar feeling, yet one she could not describe even to herself. The freshly planted grass had made remarkable progress over the past few weeks, almost concealing any evidence of the grave's existence. Her bare feet forced her to the center of Charlie's final resting place before she felt her body absorb a jolt of tension. She stood immobile as her non-manicured toes felt the cooling of the moist ground beneath her. Her limbs hung heavy, her voice was nonexistent, and her face may as well have been made of stone. Without warning, two hands shot up out of the unmarked grave and tightly gripped her ankles. Within seconds, they pulled her body under, yanking her into the dirt coffin. Her strength returned and she flailed her arms violently to break free from whatever or whoever was pulling her down.

"Let go! Let go! Leave me alone! Leave me be!"

Before she knew it, dirt filled her mouth and her breaths were cut short. She coughed and choked, gasping for air, desperate for freedom, struggling for her life. The pressure crushed her, and her body became limp.

Strangely, death eventually let go of its grip. Her eyes slowly tried to open. Her searching touch revealed that she was surrounded by cold, wet dirt. She attempted to use the dirt as leverage, and she hoped she would at least be able to stand up. Her attempts failed. She found herself encased in mud wearing a filthy, black silk nightgown. "Where am I?" she wondered as her nose captured a putrid odor.

"How does it feel?" a voice boomed.

She quickly jerked as much as she was able. Spastically, she looked around. Goose bumps laced her skin. She saw no one and felt no one. She reverted to complete stillness as she listened for more words.

"I said, how does it feel?"

"Hello? Who's there?" she asked, her voice full of fright.

"I ask the questions, Roberta. I am in control. How does it feel?"

Her teeth chattered. The chilling temperature fondled her insides. The voice rang strong and angry, surely stemming from somewhere, but mysteriously nowhere.

"What do you want from me? What do you want?" she yelled in fear. Slimy creatures crawled out of the earth and into her matted hair.

"You're still not paying attention to me, huh Roberta? You're still thinking of only yourself and no one else, not even your loving husband. Your husband who stood by you through all your neuroticism." His tone calm and his words softened.

"Charlie?"

A dim light materialized. She frantically took in her surroundings. Just as she suspected, she was surrounded by dirt. There appeared to be no escape. Worms, maggots, and dozens of other creepy crawlers continued to reach for her. Sewer water trickled by her feet with a stench of spoiled eggs and dirty feet. Heavy foot-steps pounded the ground above her.

"Welcome home Roberta. Welcome to your new home. You almost reached your salvation last time we met. Remember? You almost opened Dr. Bombay's door, but you just couldn't. You never could. You couldn't seem to ever do what's best, your sick mind didn't seem to allow it. It infected everything you touched … everything. That included me, it included Jorge, and it especially included Dillon!" Charlie's voice continued in a calmer tone. "You know, look-ing back there was nothing in my life you could just let be mine, nothing I could call my own. Seeing Dr. Bombay would have changed all of that, but you refused. There was not one little aspect of my life that wasn't infected by your voice, your grab, or your influence. Work, family, my mind, the house, my san-ity, it all reeked of you. So here you go. You can now infect the one place you have yet to really experience—my death. Welcome to my eternity; welcome to my humble little grave. You found it necessary to take over my entire life, so I think it is only fair that you take over my death as well. You can't win this time. I may be dead, but I am not gone. You will pay for my misery, all of it."

Before she could muster the courage to try to respond to her decomposing husband, there on her right stood her son, Jorge. He occupied a clear space within the once dirt-filled grave and a bright light illuminated his face. His stern expression made her cringe. At first, he said nothing at all. He simply frowned at her in disgust.

"Jorgie? Jorgie? Oh, Little Boy Blue, thank goodness you are here. Your father is at it again. You have to save me. You can help; you are strong now; you are a man now. You are all grown up. Come. Come to me. Come and carry me out of this rotten hole. You know I love you Jorgie, you know I can't live without you."

He maintained an unyielding position and continued to glare as he calmly said, "Go to hell, Mother. I am not your precious Jorgie; I am not your Little Boy Blue. It's me, Dillon. I'm the one you gave away, the one you didn't want, the one you hid from the rest of the world. Remember me?"

He refused to blink even once. Without allowing time for a rebuttal, a frightening, demon-looking creature appeared and hovered on Roberta's left. She remembered being sandwiched between two evils before, but she couldn't remember when or where.

"Who are you?" she stuttered. "What are you?" she continued.

"You don't recognize me? Are ya sure? Take a closer look," a raspy voice said. Roberta looked hard into the face of the creature. The sight made her skin crawl. Her insides felt dark and possessed and the longer she looked into its eyes, the more horrendous it became.

"I'll give you a hint, little woman. Who is the only person in your life who despises you more than the husband you murdered? Who is the one person in your life you have wronged more than the son you secretly had and gave away to the highest bidder? Think about it woman. You know me better than you know anyone else. You have tortured me. You have wronged me. Now you must face me." And within seconds, Roberta found herself staring into her very own hate-filled eyes.

"This is not happening. This has to be a dream. I gotta get outta here. HELP!"

She began screaming and flailing her arms in an attempt to get out of Charlie's grave any way that she could. Her fists pounded the seeping walls, and she roughly slapped her face begging for consciousness.

"HELP! HELP!" she screamed.

"Mother … Mother … Wake up … Wake up … You're dreaming!"

Dillon sat on the edge of Roberta's bed trying to wake her from her sleep as her movements continued to thrust in chaos and violence.

"Mother!" he yelled as he tried to grab her hands and restrain them.

"MOTHER!"

Her eyes popped open, and her erratic behavior slowed as she regained her composure. The details of her nightmare were still very fresh, as well as the knowledge that they were occurring more frequently. The covers laid mangled on her mattress. "I'm fine, Dillon. I guess I just had another nightmare."

"*Another* nightmare? Do you get them often?" he asked.

"Oh, from time to time. Don't worry about it," she said. She was still very uneasy and fear continued to pump through her.

"Do you want to talk about it?"

Dillon wanted to know the details for his own selfish reasons.

"Nope. Can't say that I remember it all that much. You know dreams."

She patted him on the leg and looked at him, clearly giving a sign that he should leave her bedroom. He half smiled back, disappointed at the lack of information, and left her room. He had reading to do anyway.

CHAPTER 44

▼

Jag spent the next several weeks gathering any information he thought would contribute to Dillon's downfall. He had put together a one-inch-thick file that included spreadsheets, contact names, phone numbers, account numbers, and shipping specifics. It included everything from port locations and content listings, to delivery times and dates. Added to the file was evidence of millions of dollars worth of contributions, all traceable back to Dillon's personal bank account. It was a great feeling to know that the plan was coming to an end. All that remained to be done was to gather the rest of Dillon's fortune. So far, Jag had managed to collect nearly four hundred thousand dollars in cash, as well as sell stocks worth nearly one million dollars. Even in his wildest dreams, it was more money than he could have ever imagined. The fact that he hadn't even come close to securing the grand total of Dillon's assets blew his mind. By next month, he would have it all: the money, the girl, the exotic lifestyle, a bungalow on the beach, and his mama back in his life. And, while he and his new family sunbathed on the sand, the real Dillon would be arrested and sent to prison. No one would ever know there had been two Dillons.

"Hey baby, how do you feel today?" Lanie asked after returning home from yoga.

"I'm fantastic!" Jag said as he leaned in and kissed her.

"Do you remember what today is, sweetie?" she asked delicately.

He knew it must be some important anniversary or birthday, but he obviously didn't know for sure.

"Is it your birthday or something, honey?"

"No, it's not my birthday. I already wrote that on the calendar and circled it in red. You can't miss it," Lanie said with a smile.

Jag smiled back.

"Seriously though, I have some bad news. Today is actually a sad anniversary. Apparently you must not remember, but exactly one year ago today, your parents died in a terrible accident," she said.

"An accident? What kind of an accident?" Jag asked, trying his best to appear shocked and upset.

"Their car was hit as it crossed some train tracks. Apparently the signal failed. The police said they most likely didn't even know the train was coming, and they died instantly. It is probably a good thing that you don't remember; you were understandably devastated and you haven't really recovered from it emotionally. I actually debated telling you, but I decided it was probably the right thing to do."

Jag stood there stunned, not sure what he should say or do. He wasn't the type to cry, especially on demand. "I would like to be alone for a little while. If you don't mind, I need a little bit of time to absorb all of this," he said.

"Of course. I understand," Lanie said.

She gave him a hug and went into the living room to finish a crossword puzzle she had been working on.

Jag headed for the den to try to muster up some emotion for the news of his dead parents. The day's mail sat in an untouched pile on the desk. "Harbor Bank One?" he thought to himself as he noticed a piece of mail from an unfamiliar bank. Excitement rushed through him at the possibility of more money.

"We have currently completed the processing of your new safety-deposit box key. If you have since discovered the whereabouts of your old key, please return it to our office for proper destruction. We would be happy to issue you your new key between the hours of 0830–1600, at the branch location where your deposit box is housed. We appreciate your business."

"Hon? I'm going to take a drive and clear my head for a bit," Jag hollered as he grabbed the keys off the hall table.

"Sure, honey. Do you want some company?"

"No, I just need some time. Are my parents buried in the cemetery across town?"

"Yes, their graves are on the north side."

"I think I will go pay my respects and get some closure," Jag said sadly.

With the help of MapQuest, he found himself in the parking lot of the local Harbor Bank One branch after about twenty-five minutes of driving.

"Why would Dillon have a safety-deposit box way out here?" he wondered aloud.

Jag approached the customer service counter and made eye contact with a woman who wore a low-cut, flowered blouse and a name tag that read "Beverly."

"Hello, my name is Dillon Andresen and I am here to collect my new safety-deposit box key," Jag said with confidence as he handed the woman his letter.

"Sure thing, Mr. Andresen. I just need to see some identification."

"Of course."

Jag pulled out Dillon's driver's license and handed it to the teller.

"Just one moment, Mr. Andresen," she said before leaving the counter area.

"Why is she leaving? Where is she going? Is she suspicious?" he wondered.

His own paranoia was getting the best of him. She returned carrying a brass key, and she placed it on the counter just out of Jag's reach.

"Just a few more moments and you'll be all set," she said.

She typed fiercely on her computer as Jag watched nervously. He was desperate for her fat fingers to hand him that key.

"Please sign here, initial here, and here Mr. Andresen," she said while pointing to the respective areas of interest.

He obliged, and moments later he was holding a key with the number 6272 imprinted on it.

"NAPA," he said quietly.

"May I have access to my box today, ma'am?" he asked.

"Of course; follow me."

Once he was securely inside the protected safety-deposit box area, he inserted the key into his box, pulled the box out, and placed it on the table in front of him. His heart skipped a beat when he saw what was inside.

"Letters from my mother? Addressed to Dillon?"

CHAPTER 45

▼

Lieutenant Steele was a handsome, well-built man who stood over six feet four inches tall. His shaved head contributed to his intimidating appearance, and he had the attitude to back it up. Although he was known to be a confident and sometimes cocky man, he was also greatly respected by his subordinates. With impeccable leadership ability, his men always wanted to meet or exceed his expectations, so it was hard for detectives Whitaker and Chase to reveal their findings, or lack thereof, to him.

"It is just like he's vanished into thin air, Lieutenant. No one has seen anything; no one has heard anything."

"What about the son? I assume you followed up on his disappearance and reappearance?"

"O'Mally handled that. He is putting the report together, probably as we speak, but no leads developed. No one in Bend has any trace of Jorge ever existing there, and he himself can't even confirm that he was there. His mind was in a state of fog and basically he just remembers her picking him up. It's odd that no one is talking, and it seems as if no one really has anything helpful to say when they do decide to talk to us," Whitaker said.

"So, the bottom line is that there is absolutely no evidence that there has been any real crime committed in terms of the disappearance of Charlie Grapler," the lieutenant said.

"True, but I suspect …" Whitaker was cut off midway through his thought.

"We don't get convictions on suspicions. I need something concrete, namely a body, a murder weapon, an eyewitness, something besides a hunch. The legal system doesn't look too fondly on hunches," the lieutenant explained sarcastically.

"We need a search warrant," Whitaker said. "I know Mrs. Grapler is hiding something. I just know it. She gets very uncomfortable and defensive whenever Chase and I grace her with our presence. She's hiding something. She has to be hiding something."

"You know I can't get a search warrant. It is not like a five-year-old child has turned up missing. This is a grown man we're talking about—a man who is three times the size of your so-called suspect," the lieutenant interjected

"I'm not claiming it's necessarily Roberta who's to blame. Maybe it was the son. Maybe they both know exactly what happened, but they're protecting each other."

"Get me some proof then, and we can take them down. But get it done already. We have wasted a lot of the time and money investigating this case, and so far it seems to be all for nothing. Take O'Mally back over there with you. From what I hear, she is more responsive to him. Flat out ask her if you guys can take a look around. We need to produce something or put this to rest. We can't keep harassing this woman. I have already received a call from the chief about that. Roberta has already called him and complained that we've been violating her civil rights. She feels as if she's being accused of committing a crime, and she says the accusation is causing her emotional distress. So, to be on the safe side, call her first, arrange a time to meet with her, and assure her the meeting is just to tie up loose ends. Coddle her a bit, let her feel that you're on her side. Don't make her feel like a criminal. This is all 101 stuff; come on now," the lieutenant said.

CHAPTER 46

▼

"Ken?"

"Yes," Ken responded to the strangers on his porch.

It was early Saturday morning when Dillon and Sam showed up at Ken's house.

"Can I help you?"

"We hope so. Hi, I'm Dillon, Dillon Grapler," he said as he extended his hand out politely.

"Dillon Grapler?"

"Well, you might know me as Jorge?"

"Yes, of course. It is certainly nice to finally meet the boy I have heard about for so many years. Charlie's son, right?"

Ken recognized him from the picture Charlie carried in his wallet, but he was still confused about the name. Was it Jorge or was it Dillon?

"Come in, come in."

Ken stumbled a bit while getting his bearings.

"Sorry to just barge in on you, but I came across your name and I wanted to get your opinion, or your thoughts if you will, on who my father really is."

"Have you seen him? Do you know where he is?" Ken asked, his face lighting up.

"No, I have no idea where he is, but I would love to find out. That's one of the reasons why I'm here," Dillon responded.

"You said you came across my name. Where? And what do you mean you want me to tell you who your father really is?" Ken asked.

"First of all, I should tell you that I can't remember my father. I was in some type of accident. I have no idea what it was, but my memory has been wiped clean. My mother tells me that my father is a terrible, terrible man. She says he's abusive to her, he's awful to me, he's never around, and so on and so on, but I just don't think I believe it. Oh, excuse me. This is Sam. She is Roberta's neighbor and my ... uh ... friend."

Dillon knew that Sam was probably more that just a friend, or at least he knew that he wanted her to be, but now wasn't the time.

"Nice to meet you," Ken said, cordially. "Your father is an amazing man. He's my best friend. He'd give you the shirt right off of his back without hesitation. I have never had a better friend. But what makes you doubt Roberta, especially since you aren't able to remember anything?"

"I found my father's journal."

"You did? Did you read it? Are there any clues as to where he could be right now? Is there anything at all that could help track him down?"

Sam stood there listening to the conversation about the whereabouts of Charlie Grapler, knowing all along that she had helped bury him on the very property where Dillon resided. Her guilt still fed off of her, but she had to know who the real Charlie was before risking everything for the good of the cause.

"I am still reading the journal," Dillon said. "So far, there's nothing about him planning a departure. Most of it is about how awful Roberta is and how he couldn't stand having her in his day-to-day life. I still have a lot more to read though. Each page is a lot for me to take; it is helping me piece together my own sense of who he is and who I was to him. What do you think about Roberta?"

"Honestly?" Ken asked.

"Yes, honestly, of course," Dillon said.

"I don't like her at all. She is a cruel lady who caused Charlie a lot of heartache. I have never heard Charlie say a nice thing about that woman. I shouldn't say that. During the beginning of their marriage he thought the world of her. They married young. They were living on love he would say. It quickly diminished though. The longer they were married, the less I heard about Roberta. I do remember when you were born though. It was the happiest day of your dad's life. Those were his actual words, 'This is the happiest day of my life.'"

"Were you there? At the hospital I mean?" Dillon questioned.

"No. Actually, your dad and I were on a job in Southern California when you were born. Your mother ..."

"Let's not call her that," Dillon interrupted. "I would rather just refer to her as Roberta from here on out."

"You got it," Ken said. "Anyway, Roberta was supposed to call Charlie if she had contractions or felt any inclination that she was going to go into labor, but there was no phone notification. I remember getting a phone call from Charlie the day after we returned from the job site. He told me Roberta had given birth to you four days prior to our return from the trip, so you had already been born when he returned home from the job. He was devastated, totally devastated. At that point in their marriage, that type of behavior was becoming more and more normal for her."

The wheels in Dillon's head turned productively. He pieced together a scenario of his own.

"So, nobody besides Roberta and the doctors were there for my birth?"

"Not to my knowledge," Ken replied. "Why? What are you thinking?"

"I may be thinking crazy, but I'm thinking twins. Is it possible that I have a twin named Jorge? Is that crazy sounding?"

Sam and Ken both had looks of surprise in their eyes.

"It would make sense," Sam said. "It would explain the baby book with Jorge's name in it and the differences in mannerisms between you and your mother, or, I mean between you and Roberta," Sam corrected herself.

"Do you know anything about a twin, Ken? Were there two babies?"

"To my knowledge, no. There was just one baby. I am sure that if there was another baby, Charlie would have told me. That is, he'd have told me if he'd known about it himself," Ken said suspiciously.

"Shouldn't we be able to look it up, trace the birth? Wouldn't there be records showing if a woman gave birth to two babies instead of just one? And wouldn't there be a record of an adoption if one had taken place?" Dillon asked.

"That was so many years ago. I would assume that type of adoption information would have been sealed. I would think that the only person who would be able to gain access or request information on it would be the birth mother, or possibly the adoptive mother. I am not sure. I will make some calls and see what my contacts can tell me," Sam said.

"Have you ever meet Roberta in person?" Dillon asked Ken.

"Well, strangely enough, no. I've never met her in person. I did speak with her over the phone a little over a month ago. It was a few days after Charlie disappeared. I was worried about him because he didn't show up for work. I called the house. She answered the phone and got all worked up about my inquiry. She said, as she continues to say, that he just took off. I just don't buy it. He wouldn't leave, at least not without telling me, or possibly you," Ken said.

"I don't think I was around. At least according to Roberta, I haven't been around for a year or so. Then again, who knows? We need to find this Jorge person though, unless of course I am Jorge. I'm so damn confused," Dillon admitted.

"We will figure this out. We will. Charlie is a great man and a great friend. If it is the last thing I do, I will find out where he is. Along the way, all the unanswered questions will surely be answered. Namely, who you are and where you've been for the past year or so of your life," Ken said.

Sam continued to listen to their heartfelt and emotional words. Her feet were moving back and fourth nervously without her even realizing it. She desperately wanted to intervene. She desperately wanted to put the question, "Where is Charlie Grapler," to rest, but she wasn't ready. And in reality, she wasn't yet willing. There was still so much to discover.

Dillon and Ken continued to talk about Charlie and Roberta and all the factors that came into play. They were convinced that a crime had been committed, and they were dead set on learning the entire story behind Charlie's fate. Knowing that the name Jorge floated around out there with uncertainty was the biggest lead they had to prove that there was, in fact, an inconsistency in Roberta's story. What had been a team of two had just evolved into a new team of three. They made a pact to stick together, avoid talking with the police, and discover on their own what the real story was.

"Roberta's phone records are supposed to arrive today, Dillon. We should get back and see if they have been delivered," Sam said.

"How did you manage to get a hold of her phone records?" Ken questioned.

"Oh, Sam used to be a reporter for a major newspaper before she moved here. She has connections."

Sam and Ken exchanged phone numbers, and each agreed to contact the other if anything developed.

"It was great talking with you, Ken. My father was right, you are a class act."

"That means a lot to me. I see a lot of your dad in you."

They shook hands, smiled, and parted ways.

CHAPTER 47

▼

Jag's emotional uncertainty soared to new heights. Never in his craziest dreams could he have imagined that his mother and Dillon actually had a relationship with one another. With a numbing sensation, Jag managed to finger through a dozen or so of the letters and randomly chose one to read.

"Please let this explain the unexplainable," he whispered to himself with the deepest hope. "Please don't let my mama be a liar. Don't let her be a liar, at least not to me."

Jag continued to talk quietly to himself as his shaking hand pulled the chosen letter from its envelope.

"Dillon,

I got my money today and I sure appreciate it, but it wasn't what we agreed on. You promised $2,000 and all I got was $800. I'll expect the rest soon. Don't make me regret all I have done for you. Don't make me regret giving you away and giving you a real chance at life. I need that money to escape, to get away from my life. You owe it to me. I am in constant torture here, and I have no one to turn to. You are all I have. Sometimes I wish I would have kept you instead of the other one, but I can't do nothing about that now. Always remember that I love ya.

PS. If you let me down, I will be forced to teach you an unfortunate lesson.

Mama"

A tear streamed down Jag's cheek. A tornado of confusion ripped through his mind. He pulled another letter out of its envelope.

"Dillon,

Hello, son. Thanks for the payment. Mama loves you. I never doubted you, not really. I would have hated to have had to punish you, after all we are family. Just keep it coming. I am starting to believe that you are the only man I can count on these days. Jorge is turning out just like his daddy. You wouldn't do that since you don't know your daddy. Looking forward to the next cash bundle. Don't forget our agreement.

Mama"

Mama's words entered Jag's mind, "Only stash cash ... no trail ..."

Jag was remembering what his mama had told him over and over again. He wondered how much money she had already stashed away. He wondered how many years she had been blackmailing Dillon. And he wondered what she was planning to do with all the money Jag was gathering.

"Why now? Why was I brought into the scam?" Jag wondered. "Did Dillon refuse to continue sending money? Did Mama not want to jeopardize her own safety and security? Is that why she misled me into finishing the job? Is she just using me?"

He had a thousand questions that needed answers. He thought back to the harsh words his mama had written with her own hand, "Jorge is turning out just like his daddy. You are the only man I can count on." Jag wondered who was going to end up with all of this money that he had been risking his life for. He began to wonder if his mama was playing him and controlling him just as she had his whole life. He began to feel less and less like the triumphant and strong man he had become over the past few months. Flashbacks of his youth began to challenge his courage.

"Jorgie is a loser, Jorgie is a geek, Jorgie is a beanpole whose name should be freak!" The words echoed over and over in his mind. "Stop, Stop! Leave me alone!" Jorge yelled, as he covered his ears with his hands and shut his eyes as tightly as he could.

The sound of a door opening jolted him out of his episode. Quickly, he glanced at the bank employee who had entered the safety-deposit box room. He immediately looked away. He grabbed the letters, put his safety-deposit box back into its place in the wall, and turned to leave.

"Are you all right, sir?" the clerk asked.

Jorge blew right past her without a word. He was desperate to get out of there, to escape his own self-destructive thoughts. He needed to be Jag again, the strong leader, the man with a plan.

"Who in the hell does she think she is playing me, lying to me," he asked himself.

He didn't quite understand what her ultimate goal was. Nor did he know if it included him or not, but he wasn't going to just sit around and find out. He wasn't going to be a victim in her secret plan, not anymore.

New questions entered his mind. "Does Dillon really have amnesia? Has he replaced me? Does she love him more than she loves me? Is she tricking him to get access to the cash? Does she hate him like she claims?"

Jag didn't know what to think or what to believe. At this point, it didn't matter. He no longer felt the strong connection for his mother that he once had. The betrayal that plagued him overshadowed his sense of devotion and love for her.

"It looks like it is just you and I, Angel, just you and I. It will be even better. It will be absolutely perfect."

He arrived home mentally exhausted from the recent events.

"Hi, hon, how did it go at the cemetery?" Lanie asked. "Are you handling everything all right?"

"I'm fine. I'm glad I went; it helped a lot," he said. "It truly helped a lot. I am going to take a hot shower and lie down for a little while. I feel completely drained."

"Sure, sweetie, it's fine. Take all the time you need."

He knew she felt bad for him and knew she was probably worried sick about his state of mind. It was just like her. It was just another reason he treasured her unconditional love and understanding.

CHAPTER 48

▼

"Sam?" Roberta asked, knowing someone had picked up the phone she was calling.

There was a long pause before Sam responded, "Yes?"

"Hey, it's me. Where ya been hiding? I haven't heard from ya. What's going on?"

"Going on? Nothing's going on. I have just been pouring myself into my work lately. It is amazing how productive I have been."

"Why haven't ya called me?" Roberta asked.

"I have just been busy; it's nothing personal."

"The police just called me again. They want to meet with me one last time."

"I really can't talk right now, I am on my way out the door," Sam said.

"Where are you going? You don't know no one around here but me," Roberta asked suspiciously.

"I don't have to know someone to go grocery shopping," Sam snapped. Realizing that she was becoming defensive, she abruptly changed her mannerisms as to not cause any hostility or mistrust between herself and her murderous neighbor.

"Can I pick you up anything while I am out?" Sam asked.

"Yeah, I could use some milk and a carton of cigs," Roberta responded. "Call me when you get back. We have stuff to talk about, important stuff."

"Sure, no problem," Sam replied.

Dillon sat at Sam's dinner table waiting for the conversation to end.

"Oh, wait Sam. You ain't by any chance seen my boy, have ya?"

"Uh, no. Dillon was it?"

"Yeah, Dillon," Roberta said.

"Have you seen him at all in the past week or so?"

"No. Why, is he missing?" she asked.

"No, but he's always gone. He says he's out walking all the time, working out, clearing his head, trying to remember his past. He ain't never asked to go and he don't ever tell me where he's going. I'm worried that he is suspicious of me. I'm worried he knows something."

"I haven't seen him."

Sam couldn't really have this conversation with her, considering Dillon was within earshot.

"I really have to get going so I can get all of my errands done before it gets too late. I'll call you later this evening."

"We can talk when you bring my groceries by," Roberta said. "It's important, Sam. The police will be here tomorrow, and I want to talk to ya about it before then."

"All right, bye now."

Sam quickly hung up the phone wondering if Dillon could see the guilt on her face. "What did she want?" Dillon asked.

"Just to chat. She thinks I am avoiding her or something, which of course I am. Good people reader," she added with sarcasm. "She did ask if I'd seen you though. Of course I said no."

Sam tore open the manila envelope that housed Roberta Grapler's phone records.

"My guys sure are efficient," she said smiling as she pulled the documents from the envelope.

"Hmm, interesting. Didn't you say Roberta claimed to have picked you up in Oregon?"

"Yes. Has she been calling there?" Dillon asked excitedly.

He needed something to work with; he needed a positive lead to follow; he needed a shred of hope that he would be able to solve the mysteries surrounding his life.

"Yep, she's been receiving calls from and placing calls to a specific number. It looks like … four, five, … seven times in the past two months. Plus, there are a couple other numbers here in the 541 area code that she placed calls to and received calls from prior to that time."

"Looks like we need to take a trip to Oregon. What do you say?"

"I'm game," Sam responded with excitement. "But what about Roberta? If we both leave, she will suspect something."

"Honestly, does it really matter?"

Sam knew that it might, especially since Roberta had something on her. She sat a couple of moments before answering. "I would just feel better if Roberta couldn't put two and two together. I need to keep some sort of relationship with her so I can get the inside scoop. She trusts me; she may confide in me. I would rather keep that relationship alive, than burn a bridge that could be useful later."

"So what do you suggest?" Dillon asked.

"I'll call her later and tell her I was unable to go to the store because I got a call from my mother. I'll tell her my father had a heart attack or something, and that I am leaving out on the red-eye tonight. Since you'll be there when I call her, she hopefully won't even think to connect the dots. She isn't the brightest crayon in the box, you know," Sam pointed out.

"Right you are. Right you are," Dillon agreed.

"I'll hide my car around back so if she drives by before we officially leave tomorrow, she won't see it, and that will jive with my story about taking it to the airport. So, why don't you come here around eight o'clock tomorrow morning? That way, Roberta will see you in the morning, and she won't suspect anything, at least until later tomorrow evening. Then, we'll go from there, depending on what we find," Sam continued.

"Boy, how did you come up with all of that in what … like three minutes?"

"I am a writer you know," she smiled.

Sam walked Dillon to the door. He leaned in and coddled her cheeks in his hands, before pulling her close. Their lips met, and this time the kiss lasted a good fifteen seconds. Butterflies bounced around in her stomach. Her eyes remained gently closed for a second or two after the kiss ended. He rubbed her cheek softly.

"See you tomorrow, Samantha Barker." He waved happily before darting into the grass to return home. Roberta's house was the last place he wanted to go, but hopefully it was also the last time he would have to go there. After all, he was a grown man; she couldn't keep him there against his will. Once he figured out his past, he would finally be able to concentrate on his future, and he already knew it would be void of her.

CHAPTER 49

▼

Jag lay still in the fetal position. He had nothing on but a plain, white tank top and a pair of gray-and-black pin-striped pajama bottoms. Helplessness pinned him to the down comforter, as tears collected beneath his chin's whiskers from the devastation of learning that his mother was a fraud. Flashbacks from his youth shot through his memory. He didn't want to remember or even think about the past, but his conscience demanded otherwise. He pictured the face of his first crush, a little girl named Naomi. Jorge considered her the prettiest little girl in school, and the distraction of sharing the same classroom with her only made his feelings for her grow. A long, thick braid always managed her extra-curly hair, and a colored bow always tied it off. The color of the blue sky beamed from her eyes and her smile never failed to craft deep dimples. She smelled of flowers, just the way a beautiful girl should smell he'd always thought. Every recess he propped his back against the brick school building and watched all the other kids run and jump with laughter. Naomi especially. He didn't dare try to join in, for fear of being picked on even more than usual. He sat alone every day in his Goodwill clothes, casually chucking pebbles in front of him and waiting for the bell to bring him back in to the safety of his own desk. He remembered his roaming eye searching for Naomi one Friday afternoon. She was nowhere to be found. Sadness overcame him. It was then that he realized that even from a distance, she brightened his day. They had never spoken, for he was much too shy and insecure to ever approach such a popular girl.

Jorge was far, far away in his thoughts that day when he felt someone tapping his left shoulder. He jumped and looked up. No words would come out of his open mouth. Naomi offered a smile to him. He gazed up at her and noticed that she wore the coolest purple shirt. It read, "Girls rule."

"Hi Jorge," she said. Her words danced into his ears.

"H … Hi Naomi," he stammered and he wondered why on earth she was speaking to him.

"Do you want to walk home from school with me today?" she asked confidently.

"Me? You want me to walk you home? But why?"

"Kids around here are jerks. I know they pick on you a lot. If you walk with me I can tell them to leave you alone," she said.

"Why would you do that?" he asked.

"'Cause you're cute, silly."

Within an instant, his face resembled a turnip and wetness attacked his palms. "Sure. I will walk you home."

For the rest of his school day, Jorge had felt that time was standing still. His telling eyes constantly watched the ticking clock. His legs fidgeted with anticipation and nervousness. Never before had he wanted school to let out, but never before did he have a cute girl to walk home with.

"Maybe my luck is changing," he'd thought to himself. "Maybe Naomi would show those other kids how nice I really am. Maybe I will have a friend to tell Mama about."

The jitters continued to invade his body until the bell finally screamed for their release. Quickly, he zipped his vinyl jacket and waited by the large tree at the curb for his new friend.

"Ready to go?" she asked.

He reached out as an offer to carry her pink book bag.

"Thank you, Jorge."

The next fifteen minutes warmed his fragile heart. No one approached him or yelled out cruel names. They just left him alone to be with his girl. It was the first time he'd felt safe, and it was all due to Naomi.

"This is where I live," she said.

"Thank you for talking to me today. No one has ever been so nice to me," Jorge responded.

He returned her bag and waved.

"I'm sorry Jorge. I really am." Her head dropped with sincerity.

"About what?" he asked.

Just then, she stepped aside as four kids raced up to him with bottles of various condiments. They shoved him up against the fence and began spewing the contents of the bottles all over him. With nowhere to go and no one to help him

Jorge had no choice but to throw his arms over his face and take it, just as he always did. The best day of his life had become the most hurtful one. Naomi had tricked him. He should have known that no girl would actually think he was cute. He should have known that no one cared enough about him to protect him, no one except his mama. They labeled him a wimpy baby because he cried harder than he ever had. Naomi ran off, clearly ashamed of her behavior, but apparently not ashamed enough to stop the attack. The humiliation of being left lying on the sidewalk threw him into a state of numbness.

Jorge finally pulled himself to his feet and slowly wandered home carrying with him the stench of tomatoes, honey, vinegar, and pickle juice. Jag remembered that day as if it had just happened, and in a way it had. His mother was betraying him, only on a much larger scale. He never talked to Naomi again, despite her few attempts to reconcile. And the same would ring true for his mama.

Patiently, he waited for the three Percocet he had just taken to consume his racing mentality. He needed to forget the letters, the deceit, the lies, and the possibility that his mother was double-crossing him. At least for the next few hours, he needed to forget. Maybe he was just an easy target, just as he had been all those years ago with Naomi.

He watched as she slowly pulled up the zipper on one of her patent leather, thigh-high boots. They were bright red and sported a three-inch heel. She stood up sharply and slid her hands down her very high-cut skirt to smooth out any ripples that may have gathered. While rubbing her lips together, she began strutting slowly away from her bedroom and down the hallway. Jorge clumsily stumbled back and quickly hopped into his broken-down single bed. He sharply grabbed and pulled his favorite cowboy-and-Indian blanket up to his neck and shut his eyes, pretending to be fast asleep. The sound of his bedroom door opening sent panic through him.

"Jorgie? Are you awake?"

He was never very good at pretending to be asleep and somehow his mama always knew when he fibbed.

"I know you're awake, little one. I just wanna say good night now."

Her voice soothed his worried mind. He couldn't help but open his eyes to her.

"I'm awake, Mama."

As his vision adapted through his waterlogged eyes, he saw his beautiful mama standing at his door. She was slowly coming toward him. She wore a pretty, baby blue dress that was trimmed with lace. Her lips shimmered with sparkles. He wondered where her scary red clothing had gone.

"You look pretty, Mama," he said with surprise.

"Thank you, honey. Now you get to sleep; it's past your bedtime. Close those eyes and have sweet dreams. Tomorrow we get to have peanut butter pancakes in the shape of Mickey Mouse."

That sounded good to little Jorgie. "Okay, Mama. I love you."

"I love you too."

She clicked the door shut and turned out the hall light. It wasn't but a matter of seconds before he heard the sound of a man's voice. Thinking his papa was home, he sprung out of bed and peeked out his door. It wasn't his daddy; it wasn't his daddy at all. Jorgie hated the constant confusion. Again, his Mama was dressed in her shiny red outfit, her hair was all stringy and straight, and her lipstick was as bright as a fire truck. She grabbed the hand of a tall and skinny young man and led him through her bedroom door. Jorge couldn't quite see the man's face through the stranger's long, stringy black hair, but he was certain the man was not his daddy. Little Jorgie angrily stormed out of his bedroom and ran over to where his mama and that man were. He sternly thrust his little fists against the door as hard as he could.

"Mama! Mama! Mama, open the door! Where's Daddy?"

After a few moments, the door slowly cracked open and she stood there with sleepy eyes.

"What is it Jorgie? What is the matter with my Little Boy Blue? Did you have a bad dream?" she asked with concern.

Jorge looked at her beautiful face and saw nothing but goodness. There was no lipstick or boots to speak of. She wore a long, white nightgown with ruffles along the neckline. It covered her from head to toe.

"I saw him. I saw a man with ya, a black-haired man holding your hand."

"Now what kind of dreams are ya having? Was it your daddy?"

"No, it wasn't daddy. It was some other guy, a young guy. Where is he?"

"Where is who? The man in your dream?"

Jorge continued to stare at her with concern and confusion.

"Well, he is probably right where you left him, back in your mind. That's the last time you eat pizza before bed. Now get back to your room and get some sleep."

He had no other choice but to oblige her. He began walking back toward his bedroom, but the more steps he took, the further away his door became. The pathway narrowed and looked crooked and distorted. He walked faster and faster, and eventually sprinted with wasted effort.

"Mama!" he yelled as he turned to run to her.

Immediately, he halted in his tracks. The evil-looking woman had returned. She stared at him with cruel eyes as she held the hand of her young lover.

"What in the hell do I have to do to get some privacy around here? I told you to go to bed, and I meant it. Get to your room NOW, young man! Right now!"

"Mama, I can't get to my room. I'm scared. Who are you? What's going on?" His cheeks were soaked with tears and his lips quivered uncontrollably.

She reached out with her long black fingernails, "Get over here!"

He turned again and ran, despite the fact that his room was apparently unreachable. His mother trailed him by one measly step. He could feel her fingernails barely touching his messy hair as she swiped for him over and over again.

"Stop, Mama! Stop! Leave me alone. Please don't hurt me! Papa! Papa!"

Just like the wind changes in an instant, so did his fearful attempt for an escape. The room spun him around, and the sound of nursery rhymes hugged his fears. A sweet familiarity coddled him. His mama was rocking him to sleep and looking tenderly into his eyes. Her beauty had once again returned.

"Hush, little Jorgie. Hush little one. Mama's here. You don't need to cry anymore, my Little Boy Blue. Mama's here. Shhh, I love you Jorgie, I love you Little Boy Blue. Oh and don't forget, I'm gonna KILL YOU!"

His eyes shot open and his little vocal cords shouted with all their might, "Ahhh!"

"Honey, what is it? What is the matter?" Lanie asked as she rushed into the bedroom.

It took Jag a few moments to realize that he had just awakened himself from a twisted and disturbing dream. He saw Lanie looking at him with concern. Sadness glossed over her eyes.

"Are you all right?" she asked again.

He took deep breaths to try and slow his heart rate. Sweat saturated his shirt, and his skin felt hot and feverish. A similar nightmare he'd had while in the hospital crossed his mind. He was the same scared and confused little boy that he had been just moments earlier. With terror brewing in the pit of his stomach, his mind tried to rationalize the contradictions in his dreams. Deep down, he believed that there was a harsh truth trying to surface, a truth that had been buried for many, many years.

"Dillon? Can you hear me? Are you alright?"

"I … I guess I was just having a bad dream."

"I guess so. I have never seen you so disoriented. What on earth was it about?"

"Well, I am not really sure. All I know is that it was way too real. I mean, look at this," he said as he pulled at his drenched shirt.

"It must have been from the medicine I took. It must have messed with my mind or something."

His medicating to rest his mind seemed to have backfired on him.

He decided that it was time to get the rest of the money, get Lanie, and to pull out of that old life and into a new one for good. It would be a refreshing change to evolve into an existence full of possibilities. He was ready to put the plan behind him. There would be no more searching for his brother's criminal background, no more fake doctor's appointments, and no more orders from his mother. She was his target now.

CHAPTER 50

▼

The summer morning came early, as Roberta rolled out of her bed. She knew the police would be arriving in a few hours to question her once again on the disappearance of her husband. She turned the monitor on one last time hoping to finally get a glimpse into the Andresen's home. Static continued to smirk at her.

"Damn it!" Fire speared through her veins.

Dillon contently remained in his bed reading several more entries from his father's journal. He'd found that they all had a very common thread, and it seemed that each entry bled right into the next. It was abundantly clear that Roberta was a woman who was able to make his father feel miserable, alone, and inadequate. She often lashed out at him with accusing words that made no sense. Charlie lived a stressful life, and according to the journal, Roberta was responsible for all of it. Dillon wondered why his father had stayed with Roberta for so long. Why stay in a relationship that brings you down to the lowest point a man can be? The question was soon answered and even understood, at least on some level. Dillon flipped to the very last journal entry to get a glimpse into how it all ended. It wasn't until then that he fully understood.

"I tossed and turned all night because of the decisions I have made. I hope somewhere within her she will know that I had no other choice. I love her, even now, no matter how warped that may seem. Somewhere deep within her shell is the woman I learned to laugh with, cry with, and love with. But regrettably, that girl vanished right before my very eyes. I need closure and need to be sure I always remember how I am feeling right now and have been feeling for so much of my past. I have decided to write her a letter, never to be sent, but always to be read by me when my compassion and guilt tries to creep back into my thoughts. This is for the best, and I have to know that, always. No more second-guessing.

Dear Roberta,

I am angry with you. Angry because you have robbed me, robbed us, of our happily ever after. The first year of marriage was supposed to be the hardest year. That's what they say, right, that the first year tests a marriage? It is supposed to be spent learning the ups and downs of one another, getting on each other's nerves to the point where you question your commitment. Dinners get burned, fights carry on through the night, and the husband ends up sleeping in the doghouse. Well that was what was so great about us; we were never like that. We were different and it was amazing. I would give up everything I have just to relive our first year of marriage. I guess for us, every day after day 365 can be considered our own hellish version of a first year of marriage. And you know what Roberta? I blame you for it, for all of it. At least I blame your mind. If only you would have kept seeing Dr. Bombay, if only you would have considered my side of it or even Jorge's, things could have been different. We could have recovered, but you refused. You and your sick mind decided against anything logical. The ironic part of it all is that you are the one who calls me 'the crazy one'. I would sometimes pray that you would be able to see yourself and somehow understand your demented behavior, but how do you convince a crazy woman that she is in fact crazy. I guess you don't, at least I couldn't.

I watched your men come and go, I saw the marks they left on you, and I tried to stop it. I really tried. You wouldn't have it. Somehow what your johns did to you was my fault. Somehow the bruises left on your body reflected my inability to control my temper. You lost your trust for me so long ago that I barely remember it myself. In your eyes, all men are bad. You use them and then toss them, only calling them back when you need them for something.

I will never understand your sickness, and I will never forgive your choices. After so many attempts to control your warped sense of reality I just couldn't do it anymore. I couldn't watch you self-destruct, mostly because of how much I loved you and how guilty I felt for not being able to fix you. Some nights I just had to escape from your mind, something you haven't been able to do for many, many years.

My cabin has become my blessed safe haven. It provides me with the freedom to be away from you, while still keeping me close enough to watch over you. I could never have abandoned you, and that is not what I plan to do now. This is all for your own good. For some reason, I held on to my own delusional thinking pattern. I always kept a little bit of hope that one day you would be the old Roberta again. I would push open that door and find you there waiting to tell me you had decided to get help. Waiting to tell me that you are sorry for the years of accusations and mental abuse. I longed for you to tell me that I was worth that. I had high hopes of saving you and saving us. I held out for so very long that my own life and my own sense of identity got buried amongst the ruins. I can't hold out any longer.

Jorge is old enough to be on his own now; he can take care of himself. I am amazed that you have been able to trap him into your web for as long as you have. He thinks the world of you, thinks you are his fearless protector. He never knew you before. He hasn't experienced the Roberta then and the Roberta now. He seems to be the only man you let in since your mental incompetence took over. I will be here for him, Roberta, if he will have me, and you will no longer have the influence to control that. You are poison to yourself and to all those around you. Don't you worry Roberta; I have been saving for this day. I want Jorge to be able to have a good start in life. He needs to start living a real existence without you. And so do I, desperately.

So, Roberta my love, this is it. I truly believe this to be tough love. So when you are lying still in your hospital bed and wonder how you ended up in such an unusual place, your misguided mind will never quite understand. I know, however, in your heart of hearts, somewhere way down deep, that you will know this is the best way to help you escape from yourself. The mental institution will provide the sanity you can no longer provide for yourself.

I will not allow myself to feel guilty. I will not allow myself to apologize. I will stand by my decision from here on out, without waiver. It is time for me to take back my life and give you peace in yours. I am giving you a long overdue saving grace and it will make you happier and better off. God Bless you my dear Roberta. I loved you then, and I still love you now. Always know that, even if it is only in your dreams."

Dillon slowly closed the journal with a new understanding of Roberta. Apparently, she was much worse off than he had assumed. He finally had a true vision of what Roberta's past was about, and it was coming from a reliable source. His heart felt sad for what his father had gone through and even a little sad for Roberta.

"What a great and compassionate man," Dillon whispered under his breath. "I will find you, and when I do, I pray you are alive and well."

With eagerness to share his findings with Sam, he quickly got up and showered for the day. It wasn't long before they would be departing for their long-overdue road trip to Oregon.

"Hello Roberta," he said with a smile as he entered the kitchen for breakfast. He had on a green jogging suit that Roberta had recently picked up for him at a yard sale, and his hair was styled with mousse to keep it out of his face.

Roberta made sure that she was there when he entered the kitchen that particular morning. It was vital that she got him out of the house before the detectives and O'Mally showed up.

"Morning, Dillon. You going out this morning?" Roberta asked casually.

"Yes, I have become quite fond of my morning walks. It is so peaceful out there. It seems like there is so much to explore and see."

"Are you going to be gone all morning like usual?"

"Why do you ask?" he questioned. She had never been so polite. Something had to be up.

"No reason, I am just making conversation. We never seem to talk no more. Can't a mama show interest in her son's life?"

He didn't believe for a second that showing interest was her intent, but it really didn't matter. Whatever she was up to couldn't have been nearly as interesting as what he was up to that day.

"Yes, I will be gone most of the day, like usual. I can't stand feeling cooped up in the house. I would rather search for my memory out there in the fresh air," Dillon said, convincingly.

"How is your memory coming along? Have you remembered anything yet?"

Roberta feared some kind of breakthrough from him at some point. It troubled her paranoid mind.

"No. Not yet, but I am sure it will come soon. I did have a strange dream last night though."

"Oh really?" she asked as she tucked her hair behind her ears while nervously waiting for the details.

"I was sitting here in this house and I saw myself from across the room, but it wasn't really me. I mean it was, but I was different somehow. It was as if there were two of me, and each of us was staring at the other."

Roberta dropped her cup of coffee in a knee-jerk reaction. Her *Mother of the Year 1989* mug broke in several areas. Her right hand shot up to her lips. Quickly, she turned her back to Dillon and searched for a towel to clean up the mess. Dillon laughed on the inside. He'd expected such a reaction.

"Do I actually have a twin brother running around?" he asked himself. He was becoming more and more convinced of it.

"Well, enjoy your outing. I'll be seeing ya," Roberta blurted out.

He could tell that she wanted him out, and he was happy to oblige. His hope for a happy ending soared higher than it had since the first day he'd stepped into Roberta's warped world.

"I will. Maybe I will come back with a memory to share. Good-bye Roberta."

His bag was already packed and stashed outside by the great oak tree. They were both getting what they wanted that morning.

CHAPTER 51

───────────── ▼ ─────────────

"Let's get out of here, Angel," Jag blurted out.

"Sure, babe, where do you want to go? You hungry?" she asked.

"No. I mean really get out of here. Ever since the accident I just don't feel like myself anymore. I don't feel like I belong here."

Lanie looked at him, confused.

"What are you talking about?"

"Think about it. Every day I roam around looking at pictures, pilfering through my office, wondering what it is I am looking at, or looking for, for that matter. I don't know who I am; I can't do the job I spent so many years learning and mastering; and I have no desire to go back and try to learn it again. Think of it as a revelation!" he said, excited.

"We can just take a year for ourselves and explore. We'll see the world and put the money we've made over the past couple of years to good use."

"You're talking crazy. You mean just pick up and go? Really? Just take off?" she questioned. "What's gotten into you? This is as far off from your personality as you could get."

"That is my point. I don't like who I was; I don't want to be that guy anymore. I want to be the spontaneous guy of your dreams, the man who will sweep you off of your feet and take your breath away every single day. I am not the Dillon you fell in love with. Let me be the new me. I know you will love him more than you ever loved the old Dillon. We can get back to us." He spoke as he paced across the Berber carpet in his bare feet.

"What about our international aid work? We have people counting on us. And what about the house? This is our dream house. We found this house and knew it was the one we would raise our children in. What about all of that?" she asked.

"I don't even know how to do the aid work. I don't remember much of anything in terms of work. I am sorry, but I will never be that cutthroat businessman you married. If that is not all right, I will understand, but I am who I am now. I believe it happened for a reason. Everything does, remember? You taught me that. You have said that to me consistently for a few months now. We don't have to sell the house. We can come back if we want, when we are ready to start a family. So, the plants will die and the corners will fill with cobwebs. It won't be anything we can't fix later. Work can wait; maybe you can recommend a temporary replacement. You are very respected at work. I'm sure something could be worked out."

"You make it all sound so fun and exciting, Dillon. It would be great. Wouldn't it? Just the two of us against the world? We could go anywhere, couldn't we? The possibilities are endless."

"We could go to the peaks of the mountains in Switzerland or inside a pyramid in Egypt. We can just go," Jag said, enthusiastically.

He knew he had to get out of there fast. His mother was obviously planning something that didn't include him, or Lanie for that matter. He would have none of it. His mother would be sorry that she had tried to scam her own son; she would be very sorry. Before she would become wise to being double-crossed herself, Jag and Lanie would be relaxing on the beach with a sweet cocktail quenching their thirsts.

"Okay, let's do it. Let's get outta here," Lanie agreed. "But I do have something to tell you, Dillon. I was waiting for the right moment. It seems like now is as good a time as any."

"What is it? It is good news, I hope?" Jag said to break the silence.

"I think it is great news. You on the other hand may not think so. Then again, your new perspective on life may prove me wrong."

"What is it, Angel?"

She raised up off of the couch and smoothed out her cotton sundress. Jag watched her moving, eager to hear what she had to say. She handed him a beautiful, red-laced box with a velvet bow tied around it.

"Open it," she said with a smile bigger than happiness.

"Is it an anniversary of something?" he asked.

"Just open it," she said.

He pulled at the ends of the bow until they released; he then gently lifted the lid. He looked up at her with disbelief in his eyes. She returned his luminous stare, while waiting for a reaction.

"We're going to have a baby?" he asked with a joyful heart.

"Yes, we are going to have a baby," she said.

The little plastic stork wrapped so neatly in the box represented the most precious gift he could have received. Jag was going to be a daddy.

CHAPTER 52

▼

"Come on in, officers," Roberta said, begrudgingly. She opened the squeaking door wearing quite a peculiar ensemble—a short jean skirt that barely covered her upper thighs and an orange tube top that left a small area of her stomach exposed. And she'd added a pig-shaped broach to top off her outfit.

"How do you like my pin, fellas?" she asked with a smirk.

"It's lovely Mrs. Grapler. It suits you just perfectly," Chase replied quick-wittedly. She shot a glare his way and turned to shut the door.

"I figured I'd dress up and look nice for our last day together. I suppose a party dress would have been more appropriate though," Roberta snapped.

"I guess we can get down to business then," Chase said in an attempt to end her unnecessary banter.

"What now? What do ya want from me this time? You'd better make it good. After all, it's your last shot at this."

"First of all, why don't you have Jorge come on out too, that way we can kill two birds with one stone."

"Oh, you'd like that, wouldn't you," she exclaimed. "Sorry, that wasn't part of the deal. He don't wanna see ya no more than I do."

"Do you mind if we take a look around, Mrs. Grapler?"

"Why would I want you pigs snooping around my home?"

"Oh, no, Mrs. Grapler, it's not like that. We aren't suggesting that we open drawers or look in closets; it's not that kind of looking around. We just want to take a glance. You know, look at the wall hangings, see what types of things Charlie likes. We need to get a feel for who he is, just as a last-ditch attempt to learn a little bit more about him. It can only help in our investigation. You aren't a suspect, Mrs. Grapler. It's not about that. We are starting to realize that maybe you have been right all along. There isn't one shred of evidence to suggest that there was any suspicious activity."

An I-told-ya-so smirk radiated off her face.

"I've been telling ya that all along. It's about time ya started believing me. So then, why the hell do you wanna look around?" she asked rudely.

"Mrs. Grapler, we want this investigation over as much as you do. We are trying to wrap things up, but the report needs to be complete or the captain won't sign off on it." The detectives would have said just about anything to get Roberta to cooperate.

"Ya got five minutes to look. No touching!"

"Can I use your bathroom, Mrs. Grapler?" Officer O'Mally asked.

"First door on the left," she barked.

Detectives Chase and Whitaker took a look around as Roberta watched their every move.

"How come Charlie isn't in any of these family pictures?"

"He was a bastard who wasn't around much, why would I wanna look at his face every day?" she responded.

"Do you or Charlie own any guns?" Detective Chase asked.

"You should know the answer to that. I'm sure ya checked the state registration records. So you tell me. Do we own guns?" Roberta asked snidely.

"The State of Idaho shows that neither you nor Charlie own a gun."

"Well then, I guess there's your answer."

As Officer O'Mally exited the small bathroom, he noticed a small window at the end of the hallway. An impulse drew him to it as his radio quietly released police conversations. O'Mally's eyes were immediately drawn away from the rustic environment to an unusual patch of freshly planted grass that covered what appeared to be an eight-by-six plot of land. It was a much lighter shade of green than the rest of the grass that dressed the property.

"Oh, Roberta," he sighed.

"Your five minutes are up guys. I guess you'll be leaving now."

At this point the detectives had no idea what was going through O'Mally's mind or what he had discovered. He returned to the living area without saying a word. It wasn't the right time.

Another twenty minutes passed before Roberta practically threw the men out. The stench of death was long gone and Roberta knew she had literally gotten away with murder, or so she thought.

CHAPTER 53

▼

The roads were congested, surely due to the typical rat race of life. People were coming and going in all directions, desperate to get here and there as fast as they possibly could. Travelers eyed the lane next to them as car horns beeped and drivers tried to pass one another just to get a single car's length ahead of the next guy. It was as if they thought a one-second head start would make a difference.

"This is the very reason I moved to the country to write," Sam said. "I can't tell you how many times I was in one of those cars, racing to get where everyone else was going. Never again."

"It sure raises your stress level. The world would be a much happier place if everyone would just stop to breathe and take a look around them," Dillon replied, not realizing the irony of his statement.

"It's just too easy not to," Sam said.

Although they were in her Jeep Grand Cherokee, Sam enjoyed that Dillon sat behind the wheel. She kind of felt like they were on a date. She dressed up more than usual, especially considering they had a long road trip ahead of them, but she wanted to look nice for Dillon, even if he didn't realize she was doing it. She was hoping that her black, flowing skirt and pineapple yellow blouse had caught his attention.

She reached over and tuned the radio to her favorite soft rock station.

They had been traveling for a few hours, chatting about Charlie, Roberta, and the whole twisted scenario they were in the midst of.

"I'm starving, Dillon. Are you ready to stop for some grub?" Sam asked.

"Well, since you put it so eloquently, how can I refuse?" Dillon said with a chuckle.

They were past the pleasantries of proper conversation. The comfort level of their relationship had blossomed immensely since that first day they'd sipped tea in Roberta Grapler's kitchen.

"What do you feel like having?" Dillon asked.

"Something sit-down, but that won't take a long time. I am dying for a chance to read that journal entry you were telling me about, the last one you read about Charlie's letter to Roberta," Sam said. Reading in the car wasn't something Sam's stomach agreed with.

"How about a buffet? It's both sit-down and quick," Dillon suggested.

She grinned, "Perfect."

As she sipped her coffee, she opened the journal to the page Dillon had marked for her. Her nerves spiked. So many words stared up at her. The last thing she wanted to learn was that her instincts were right on target. She didn't want to know that Charlie was in fact victimized, and that she had helped cover up his murder. She secretly wished the next few pages would be filled with some form of cruel depiction on Charlie's part. Only then would she possibly have a chance at redemption in Dillon's eyes, as well as in her own.

Her self-respect plummeted as she concentrated on every word, every sentence, and every emotion that created the last known thoughts of Charlie Grapler. He was a good man, better yet, he was a great and compassionate man, just as she had begun to assume. He sacrificed his own happiness and his own freedom to give Roberta the space she felt she needed, despite her disillusions of reality. He let his own status of husband go so that his son could have a mother and his wife could have a son. Despite his own pain and suffering, he watched from a distance and suffered the verbal and emotional abuse for years on end to give his family what they wanted. Sam couldn't hate herself anymore than she did at that very moment. She knew most of the mystery of Charlie and Roberta's life was now solved. With her confirmed knowledge, she remained silent. Dillon needed her now more than ever. They were on a mission to find out who Dillon was in this world. This task was first and foremost; it was more important than relieving her conscience of guilt. Losing Dillon's trust and affection was inevitable, but it was going to be lost on her terms. Dillon would discover his past, his identity, and the identity of Jorge before he would learn about the whereabouts of his father. The puzzle would then be complete, and he could carry on with his future without having unanswered questions lingering from his past.

"Sooo … what do you think, sweetheart?" Dillon questioned.

That wasn't a name he had ever called her before. It only exacerbated her already tormented conscious. Water lined her tear ducts, partly out of tenderness, but mainly out of sheer remorse. Ironically, she felt Roberta slowly emerging from her own self with each lie she spoke.

"I think Charlie is an amazing man, and I see a lot of you in him," she responded truthfully.

"You know, I think he's a great man, too."

They finished their meal with little conversation as if satisfied with the words Charlie had left them to ponder. It wasn't long before they were on the road again, headed for the great city of Bend, Oregon. St. Charles Medical Center would be their first stop. Hopefully there was some significance as to why Roberta called there just days after Dillon began staying with her in Idaho.

Their questions were simple. If Dillon was picked up from Oregon on May 13, then why was Roberta calling the hospital there days later? And why was it that when Dillon called the hospital himself, there were no records of a Dillon Grapler or a Jorge Grapler having been a patient there? What was Roberta's connection to Bend in the first place?

The minutes turned into hours as they effortlessly chatted about aspirations and first times. They were amazed at how fast the six-hour drive had flown by as they noticed the road sign reading "Bend 24 miles."

"Well, we're almost there," Dillon said. It wasn't until he saw that sign that his anticipation grew and gripped him tighter than ever before.

"Wow, we are really here. There is no telling what we are about to discover."

"I know, I am nervous for you, Dillon. I know we are doing the right thing, though. It is better to know the truth, even if it is something unexpected or bad, than to not know at all."

As she heard the words coming out of her mouth, her crime flashed through her memory.

"Hypocrite!" she crucified herself silently.

"This is one of the most important journeys I will ever take; I am sure of it. Thanks for being with me on it, Samantha. I have a feeling we will be taking a lot of journeys together," he said with a smile as he put his hand on hers.

She smiled back with tenderness, knowing it probably wouldn't happen, but desperately longing that it would.

She pulled out the city map she had picked up at the last Chevron station they'd stopped at, and began to navigate them to the first stop in their investigation.

"I wonder if Roberta realizes I left?" Dillon asked.

"If not yet, surely by bedtime," Sam said.

"I can only imagine. Her mind will be frantic wondering what I am up to. She'll be crazed at not knowing my intentions or my whereabouts. Do you think she will piece it together? I mean you and I?" Dillon continued.

"I am sure she will have her suspicions. Her mind runs ninety miles an hour. She may wonder, but I don't think she will actually believe it. I think she trusts me," Sam responded.

The hospital turned out to be just a few blocks off of the freeway. They pulled into the first parking spot they saw and walked into the emergency room with determination. They approached the counter.

"Well, hello there, Dillon," the attractive nurse said from behind her desk. Her long face offered soft features. "You are looking like a million bucks. How are you feeling?"

Shock knocked the words right out of Dillon's mouth. He had planned to approach the counter with a scripted story, a story that told the truth about his situation. It was a story that explained that he'd come from Idaho to find answers, that he remembered nothing of his past, and that he was told he had been treated here. It was simple; the truth usually was. Apparently he didn't need to say anything.

"You remember me?" he responded, not knowing what else to say. He had no idea what kind of man he was. Nor did he know what he may have done, or not done, here in Bend, Oregon.

"Of course I remember you. You were a memorable patient," she retorted.

"I hope that is a good thing," he said smiling.

She chuckled.

"What can I do for you. Is everything all right this evening?"

"Yes, everything is fine. I have been meaning to stop by for quite a while to get copies of my records. I can't seem to find them anywhere, and I really think it is important to keep track of it all."

"Well, sure, I can take care of that for you. I can get them into the mail by tomorrow, if you would like."

"Well, I hate to impose, but I can wait if you can get them for me now? Do you have time?"

"You know, actually I can probably swing that. It's been slow around here today. I am sure it won't take me but a couple of minutes. Let me just take a look."

She began typing away on her computer, apparently scrolling through screens and printing out document after document. Within minutes, she was handing him a small pile of papers. His core stacked full of curiosity.

"How is Lanie doing?" she asked.

With no knowledge of who that might be or how she may be doing, he responded safely, "Oh, fine. Thanks for asking."

"She was so worried about you. It was awesome to see such a strong bond between two people. I don't think an hour went by that she wasn't by your side," she responded.

Sam smiled artificially as she listened to the nurse go on and on about this Lanie person. After the gushing came to an end, Sam reached out her hand and said, "Oh, I'm sorry. How rude of me. I'm Samantha, a second cousin."

"It is a pleasure to meet you, Samantha."

They ended their small talk with pleasantries, and it felt like they couldn't get to the car fast enough. The pair hoped they'd just secured a gold mine. The name on the medical reports read "Dillon Andresen."

"Dillon Andresen. Dillon Andresen. Is that my name? Dillon Andresen?" he repeated enthusiastically. "I am not Dillon Grapler or even Jorge Grapler, I am Dillon Andresen."

"Yes, and apparently you are married or at least have a lady in your life," Sam added.

Sam hated the idea that another woman existed in Dillon's life. It had never even crossed her mind that such a discovery would be made. She should have known that such a remarkable catch would be taken.

"You don't deserve him anyway," she reminded herself.

"Lanie. Dillon said. I don't remember that name at all, which doesn't really surprise me. I guess our journey is going to be full of surprises: good, bad, and especially eye-opening. I say we just take it one day at a time, one discovery at a time. As of now, you are my girl, Sam. You are the only certainty in my life."

"Talk about an eye-opening discovery," she thought.

"You want me to be your girl?"

"Don't you want to be?" he asked.

"I absolutely do," she gleefully answered before leaning over and pressing her lips to his.

She wondered if, in the end, she could somehow keep her guilt at bay and never reveal what she'd done in the backyard of Roberta's home. Her mind forced her heart to remain in limbo. She supposed she would never really know how it would play out until the moment of truth presented itself. For now, however, she would enjoy the moment. She would follow through with what they agreed on. They'd agreed to take it one day at a time and one discovery at a time.

CHAPTER 54

▼

Jag and Lanie sat in the fanciest restaurant in town in order to properly toast their good news. The lights dimmed the atmosphere just enough to put a romantic glow on everyone within. Cream linen tablecloths draped delicately across each table, and each was accented with shimmering red cloth napkins. Their impeccably dressed waitress competently discussed the menu with the couple before taking their orders and disappearing. They sat side by side holding hands, waiting for their sparkling cider to arrive. Lanie wore a black sequined gown that skimmed the floor when she walked, and one-karat diamonds decorated each of her earlobes. A clear polish covered her recently manicured nails.

"You look stunning," Jag said. He then subtly leaned in and rubbed his lips across her neck, smelling the soft fragrance of her perfume while he was there. A smile warmed her radiant face.

Their waitress, Isabella, arrived promptly with two wine glasses of sparkling cider and a porcelain bowl filled with homemade honey bread drizzled with cinnamon butter.

"That smells amazing," Lanie said.

Lanie thanked their waitress before ordering lemon pepper salmon with angel hair pasta in a creamy garlic sauce. "I'll have the same," Jag said.

"To our future: May each day bring with it new and exciting adventures. May our love flourish with every passing moment of time. May our baby grow healthy and strong from inside your beautiful body." Jag smiled and paused for a brief moment. "And may I never take you, our love, or our good fortune for granted. Here's to the excitement of the unknown."

They clanked their crystal glasses together delicately and each took a sip of their beverage.

"So, where do you want to go first?" Jag asked. "A beach, a lake, another country, the end of the earth? It's your choice baby."

Elation escalated within him. No longer would he be bound by the power of his mother's manipulation.

"I would love to go to New England. I have always wanted to go there. With autumn coming up, it will be beautiful. The leaves will be changing colors soon, which will only make it even more breathtaking," Lanie gushed as a bite of bread melted on her tongue.

Jag had never been to the East Coast, or anywhere east of Idaho for that matter.

"Sounds good," he said.

They casually made plans for their trip throughout their delicious dinner. Each morsel of his thirty-five-dollar meal reminded him of what was to come. His old life of poverty and loneliness faded farther and farther from his mind, as did his need for his mother's approval and companionship. With Lanie as his new leading lady, his mother would only get in their way.

"So, when do you want to leave? How about the day after tomorrow?" Jag said.

"The day after tomorrow? I think that cider has gone to your head. We can't leave that soon."

"Sure we can. I have a few loose ends to clear up at the bank, mainly quitting, and then we're off."

"I have to talk to my boss. We just talked about this, remember? I need to try and get a replacement to fill my shoes so there is no break in responsibility." The surprise sprung from her expression.

"You always tell me what a jerk he is to you, why are you feeling obligated to let him down easy?" Jag asked as he casually wiped cream sauce from his white tie.

"I don't know. I guess I feel that I have a professional responsibility not only to him, but to my co-workers and to the millions of starving people," she said.

"If you think about it, what do all those starving and impoverished people want and need? They need money. What do you say we give your organization a large donation? They can use it to send that much more needed aid. It will feed thousands and provide medical care for just as many. In the end, helping them is what matters, right? I say, if we are going to do this, and I mean really do this, we just need to go for it. We can make excuses for staying and putting it off every day for the rest of our lives, but I say let's just do it. Life here in Bend will go on without us."

Jag impressed himself with his speech. Hopefully he'd impressed his lady as well.

"So what do you say? Are you with me?"

"You bet I'm with you!" Lanie responded with excitement. "That was quite a pep talk, Dillon. I bet you could talk me into just about anything." They both continued on with their delicious meals and just enjoyed the moment.

The phone was ringing as they entered their beautiful and well-maintained home. The scent of blossoms blessed their noses as they passed a bouquet of recently picked wild flowers that stood at attention in a crystal vase they had received from an antique shop a week or so before. Jokingly, they both raced for the phone, trying to see who could get to it first.

"Hello?" Lanie asked while laughing as Jag fell onto the couch.

Click.

"Hmmm, they hung up." She plopped down next to him and rubbed her nose against his.

Jag had a pretty good idea that it was probably his mother trying to hunt him down so she could play mind games on him. His happy mood died. His hatred for her flared to new heights. He still couldn't figure out the logic behind her deception, but he also couldn't deny the telling letters. He yearned to ask his mama about them, but knew nothing but suspicion would result from it. He wondered if his own deception would ever come back to haunt him, if somehow Lanie would ever discover the truth. Staying far away from Bend, Oregon, and Emmett, Idaho, had become priority number one. He walked over to his Angel, touched her stomach to feel close to his unborn child, and wondered silently if it was in fact his flesh and blood in there, or actually the flesh and blood of his despicable twin brother. Jag vividly remembered the night he'd watched Dillon and Lanie making love on the living room floor before he was able to infiltrate his way into her life. Jag didn't want to know the due date, and he didn't want to know exactly when the doctor claimed the child had been conceived. He just wanted to believe his version of their reality. The phone rang again, but Jag had no intention of answering it. Surely if it was his mother, she would hang up once again if Lanie answered the telephone.

"Could you get that for me, hon? I am expecting a call from Rachel," she said as she was on her way to the bathroom.

He walked to the telephone, hoping and wishing it was not who he thought it would be.

"Hello?" he said with hesitation coating his voice.

"Hey, it's me, how are things going?"

"Are you crazy calling here? Lanie is just in the other room. I'll call you another time."

"Don't you dare hang up on me. I am still your mother, and I need to talk to you."

Jag wanted nothing more than to tell her a few choice words and then simply hang up the phone, but he knew he couldn't do that, at least not now. Plus, he felt guilty. He still wondered in the back of his mind if she was actually conspiring against Dillon and not him. Then again maybe she was playing them both. He pressed the receiver tightly to his ear.

"Sorry, Mama, what is it that ya need?" he said in his normal, obedient fashion.

"I'm just wondering how things are going. I haven't had no update, so I's just worried about ya."

"Things are fine. They're just as we planned."

"Time's running short, I gotta get outta here; I mean *we* gotta get outta here," Roberta said. "Dillon up and left; he just disappeared. I ain't seen him since early this morning. I think his memory came back or something, but I ain't sure."

Jag didn't know what to think or what to say.

"Gosh, Mama, I am sure he is just on one of those walks you say he takes. Don't worry. I'm sure if his memory came back he would have had said something to say to you. After all, you did kidnap him. He wouldn't just walk away quietly."

"You're probably right, but I'm really worried. Let's get our plan going and get outta here. Where have you been hiding the money, Jorge, and how much is there? I can meet ya somewhere and we can take off together. Just tell me where it is. I can pick it up, then I'll pick you up, and we can disappear," Roberta continued. "Just you and me."

Jag just felt it in his bones that something wasn't right. Her concern for the money and a quick departure created even more suspicion. The irritating sound of her demanding voice picked at his nerves. He wasn't sure he could stand to hear another word come out of her uneducated mouth.

"Oh, Lanie is coming. I have to hang up. I'll call ya as soon as I can. We can make plans then. Sorry, Mama; talk to ya soon; love ya."

Jag spurted it all out at rapid speed so she wouldn't have a chance to interrupt him. He'd lied of course. Lanie was still in the bathroom, probably taking a bath by now. In the big scheme of things, it didn't really matter.

Anger and panic gripped Roberta. She sensed her control fading. She craved reassurance. Just yesterday it seemed like she controlled the world. Everything flowed like clockwork. The police investigation had hit a dead end, Dillon sat in stupidity unaware of his true identity, Jorge had thousands of dollars stashed away for her, and Sam did whatever she was asked. Now, nothing but uncertainty tormented her sanity.

"I need to be in control. How dare they put me off? Damn them all!" she screeched as she grabbed the phone and dialed Chuck, one of her favorite and most cooperative and aggressive johns.

"Get over here now! I don't care what you are doing or who you are with; just get here."

He always came to her when she called, just like most of her men. Many seemed to enjoy her dominating mannerisms; others were stuck under her thumb because of something she had over them. It didn't matter to her if they wanted to be there or not, as long as they cooperated when she needed them to. She changed into something provocative and watched the clock. It never took Chuck long to get to her house. As for Dillon, she had had it with waiting on his return. She wasn't going to curb her urges until he decided to show himself. If he returned during her escapade, then he could just listen to her call out another man's name, a name other than his daddy's. It would serve him right for selfishly abandoning her for the day. Thoughts of what he could be doing stormed through her head. She wondered if he was out with some slut or bad-mouthing her to someone in town. Maybe he was remembering things and talking to the police about her or stealing money from her bank account. "He is just like his daddy, the bastard!" she thought. And just as her frenzy had reached its peak, Chuck pulled up.

"It's about damn time!" She grabbed him by the hair and led him into her bedroom. Her black see-through nightgown went all the way to the floor. She had nothing on underneath it but thigh-high stockings. It was a typical ensemble for her almost-weekly habit, a habit she'd been forced to curb since Dillon's arrival. "Hit me!" she commanded. Chuck knew the drill as he raised his hand and slapped her across the cheek. "Again!" she yelled. Once more, he raised his hand and struck her in the same spot as before, only harder. He grabbed her, threw her on the bed forcefully, and had his way with her just as he had on so many other occasions. She reciprocated the masochistic behavior, and from time to time she even managed to release most of her aggressions. It was just what she needed. She'd sunk her teeth into Chuck's skin on more than one occasion, and often left his wrists with marks of strangulation from the metal handcuffs she had purposely put on too tight. Once she grew tired of his presence and she'd gotten as much pleasure from him as she needed, she kicked him out without a second thought.

"All right, now get the hell outta here. I don't need ya no more," she'd casually say.

"See you next time," he'd say with a smile.

"You disgust me!" she would shout out as he walked away.

Tonight had been no different.

It wasn't a secret that she hated men; she hated everything about them except for what they could do for her. If an encounter involved money or sex, she would use them, abuse them, and then discard them. Chuck got exactly what he wanted; she knew it, and so did he.

The door closed behind him, and she quickly jumped into the shower to wash off the filth of a man. She threw her sheets into the washing machine to give them a proper cleansing, which reminded her of the night that she had killed her husband. The pleasant memory brought a slice of happiness to her dismal mood.

Dillon still had not returned from wherever he had disappeared to, and Sam wouldn't be back for at least a week.

She crawled into bed and laid her head on the ten-year-old pillow after taking two sleeping pills.

CHAPTER 55

▼

Sam's Cherokee pulled slowly into the dreary motel parking lot as she and Dillon looked at each other with similar thoughts of apprehension.

"I wonder who she called here?" Sam questioned while holding Roberta's phone records. They parked under one of the dim lights near the junky reception area.

"Be sure to lock the door," Dillon reminded her as they stepped out of the car.

"What have we gotten ourselves into?" she whispered to him, while walking quickly toward the entrance.

"Good evening," she said to the slender man behind the counter. His stubble well exceeded a five o'clock shadow, and his odor reminded her of spoiled milk. He sat on a metal folding chair behind the counter eating chips and beans. Piles of papers cluttered the counter.

"Back so soon? You come to settle, I'm hoping?" the motel receptionist blurted.

Chills blazed through Dillon's body. He searched for a clever retort.

"Am I that memorable?" Dillon spoke with a smile and a racing pulse.

"Well, you were here long enough, how could I not," he responded.

Curious thoughts splashed around in Dillon's mind.

"Actually, I would like to stay a few more nights," Dillon said as he put his arm around Sam and gave her a little squeeze.

"How much do I owe you from last time?"

"Twenty-one fifty," the man said.

Sam pulled some bills out of her front pocket and handed them to the scrawny man.

"Can I have the same room as last time?" she asked

"Sure, it's open. How long ya plan on staying this time?"

"Oh, just a few days. I got some loose ends to tie up. You by any chance have a copy of my last bill?"

"I can probably find it somewhere round here. I can bring it to ya in a few minutes, unless you wanna wait."

"I can wait. Got nothing to do but hit the sack." Even though the motel lacked any sense of style or charm, Sam and Dillon welcomed a good night's sleep.

Within a few minutes, the motel clerk pulled a piece of paper out of the stack of unorganized records. He handed it to Dillon along with the key to room 119.

Dillon and Sam sat together on the tacky, polyester comforter, and together they examined their less-than-adequate sleeping quarters. A few minor holes embellished the popcorn-textured walls and a large yellow stain covered an entire corner of the room's carpet. The odor of stale tobacco and mildew assaulted their noses, triggering Sam to spray her very favorite and very expensive perfume throughout the room.

"It's just a few nights. It will be just fine," Sam reminded him.

"I am not going to let a bit of toxic fumes and an inevitable rodent run me out of here," he said with a grin.

They unfolded the old invoice.

"Jorge Grapler?"

"Look at the dates," Sam suggested. "It looks like you stayed here for several months right up until the time Roberta took you to Idaho."

Dillon continued to run a question-and-answer session with himself. He was trying to make sense of everything. He was Dillon Andresen according to his hospital records, yet he was Jorge Grapler here at dump-town USA.

"I don't know what to think, Sam. Who the hell am I?"

"Let's take this one step at a time, Dillon. We know you stayed here for a few months; we know you checked out of this motel on the very same day that you were admitted into the hospital; and we know that you arrived at Roberta's house in Idaho one day after you were supposedly admitted into the hospital. We also know that the entire time you were supposedly in the hospital, you were actually in Idaho with Roberta, and without a memory. There is no way you could have been in two places at one time, let alone two states at the same time. You have to have a twin out there somewhere. It is the only logical solution. We just have to find him."

"I just wonder which one I am. Am I Dillon Andresen or Jorge Grapler? I am willing to bet that I am definitely not Jorge. I am too much the opposite of Roberta Grapler to be Jorge. I have a feeling I am Dillon. I am used to that name; it seems to suit me. Don't ya think?"

"It doesn't matter what your name is, honey. You are who you are. And I adore you just as you are, memory or no memory."

"I wonder what the hell it's all for. What is the point behind all the lying? What is the big secret?" Dillon asked.

"I am sure it has something to do with money or property or something valuable," Sam replied.

"I wonder who I was. Maybe I was a bad guy. Maybe I deserve the uncertainty that life has brought me."

"Or maybe, just maybe, you are the victim," Sam countered sincerely.

"You know, I have nothing to lose. I am going to go talk to 'Mr. Scruff' back in the motel office. I am just going to lay it all out. I'm just going to flat out ask him what all he knows about me."

With that, Dillon exited the room and headed for the motel office.

On his way to the office, he heard a voice ask, "Where's your fancy Beemer?"

Dillon turned and saw a man leaning against a pole across the parking lot. He held a cigarette in one hand and a bottle of something dark in the other.

"Excuse me? Do you know me?"

"You mean to tell me ya don't remember our little encounter?" he asked in a harsh and monotonous voice. Dillon had had just about enough of being in the dark about everything. He aggressively approached the bold man.

"What do you know about me? What happened during our encounter?"

"You off your rocker or something? I'm the guy you grabbed by the throat and threatened to hurt if I didn't leave ya be."

"Well, don't make me do it again. I've had a bad couple of weeks, actually a bad couple of months for that matter. I can't remember anything, not even my name. So, since you went out of your way to holler at me from across the parking lot, I must have made quite an impression on you."

The unknown infuriated Dillon. He needed some answers, anything that could provide some insight.

"I'm not going to ask you twice. Just tell me what you know. Anything … anything at all!"

He handed Dillon his bottle and told him to take a seat.

They sat together in the misty night air discussing the events that had occurred on May 13 of that year. The stranger may not have had all the answers, but he was able to paint a vivid picture of an event from Dillon's past.

CHAPTER 56

▼

Roberta rolled herself out of bed at around 8:00 AM. Without an extra second ticking on the clock, she propelled herself toward her ungrateful son's room.

"He had better be there!" she thought.

She flung the door open, only to find a neatly made bed, that looked just as it had when she'd gone to bed last night. Her temper flared, not just because Dillon had failed to return home the previous night, but mainly because she knew she had lost all control. It seemed as though all the men in her life were turning on her, and she would have none of it.

"I should have known better than to trust any man, especially Dillon," she thought.

In her own warped thinking pattern, she believed she had been deeply wronged. The fact that her thumb no longer rested upon the shoulders of her unsuspecting son was, to her, a betrayal on his part. There was one man left in her lonely life that she could count on. Her thick fingers hastily dialed the same number they'd been dialing for more than a year.

"Officer O'Mally, can I help you?"

"Oh, cut the BS. It's me. We got a problem."

"What would that be, Roberta?" he asked, annoyed.

"Dillon didn't come home last night. I ain't seen him for almost twenty-four hours. I'm worried his memory came back."

"What exactly do you want me to do about it? You're supposed to be handling Dillon. I'm in charge of handling the investigation."

"What … you ain't gonna help me? You got nothing to say about it at all? Ya know what? Fine, you son of a bitch. Just sit there in your cubicle stroking your little pencil, I'll do the rest!" Roberta screamed. "You're just like every other man!"

"Pull yourself together. Damn it Roberta; calm down! You are an awfully unappreciative woman, you know that, but that is one of the things I like about you, I guess. You are a challenge."

Tate O'Mally had a way with words. He managed to not only insult a person, but to also make them feel good about themselves at the same time.

"First of all, I have gone above and beyond the call of duty, like the good policeman that I am. If it wasn't for me, Investigations would know about Jorge's stay at the hospital; they'd know about Dillon's real residence and life in Bend; they'd know that Jorge is there posing in his place; and they'd know that you had basically kidnapped your own son. And what about Sam. Let's talk about her for a minute, shall we? We both know that if someone had actually questioned her, she would have cracked and the case would have been blown wide open. Surely you are aware that I have fudged just about every report that has been submitted on you and on this case. Oh, and one more thing, it doesn't take a genius to figure out that the body of your late husband is buried out behind your house. You may as well have just put an arrow out there with the name CHARLIE written in big bold letters. That would have been just as inconspicuous. You know, you took a simple kidnapping-and-theft operation and somehow twisted it into a messy murderous plot. None of that was part of the plan, the fact that you murdered your husband only complicated matters. If you would have stuck to the plan, Dillon would be locked up right now, Charlie would be alive, and no one would be the wiser. You know the original plan! You have put us all at risk. So before you start jumping on my case because your crazy mind tells you to, think about how I have done nothing but go above and beyond for you," he said, smugly.

"You ain't doing it for me. I ain't stupid. You're doing it for the money. I just happen to be the one thing between you and the cash, so you have to protect me. You have to be on my side. And if where I buried Charlie was so damn obvious, why ain't no one so much as blinked an eye at it?"

"I can't explain the stupidity of others, just the brilliance of myself."

Roberta may not have been able to see his face, but she knew without a doubt that he smirked in self-satisfaction.

"Let's just get to the point, Roberta. When is Jorge going to have it all?"

"I ain't sure. I think any day now," Roberta replied.

"Any day like tomorrow? Any day like next week? When?"

"I dunno!"

"How much has he gotten so far?"

"Ain't sure exactly."

"What do you know, exactly?" O'Mally asked as irritation cursed his voice.

"I know that last time we spoke, he had seventy-five thousand, plus access to lots more."

"Seventy-five thousand? That's it? There are millions at his fingertips! I could blow my nose with seventy-five thousand," O'Mally snapped. "It sounds to me like you don't have a handle on anything. Maybe that's because Jorge doesn't want you to. Maybe he has a little plan of his own."

"Well, there is one way to find out. I am heading to Oregon just as soon as I can get myself packed," Roberta said.

"What do you plan on accomplishing there?" he asked.

"A whole hell of a lot more than I'm accomplishing here. I think Dillon's memory must have come back or something. He's probably a loose cannon. Who knows what's going on in his head. I ain't just going to sit around and do nothing," Roberta said.

"You know, moving on doesn't sound like such a bad idea. I have pushed my luck here, and am actually amazed at how much I have gotten away with. I suppose it only makes sense to move on before anyone puts two and two together," O'Mally said.

"That's just stupid. They's really gonna think something is up if we both just disappear, Dillon too for that matter."

"Roberta, use your head here. I am not going to just disappear. I'll take a leave of absence, maybe make up a family emergency … something like that. Don't worry. Just drive your truck to the train station and park on the west side of level two. I'll pick you up in a few hours. Be ready."

"Fine, but make it two hours," Roberta snapped.

O'Mally sighed, knowing that she always had to have the last word.

"All right, Roberta, I'll try to make it there in two hours. Hey, put something on your machine that says you're visiting family out of state or something. Be convincing and breezy about it; just don't sound suspicious."

The two of them hung up; each irritated with the other. Nothing good was to come of the next twenty-four hours, at least not for the two of them.

CHAPTER 57

▼

The maddening sound of the alarm blared incessantly as Dillon struggled to open his eyelids.

"When did you make it in? I waited up as long as I could, but apparently I fell asleep long before you got back," Sam said.

"I don't even know. One thirty or so, I think," Dillon responded.

"So, who was that man you were with last night?" Sam's mouth opened wide to exhale a strong yawn.

"He supposedly knew me, or at least someone who looked like me. I think my brother and I were both here at the same time, together. I also think a third person was here as well, and I would bet that person was Roberta."

"Does that guy know them or something? Did he see you all together?"

"Boyd, that's his name, said I was here on May 13, and I was trying to carry a drunk man into this very room. I apparently asked Boyd for assistance. So we both ended up hauling the drunk guy in and plopping him onto the bed. Boyd also said that as soon as we entered the room he noticed a cloud of fresh cigarette smoke lingering in the air and he could also smell strong perfume. So, the way I see it is that there was someone in the room before we got there," Dillon said.

"Did Boyd see Roberta?" Sam asked.

"No, he only saw the two men, one of them being me. But if you think about it, Roberta smokes and isn't all that subtle with her perfume. I'm sure it was her; it had to have been. Oh and there was also a white truck parked out front, along with the BMW that the two guys arrived in. I'm assuming those two guys were me and Jorge. I am convinced Roberta and Jorge are in on this together. They must want something from me."

"Like I said, money is the root of all evil. Maybe the BMW is yours. Maybe you are rich, but just don't know it because of your memory loss," Sam suggested.

"It would make sense. Not to sound conceited or anything, but I think it is obvious that I have been well educated, I have a good head on my shoulders, and I seem to generally like sophisticated things. I guess I don't need a memory to know that."

"You're right, it was apparent the first time we met," Sam said, as she yawned for the third time since their conversation had begun.

"Hey, let's get some coffee in us and get on the road. I think today is going to bring with it a lot more pieces of the puzzle." She crawled out from the warm covers wearing cotton shorts and a large Harvard T-shirt. She traced a comb through her rumpled hair and pinned it back nicely with a few bobby pins.

"I'll change in the bathroom," she offered.

On their way out, Dillon gave his new acquaintance a sincere "thank you" for providing him with what no one else would, the honest and raw truth.

"I hope to repay you someday."

Boyd tipped his hat in appreciation and waved good-bye to the couple.

After stopping for a quick bite to eat, it only took the couple about ten minutes to arrive at their next destination.

"What an exquisite home," Sam said with admiration.

"I wonder if it is mine?" Dillon uttered.

His eyes scanned the property closely, using a pair of Roberta's ancient binoculars. His heart fluttered when he saw the name inscribed on the wooden mailbox.

"Andresen," he said aloud.

Sam looked at him and then took a hold of the binoculars to see for herself.

"I guess this is your house, Mr. Dillon Andresen. It's remarkable."

While so happy for him and his discovery, she also secretly resented what she was witnessing. The beautiful home, the white picket fence, a woman named Lanie probably inside.

"I bet you have a dog too," she said, as she looked at him and smiled. "It looks like you already have everything else."

"Remember, honey, one day at a time, one discovery at a time."

She smiled, despite her worried heart.

"So what now, Dillon?"

"I guess we wait. We'll wait and watch at least until it's a decent enough hour to where you can go and knock on the door."

"Knock on the door? Me? And say what?" Sam asked.

"I don't really know. I guess you can leave it up to your reporter side," Dillon said.

"Do you think my brother is inside? Do you really think I have a twin?" Dillon wasn't sure what to truly believe. He asked again, "What do you think?"

"I don't know, hon. I think it is very much a possibility. I think all of the evidence we have found so far leads to there being two of you. It is the only explanation for people thinking you were here in Bend at the same time you were actually in Emmett with Roberta. There is really no other explanation that could make more sense. Let's just watch and wait. I think we will have it figured out soon, I really do."

Sam prayed for a happy ending, but each step they took that brought them closer to discovering the truth about Jorge and Roberta meant they were also another step closer to Dillon discovering the truth about her.

It wasn't but a couple of hours before the two of them witnessed a beautiful woman exiting Dillon's house. She pranced down the steps in what appeared to be a pair of black yoga pants accompanied by a soft, pastel-pink stretch top, and she had a bag slung over her right shoulder. Her carefree energy exuberated off her. Both Dillon and Sam felt mesmerized by Lanie's carefree presence. Neither of them said a word as they watched until her car drove out of sight. Their next few seconds of silence lasted forever and a day. Sam campaigned against her instincts over whether or not that woman was Lanie, the wife of her current love.

CHAPTER 58

▼

"You were right, one hundred percent right," Detective Whitaker confessed. "That little bastard! I hate to admit it, but I didn't even see it coming."

Chase and Whitaker sat behind closed doors in their lieutenant's office. Indignation and disgust consumed them.

"How did I not see this coming?"

"Damn it!" Whitaker continued. His lack of insight blew him away.

"There's more," Lieutenant Steele said. "A lot more."

His large pointer finger pressed the play button again as the room fell silent.

"First of all, I have gone above and beyond the call of duty, like the good policeman that I am. If it wasn't for me, Investigations would know about Jorge's stay at the hospital; they'd know about Dillon's real residence and life in Bend; they'd know that Jorge is there posing in his place; and they'd know that you had basically kidnapped your own son. And what about Sam. Let's talk about her for a minute, shall we? We both know that if someone had actually questioned her, she would have cracked and the case would have been blown wide open. Surely you are aware that I have fudged just about every report that has been submitted on you and on this case. Oh, and one more thing, it doesn't take a genius to figure out that the body of your late husband is buried out behind your house. You may as well have just put an arrow out there with the name CHARLIE written in big bold letters. That would have been just as inconspicuous. You know, you took a simple kidnapping-and-theft operation and somehow twisted it into a messy murderous plot. None of that was part of the plan, the fact that you murdered your husband only complicated matters. If you would have stuck to the plan, Dillon would be locked up right now, Charlie would be alive, and no one would be the wiser. You know the original plan ..."

Every single person in the room stood shell-shocked at the recorded words.

"How did you get this information, Lieutenant? I mean, how did you get a warrant to tap Roberta's telephone? I thought it was impossible due to the circumstances of the case and, of course, the lack of evidence?" Detective Whitaker questioned.

"I didn't tap Roberta's telephone, I tapped O'Mally's," he said. "Things just weren't adding up. He seemed quite involved in the case, but yet brought nothing to the table. His reports were filled with fluff. There were very few specifics. There were no point-of-contact names on any of the searches he supposedly accomplished; he turned in nothing in writing from the sheriff's office in Bend; there was nothing that really proved he accomplished even an iota of what he claimed he did. So to make a long story short, I called Bend myself. My gut was right, he'd never even contacted them."

Detectives Whitaker and Chase lowered their heads in unison.

"Did either of you check out any of the leads?"

They didn't dare answer his rhetorical question.

"You two are the lead detectives on this case. The lead detectives! That means you lead! You don't follow the lead of a beat cop who has had no formal detective training and who is supposed to be assisting you. If that were the case, you two would have been the assistant detectives, now wouldn't you? If you want to assist, I can arrange that. Now I know you guys are capable of greatness. I also know that you have brains somewhere in those thick skulls of yours, and I definitely know that none of you are going to let a crooked cop get the best of you. However, I am utterly disappointed that it took me less than forty-eight hours to solve a crime that you've been working on for weeks!"

Lieutenant Steele's hand hammered down forcefully onto the old oak desk. His heavy footsteps echoed as he paced the room, and he ran his hands across his shaved head.

"So, ladies, the question still remains. Do you want to assist, or do you want to earn your paychecks and actually lead this investigation?" the lieutenant asked.

Chase and Whitaker continued to sit quietly and respectfully, while accepting their lashings like men.

"Well, which one is it?" Steele asked again in a loud, firm tone.

"Lead sir," the two of them shouted in unison.

"Well, your ass chewing is going to have to wait until later then. We have a dead body to dig up; we have Roberta and O'Mally heading to Oregon; and we have a ton of unanswered questions to resolve. Let's get moving." The two detectives efficiently rose up and dashed for the exit.

"And Whitaker! Tuck your shirt in. You look like a slob!" Steele yelled after them.

CHAPTER 59

▼

"Hello?" Sam paused.

"Really?"

Dillon attentively listened to her one-sided phone conversation; knowing it was probably news he would be interested in as well. He waited patiently for the call to end, eager to hear any news that would help them in their search for the truth.

"That was Lou, my friend and contact from the newspaper. He's been doing some digging for us. Apparently, Roberta's medical records indicate that she only visited the doctor three times during her pregnancy. The last time was at three months, and apparently the annotations suggest there were possibly two heart-beats, but the records end there. She never returned to the doctor, at least not one Lou could find. And let me tell you, Lou seems to have the key to the country. I don't know how he does it, but he's so good, he could track down Big Foot for the right price."

"Did he look into adoption agencies? Did anything show up about adoption?"

"Nope, there was nothing specifically on adoption; but get this …" she couldn't wait to finish her dishing. "… last night when you were talking with that man out in the parking lot, I called Lou. I gave him all the information we had so far, most importantly your last name, Andresen. Turns out, there was a couple who used to live in Central Idaho who up and left about twenty-four years ago. They moved to a place called Crescent Lake, which is only a couple of hours from Bend. They had a baby in tow, but there was no record of a birth."

Dillon continued to listen, wondering what she was getting at.

"So, I think it was you. You were that baby. Their names were Sharon and Cliff Andresen. Sharon was a nurse, a midwife." Sam looked at Dillon with such enthusiasm. "We are finally putting all of the pieces of the puzzle together," Sam continued. "She must have been the one who helped Roberta deliver. They probably knew your whole story."

"What do you mean knew? Past tense?"

"That is the horrible part of it all. They were in a tragic accident. They both died when their car was hit by a train."

Dillon sat a moment and tried to absorb it all. It was so much to think about. Even though he didn't know Sharon and Cliff, or at least didn't remember them, his heart ached. He wondered how he could miss people he never even remembered knowing. At the same time however, his heart overflowed with gratefulness and hope. He had discovered that a real piece of his past was alive and well, and that there was more to Dillon Andresen than what Roberta had claimed.

"Sharon and Cliff, those are good names, huh? I bet they were good people," Dillon said.

"I am sure they were great people," Sam replied.

They took an unplanned pause.

It was time.

Sam's brown, lace-up sandals swung out onto the pavement and began dragging her toward the front door of the yellow house. One by one, she yanked out the pins that held her hair hostage.

As she walked up to the house she gave herself a pep talk, "Imagine you are a reporter again. Get the story! It's all about the story!" Her self-coaching bullied her fears. Each approaching stride became easier and easier.

"Do it for Dillon. You owe him that much," she told herself.

Dillon sunk low into the Cherokee's leather bucket seat. Eagerness consumed him. The temptation to look at who opened that door monopolized his voice of reason. His resistance stayed strong. Hastily, Sam activated the doorbell. "There's no going back now," she thought. Her stomach twirled with each passing second. She briefly scanned the neighborhood.

A dark-haired man discreetly eyeballed her from a side window. With a smile and a wave, Sam made it very obvious that she had seen him. Her SUV sat across the street with its hood propped up. Her hazard lights had been activated and were actively screaming for help. Without thinking twice, Jag unlatched and then opened his door to her.

There, before Jag, stood a nice-looking woman, most likely in her mid- to late thirties. She had a winning smile with very distinctive dimples on each side of her pale cheeks. The color of her hair shared a striking resemblance to that of a perfect cup of hot chocolate. A simple pair of loose jeans and a frilly, white blouse made her femininity shine.

"Can I help you, miss?" Jag asked, politely.

Her mouth refused to open. Tingles surged through her. Her eyes traced his every feature. "Ma'am? Did you need some help? Are you having car trouble?"

As if starstruck, she maintained her stare for a moment longer as she looked into the face of Dillon. She slammed her eyes shut, took a lengthy breath, and proceeded.

"I'm sorry, I am pretty shaken up. My car broke down right over there. I thought it was going to catch on fire or something." A slight weep sneaked out of her mouth. "I am hundreds of miles away from home and it's just unsettling."

"Do you want me to take a look at your car for you?"

"Ahhh, no. That won't be necessary. I just wanted to know if I could use your phone and possibly your bathroom? I have Triple A. They'll be out here in no time. I figure I pay for the service, so I should take advantage of it when I can," she said.

As she entered the immaculate home, she noticed that boxes cluttered the floor.

"You moving?"

"I guess you can call it that."

"You must be going some place pretty special to be giving up such a beautiful home."

He just looked at her and nodded in agreement. His clothes shouted sophistication; she could definitely imagine Dillon wearing the same khaki slacks and burgundy cashmere sweater.

"The phone is right over there," Jag said as he pointed.

Her eyes discreetly roamed as she approached the bar that linked the cushy living room to the spotless kitchen. She picked up the receiver and dialed a 1-800 number, leaving off the "1." She continued her inspection. She thought she remembered this same home in an issue of *Country Living*, but she decided against it. Skillfully crafted woodwork, quilts, pillows, and furniture that looked aged, but surely was not, offered a warm and unpretentious environment. Thoughts of her and Dillon sitting at the table or opening the huge silver refrigerator for a beer invaded her quick daydream. The idea of them sitting in this comfortable space together heated her heart. It was a dream that would surely never exist due to her soon-to-be announced betrayal. As she hung up the telephone, Jag pointed in the direction of the bathroom and she proceeded on with her mission. The reporter in her scanned the hallway, quietly opening doors as she passed them. The medicine cabinet revealed nothing except prescription bottles that listed the patient as Dillon Andresen, which she'd basically figured out on her own. Without a true understanding of what she hoped to find, she left with the best piece of information available—confirmation.

He offered to let her wait inside for the tow truck to arrive. She insisted, however, on waiting with her vehicle. She claimed that she had a good book waiting to be finished in the glove box. She heard the door latch behind her as she skipped down the steps.

"So, what did you find? Who was inside?" Dillon asked with anticipation.

Shock still mauled her mind.

"It is true; it is all true. He didn't give his name, but he's your identical twin," she blurted.

"What in the world is going on here, Sam? Why are there two of me? Why is it a secret? Why would Roberta, my apparent mother, do such a thing? What are they possibly gaining from all of this?"

"I wish I could answer all of your questions, honey, I do."

She compassionately put her hand on his knee.

"What now?" Dillon asked. "What now?"

"Oh, and there were prescription painkillers in his medicine cabinet. They were prescribed after you started living with Roberta. Somehow he managed to swap lives with you."

His stillness and blank stare revealed his racing mind, as Sam placed a quick call to Ken to share the news they had gained so far.

"… and this is the address we are at in case anything goes wrong. I'm not sure what we are about to get into, but it's bound to be explosive on some level," Sam said as she ended her call.

"Ready?"

"Ready," Sam said.

They exited the car, grabbed one another's hands, and walked directly up to the front door. Dillon moved over to the side of the porch in order to remain undetectable until he was ready to show his face.

CHAPTER 60

▼

While biting into a piece of apple streusel pie, Roberta's stare anxiously scanned the dining room. Roberta detected watchful eyes and knowing minds within the truck stop restaurant. She softly, and as inconspicuously as possible, signaled to O'Mally that they had to get out of there before it was too late to do so.

"I'll hit the john, you hit the gift shop, and we'll meet at the car in exactly four minutes."

"You're acting crazy. If people are staring, it is only because you are acting like a loon. Just eat your damn pie and be quiet."

Her eyes cursed at him in utter disapproval.

"The last time a man tried to shut me up, he ended up six feet under," she said with assertiveness. "Remember that the next time you're opening your mouth to me," she added.

He shook his head in annoyance, but humored her.

"All right, Roberta, you've made your point. I'm sorry. Let's just get the check paid and get back on the road."

They proceeded to the register, before heading out to the car.

As they exited the building, quick chaos exploded. The vibration of stomping boots shook Roberta to her core. Her rage blazed like the blue flames of a burning house.

"Stop!"

The three men she could see all wore black jumpsuits and held handguns that were pointed at her demented brain. She knew that shooting a woman in the back was the best way to get kicked off of the force. With that in mind, she quickly grabbed O'Mally's arm, turned, and ran to the side. She would have left him for dead, if only he hadn't possessed the keys to both the car and her future wealth.

"STOP! I won't say it again!" one of the officers yelled.

"O'Mally broke away from her, stopped dead in his tracks, smirked, and pulled his own gun on her.

She looked back, "What are you doing, you good-for-nothing son of a bitch? You're in on this?" she asked in disbelief. "I should've known! I should've known! No man is worth nothing! You'll pay for this, just like all the men in my life!"

She turned back around and began her sprint again. Her leopard-print high heels and her skintight black jeans hindered her getaway, but her efforts continued nonetheless. The sound of exploding gunfire resonated in her ears. She knew, without a doubt, that the bullets were aimed at her. They were out to get her just like all the rest of them. They didn't get it; they didn't understand. She was hit square in the back. An instant and intense burning swelled through her body. She imagined a hot iron rod being jabbed into her flesh, then being turned and turned as it created a larger and larger gaping hole in her spine.

At that moment, she knew how Charlie had felt the night she'd shot a bullet into his head. It actually soothed her some. Her palms smashed into the pebbly ground before her face skidded across the pavement. She used all of the strength she had left to drag herself as best as she could. She didn't know where she was going. She wanted to go somewhere, anywhere, as if she could somehow hide from the all-knowing and all-seeing eyes. Her time appeared to be up. She felt a pull at her shoulder and she rolled over onto her back. Blood and road rash branded her face. She squinted, trying to focus in on the man who'd taken her down, convinced it was going to be her deal-breaking partner, O'Mally. But it wasn't. Instead, Charlie shadowed her size-twelve body. A hard gasp released from her lips, her eyes popped open, and her body jerked in shock. It took her a moment to gain her composure and regroup.

"Did you have a nice nap?" O'Mally asked.

She just looked at him with a blank expression. To her, the dream had been a warning. It was a clear message that O'Mally was going to turn on her. Her instincts never lied.

"How much longer before we get there?" she asked, roughly.

He looked back at her, "Not a morning person, are you?"

"How much time?" she yelled.

"We have about eighty miles to go. Calm down."

O'Mally had had just about enough of her attitude.

"Why are you always in such a bad mood? You are absolutely no fun to be around," he said calmly.

"Don't get no ideas. Without me, Jorge ain't gonna help you. He don't even know you's involved. You show up alone and you're back to square one."

"Don't *you* get any ideas, I have a lot of secrets tucked away in a little book hidden somewhere very special. You don't want it to fall into the wrong hands now do you?" O'Mally retorted pleasingly.

"What's that supposed to mean? You blackmailing me or something? I cooperate or ya tell on me? That's original. We'll both be jailed if this gets out, so let's just get back to business and stop yammering about it all."

They sat silently, pressing on with the drive and their final eighty miles to riches.

C H A P T E R   61

▼

Flashes went off left and right as the camera continued to stare into the dark and somewhat shallow grave Charlie's contorted body rested in. Bright yellow police tape blockaded the land, and police cars littered Roberta's property. A silver-haired man hoisted the body up with a large mechanism and gently situated Charlie on the ground beside his burial vault. His decomposing frame reeked of rotten eggs and stale urine, forcing the officers to yank their shirts over their noses and mouths. Maggots fed on his rotting flesh, crawling in and out of his orifices. A crusted bullet hole answered the obvious question of how Charlie Grapler died.

"So, other than the obvious, what else can you tell us?" Lieutenant Steele asked the on-site coroner.

"Well, Charlie has probably been dead for about three months. Based on the severity of the exit wound, the weapon was probably a handgun, possibly a .38. One can tell this by the effects a blunt bullet, or a handgun bullet, has on a wound. It causes an explosion upon entering and exiting the target, which is what seems to be the case here. There could be a bullet floating around this crime scene somewhere just waiting to be found. There don't seem to be any apparent signs of a struggle. The body has no broken nails, no ripped clothing, and no obvious injuries other than the gunshot wound. It could be inferred by the corpse's attire—sweatpants and a T-shirt—that the shooting likely took place either after the victim returned home from work, or possibly on a day that the victim didn't work at all. So, it's likely that he was murdered in the evening or on a weekend. There seems to be some trauma to the back of his skull above the exit wound, possibly occurring from a hard fall, or a blunt blow to the head. Further examination will determine for sure. But I just don't see him getting hit over the head and then shot. It wouldn't make sense. My guess is the bullet entered and then exited the skull producing a force that pushed the victim backward, causing him to fall back on a hard surface. There is no type of flat surface anywhere surrounding this grave, so that had to have happened somewhere else. This leads me to conclude that a third party was involved in this murder. There is no way that the victim's wife could have drug his huge body all the way out here by herself. It would be very unlikely. With the deadweight factor, even a large man would have had trouble."

"According to O'Mally's so-called reports, a woman named Samantha lives a couple miles over. We think that was Roberta's accomplice. Samantha served as Mrs. Grapler's alibi, and Samantha was also the person O'Mally cited as Mrs. Grapler's helper when they were arguing on the telephone earlier today. Roberta called her Sam. It all seems to point to the two of them."

"Have you spoken to this Samantha?" Whitaker asked the coroner.

"Not yet; she isn't home and hasn't been for hours. I have some officers watching her house. We are getting a search warrant as we speak."

"Have O'Mally and Roberta been arrested yet?"

"Nope, but they are being tailed. They are more useful to us this way. Apparently, their plot entails a kidnapping, money laundering, murder ... who knows what else. They are so cocky; it's going to be rewarding as hell when we bust this case wide open. As soon as we know O'Mally's exact destination, we all will be catching the first flight out. This is real life you two, start treating it as such," Steele said sternly.

Lieutenant Steele and detectives Whitaker and Chase continued their walk toward Roberta's home.

"Boss, check this out," an officer signaled to Steele as he approached the run-down residence.

"It's just right here in the closet. It's not hidden or taped to the ceiling or the wall. It's just out in the open."

"Yep, it's as if she felt she had nothing to fear," Steele replied.

"Bag it and tag it. I am sure that's our piece."

The old .38 Smith and Wesson was dropped into a plastic bag. Apparently, Mrs. Roberta Grapler wasn't as smart as she thought, for she'd made the biggest mistake of all, she left the murder weapon behind. As a bonus, the inside of the gun still had residual brass left over from the last time the gun fired.

"It's like she wanted to get caught," Steele mumbled to himself.

Roberta's home and property turned out to be a gold mine of evidence: the dead body, the possible murder weapon, medical records, building permits for a certain cabin in the woods, and surely much, much more was to be revealed.

"I think you are going to find this interesting, Lieutenant," Chase proclaimed.

Steele opened the worn cover of a small red book kept nestled within her lingerie drawer. He fingered through the pages and found several familiar names listed boldly in fierce red ink. Under each name were hash marks, some with only one and others with up to twenty-five. He glanced up and shot Chase a look that reinforced his own suspicions. As he flipped through the pages, he saw several prominent names. Shock and disbelief gorged his mind.

"If this is what I think it is, she was sleeping with half the town of Emmett. Brent Thorton, Judge Almond, Charlie's co-workers, Dr. Mets … Holy shit! This is outrageous," Steele exclaimed as he paced the floor.

"Talk about motive."

"Why on earth would these men want her? She isn't the least bit appealing. In fact, she is repulsive."

"Obviously she is giving them something they don't get elsewhere," Steele said as he pulled a leather whip out from under the bed. Their surprised eyes stared at one another.

"I guess there is a lot more to Roberta then we all thought," Whitaker said to Chase.

"I am sure her escapades are agenda-driven. It doesn't take a rocket scientist to figure out why, for example, she would want to pleasure the judge. She must have dozens of dirty little secrets."

CHAPTER 62

▼

The sound of the doorbell roared in Dillon's head. He wanted to throw up. His fingers fidgeted against his leg, and his heart tried to bully its way out of his chest as they waited for Jorge to answer the door. A cloud cover loomed overhead marking the mood.

Questions came fast and furious in Dillon's mind: Was he ready for this? How would it end? Was Jorge living his life? How had he ended up in Emmett, Idaho?

The sound of the doorknob turning brought him to the here and now; it was the moment of all moments, the one day that would change the course of his future.

"Well, hello again," Sam said, as she remained on high alert.

Jag bowed his head and smiled, "Well, hello again. What can I do for you?"

"I was wondering if I could use your phone again … uh, to call my brother. I am sure he is worried about me. Do you mind?"

"Of course not."

Jag thought nothing of it and opened the door wider for her to enter his home once again. As she brought her right foot over the threshold, her cell phone rang. He looked at her puzzled, and she looked back at him with widened eyes. Their silence carried on for few seconds as the phone continued to ring. "I don't understand," Jag said. "Why do you need my pho …" Suddenly, his manners disappeared.

"I think you should go now!" he said sternly, as he attempted to close the door. His motion ceased instantly as Dillon made his presence known right then and there. He used one foot to keep Jorge from being able to close the door. Within seconds, the past six months flashed before Jag's eyes. He had come so close. He was one day away, one measly day away from freedom and a life he never dreamed he could have.

"Hello, Jorge!" Dillon said.

He couldn't let this happen, he couldn't allow for his insignificant, good-for-nothing brother to come in and swoop up what he'd worked so hard to put in his own grasp. He clenched Dillon's shirt into his fist, forcefully pulled him into the entryway, and followed it up with a left hook. Dillon went down quick and hard from the unexpected punch. Jag meant business.

"How the hell did you find me? Did Mama send you?"

Jag's feet shuffled from side to side, waiting for Dillon's retaliation. Dillon kept eye contact with his crazed brother as he pulled himself up off of the floor.

"I came here looking for answers. Nobody sent me, especially that insane woman, Roberta, if that's who you mean."

"Bullshit!"

Jag lunged forward and swung hard, landing an uppercut and a good solid hit in the stomach. Dillon dropped to his knees.

Jag continued to jump around, alert and ready for a counterstrike.

"Apparently you are the fighter in the family," Dillon said with irritation.

"Now just stop a minute. Just STOP! First of all, if you do that again, I am going to hit you back. Second, I came here to talk and get some answers. If you want to do it the hard way, that's fine by me, but in the end we are still going to have a conversation about who the hell I am, and what the hell you are doing in what appears to be my home."

Jag ran toward Dillon, disgusted by the very sight of him. This time however, Dillon did the same. He didn't think he was the fighting type, but then again, maybe he was and he just didn't remember. Sam backed away and allowed the duel to take place. Dillon finally struck back and the twins punished each other for a good fifteen minutes. Grunts and curses accompanied the chaos until fatigue began winning the match. Blood oozed out of Dillon's nose, while Jag sported a large cut on his forehead from landing on the corner of the end table. Sometime during the fight, an elbow punctured the wall and two vases crashed to their death. They were getting nowhere; they were accomplishing nothing.

"Stop already! Just stop!" Dillon blurted.

The pressure of Jag's body continued to weigh Dillon down.

"Stop I said! Get off!"

Dillon struggled to push him away.

"Damn it Jorge, I just …" He panted a few moments before continuing. "… I just want to talk to you! Just talk!"

Out of sheer exhaustion, Jag pulled himself off of his repulsive, undeserving brother, and lowered himself onto the floor to rest. He had nothing left, but maintaining strict eye contact.

"Talk? You just want to talk? Yeah, okay big brother. Let's talk," Jag said harshly. "What do you have to say to me?"

Dillon didn't know where to start, he couldn't get the words out, couldn't pick out a clear question.

Sam stepped in and said, "Let's start with how you ended up here, in Bend, Oregon." "Who the hell are you, anyway?" Jag demanded.

"I'm a friend of Dillon's. Now answer the question," she said with spunk.

"Why don't you tell me what you know *bro*, then maybe I will answer your questions," Jag replied.

"I don't know anything. That is the problem," Dillon said. "I know I woke up in a strange place in Idaho. I know Roberta is apparently my mother. I know you are my brother. I know there is something very sneaky going on, and I sense that I am the pawn in the entire matter," Dillon retorted. "You know what else I know?" he said loudly. "I know I can't remember a damn thing about my life before Idaho, and I am sick and tired of being deceived. I'm so damn tired of being in the dark that I may just step over this line and do what I have to do to get some answers."

Jag looked at Dillon, then at Sam, and then back at Dillon. He truly believed Dillon's claims of stupidity. It made no difference to Jag, though; he wasn't scared of his brother. In fact, he had waited a long time to get a few things off of his chest. It really made no difference what he revealed anyway. He would be out of town by morning, with Lanie and the money.

"You know, it's funny Dillon. So many years went by when you had absolutely nothing to say to me or to Mama. And all of a sudden you want to have a nice brotherly talk because you finally need something from me. Well, I am going to do exactly what you did to us all those years ago. I'm going to turn my back to you. But before I do that, I think it's only proper to give you a few facts to dwell on. I'll just give you a few things to keep you up at night and make you question yourself from here on out, but at the same time, I'm not going to give you enough information to aid you in your quest. Hmmm, where do I start? You're despised by your mother and pitied by your father; your greediness is one of your better personality traits; you're a hardcore criminal, who's about to be exposed by the way; you're a snob; and your wife couldn't even stand you!"

Jag immediately got quiet. He knew he had said too much, he had revealed Lanie's existence.

"You are such an idiot," he told himself.

Dillon had already assumed that Lanie was his wife; all the cards pointed to it. Deep down, Sam knew it as well. However, hearing it confirmed made it a suspicion no longer and her heart silently imploded. Regrettably, she knew where Dillon would rest his head once the truth came out. The awkward moment was soon cut off by Sam's responsibility to the situation; she was selfless enough to remember that this whole journey wasn't about her pathetic feelings, it was about Dillon.

"Listen here, Jorge," Sam said calmly. "It's obvious that you are trying to leave town in a bit of a hurry, which tells me the move was a spur-of-the-moment decision. That likely means you are probably running from someone or something. So, you may as well just answer a few questions so you can be on your way. Then whatever it is you are running from won't have time to catch up to you."

She had a way with words. Jag knew he had to have them out of there by the time Lanie got back or disaster would reign.

"So, I answer a few questions, and you two will leave?" Jag asked, suspiciously.

"Yes, we will go if you help us out," Sam replied.

"It seems a bit too simple. I don't buy it," Jag said.

"Not everything in life has to be difficult; you are not that important. We just want information," Sam desperately hoped her approach would sway him.

"What do you want to know?" Jag asked.

"Why do you hate me? What did I do to you?" Dillon asked.

"You're a bastard; I already told you that."

"Now if you want us to go, you'll have to answer the question seriously," Dillon retorted.

"Mama and I have always been very poor. You have always been very rich, and despite our cries for help, you told us we were trash and you wouldn't lift a finger to help us. You were ashamed of us and basically disowned us. You scoffed at us."

Dillon feared such an answer.

"Did Roberta raise me?"

"No, you were raised by a rich couple," Jag responded.

"Why was I given away and not you?" Dillon asked.

"In Mama's eyes, Papa was an awful man. She claimed he was abusive and uncaring. When Mama found out she was having twins, she decided that she didn't want to expose two kids to her husband. You just happened to be the lucky one who was saved. I, on the other hand, was the apparent sacrifice. Mama used to tell me that she loved me more and that's why she kept me. She said that she wanted to protect me, but it turns out that I got the short end of that deal."

Jag became more upset with each question. "Are we done now?" he asked curtly after regaining his composure.

Dillon continued on. "What did Charlie think of giving one child up for adoption?"

"He didn't know. Hell I didn't even know any of this until recently."

"How did he not know?"

"I don't know. She kept it from him. She had us when he was out of town. He was always out of town. Well you know, you spent some time there recently. I am sure you rarely saw him yourself."

"I never saw him," Dillon said. "He turned up missing before I even got there. The police are involved and there is an investigation," Dillon said.

The wheels in Jag's head spun. "Have the police come up with anything?"

"I don't think so, but Roberta is acting very suspicious about the whole thing."

"How is your relationship with Roberta?" Dillon asked.

"Fine," Jag replied, quickly. Dillon knew by his tone that he was lying.

"I want you to read something." Dillon handed him his father's journal. "I found this in the cabin on your property."

"What cabin? There's no cabin."

"There is a cabin, it was where Charlie went to get away from Roberta."

That comment unexpectedly pierced Jag's ears. Roberta was the only constant person in his life as he grew up, and despite his current feeling for her, she was still his mother.

"Get the hell out of my house! You don't know about my mama, and you sure as hell don't know about my papa. I don't know what you're trying to pull, but it ain't going to work here. My mama may be rough around the edges, but she tried her best to protect me and raise me as best she could with what she had. I didn't have no silver spoon crammed into my mouth like you did!"

"Calm down, I am trying to help you understand who your mom really is," Dillon said.

"You have no right coming in here, making judgments on a family you abandoned!" Jag shot back.

"I didn't abandon you; she abandoned me. How can you blame me for a choice I had no say in? I was a baby for goodness sake. Roberta is the one who gave me the silver spoon; she allowed me to have it, and now you are punishing me for it. Your anger is directed at the wrong person."

"Go!" Jag yelled, furiously.

"Okay, okay, we'll go, but think about this Jorge. You are leaving us no choice but to go to the police. Don't let your emotions control your judgment. That is how people get into trouble. Use your head!" Sam shouted. "Here is the number where we can be reached. Call if you come to your senses."

The door slammed shut behind Dillon and Sam.

Jag was left alone to think. He couldn't help but hear Sam's departing words over and over in his head. He knew Jorge would let his emotions run his life. On the other hand, he knew that Jag would make smart and tough decisions based solely on what needed to be done. He didn't want his old patterns to creep back into his life, but he wondered if it was inevitable. Maybe after all of this, he was still in fact, the same old pathetic Jorge. He thought long and hard about which path he needed to take.

CHAPTER 63

▼

"Where have you been? I have been trying to call ya. We have problems! Dillon was here! At my door!" Jag yelled.

"I figured as much. I knew he was up to no good. Damn it! What did he say? What does he know?" Roberta asked.

"He was talking trash about you and trying to get me to turn against you. Where are you?"

"I am here in Bend. Things were getting hairy back home, too. Dillon turned up missing, and I had a gut feeling he was coming here," Roberta said.

"Dillon told me he was going to go to the police. I think he was bluffing, but I can't know for sure. We gotta get out of town, Mama. And fast! It's going to be tricky though. I'm worried that Dillon might follow me," Jag said in a panic. "Mama, I can trust you, right?"

"Of course you can. Don't ask stupid questions. I's your own flesh and blood. If you can trust anyone, it's me," she said.

"All right, I thought of a way to make this work. I have the money stashed at that hotel I stayed at. Go to the bathroom around the side of the manager's office. If you stand on the toilet and reach up, one of the panels in the ceiling pushes up. There is a metal box up there full of the cash you had me get, Mama. It's locked up tight, but don't worry I have the key to unlock it. I'll meet you at the train station in one hour. Buy a round-trip ticket to Vancouver, sit in the last box car, and I'll meet you back there once we are in motion and I feel it's safe. No one here can connect us, so don't approach me. I'll come to you."

"Sounds like you got it all figured out. So, how much cash we talking about, Jorge?"

"Two million cash and about another two million in traveler's checks and bonds."

Roberta fumbled the phone. "All of that is in the box?"

"I swear, Mother, if you're lying to me I will find you, I will!"

"Are you trying to piss me off? How dare ya question me after all I've done for ya. Stop being paranoid, and be the son that I raised ya to be! What kind of mama do ya think I am?"

"I'll see you in an hour then," Jag responded.

"Angel,

Hi, sweetness. I'm having some last-minute issues with our travel arrangements. I'm off to straighten them out. Will be in touch. Miss you.

Love, Me"

Lanie was far from a distant memory, and Jag had every intention of covering his tracks and summoning her as soon as it was safe. He planned on taking his last-minute plan one hour at a time to ensure that in the end, it would be a success.

He placed the note on the table, grabbed a few items of importance, and drove off.

Time seemed to stand still as Jag watched the glass door to the hotel manager's office. He waited to see if and when Roberta would show her face. His eyes didn't falter. He continued to linger anxiously. His feet tapped against the vehicle's floor. Like clockwork, his mother appeared. She toted the shiny metal box with both hands. "Who is that?" Jag asked himself. A man he didn't recognize was walking alongside his mama. "Who on earth is that?" he asked himself again.

"Come on, Mama, come through for me. Don't make it true. Head toward that train station," Jag pleaded to himself.

Jag pulled out of the motel parking lot, maintaining a safe trailing distance from the car that transported his mama. Only time would tell if she intended to follow through with their escape plan. Unbeknownst to Jag, his teeth munched on the edge of his lip, as he stared continually at their car. His fingers tapped the seat as they passed Exit 85, then Exit 86. He resituated himself. Doubt hovered over him. Exit 87 flew past, then Exit 88.

Jag kept asking himself, "Who is that man? Who is he? He isn't part of our plan."

The wait played torture with his faith in his mama. He feared that this freeway was going to turn his world upside down in a few short minutes.

"Come on, come on. Get ready to exit. Get over," he mumbled. Whoosh, there went Exit 89, then Exit 90. The blinker on the car she was in began to flash to the right.

"That's it, Mama, your exit is coming up. We're nearing the train station, Jag thought to himself.

He intensely watched her; desperate for the only gesture of good faith she could offer him at his point in the game.

Exit 91 passed with only one half of a mile to go. Exit 92 came and … went, along with any credibility his mother had still possessed. From the second he saw that strange man with his mother, he knew he had been replaced. He didn't want to believe it, but he knew.

"I defended you! I put my neck on the line for you! I practically killed myself in that car accident … for you!" he shouted to no one in particular.

Jag put his hands up to his face and took a moment to grasp what had just happened.

"No! No! This can't be happening. She just missed her exit; she'll get off and turn around. She will. She has to." Jag told himself. "She's my mama. She's always been there for me. She took care of me when no one else would!"

His heart, as well as the idea of what was real in his life, shattered into a million confusing pieces. His mind took him back to his early childhood, to a time when no one would play with him. Kids would call him names and push him down, and even then, his mama stood by him. She was far from perfect, but she was his mama and somehow that always made everything okay.

This very moment in time would surely go down as the loneliest moment in his life. It was over. The scheme, the thrill, and the revenge that went right along with it. Now everything meant nothing; he'd done it all for nothing.

"I was doing it all for you, Mama, to give you back the power you thought that you lost in your life, to give you a quest, a purpose, and a better life. It was supposed to be me and you against the world. It was always supposed to have been you and me against the world."

He ended his outcry and calmly turned to the passenger in his car and said, "You were right. You were absolutely right."

"I'm sorry, Jorge; I truly am," Dillon replied. And he truly was sad for his brother's reality. You did the right thing, calling us back today. You did the right thing. It was the only way to show you who she really is," Dillon said. "It was the only way to prove once and for all where her loyalties actually lay."

"And I thought I was going to be proving you wrong today. At least I hoped I was," Jag replied. "It's ironic if you think about it," Jag continued, "she chose money over her family, the exact scenario that inspired our adventure of revenge here in Bend, Oregon." His head shook with disbelief. "So, here I sit with the brother I was taught to hate, who also happens to be the husband of the woman I love. We are in a car with your mistress, following our mother to the depths of the unknown. It doesn't get much more ambiguous than that, now does it," Jag said.

"You know, it only adds to it that I have no idea what you are really like. You could either be the good-for-nothing heartless scoundrel that our mama claims you to be, or you could be the complete opposite. I guess neither of us will ever know," Jag said.

"Well, apparently I have some kind of a bad streak in me. After all, you have an entire folder of my apparent questionable importing and exporting dealings, not to mention, proof of my bank accounts abroad. Americans get foreign accounts for one reason and one reason only—to hide money, stolen money."

"Well, it looks like we are both screwed then. Maybe we can be cellmates," Jag suggested.

Sam continued to listen as the two brothers conversed back and forth. Her secret was still one that needed to be told. She just couldn't seem to find the right moment, not that there would actually ever be a right moment.

"Well, where do we go from here, Jorge?" Dillon asked.

"Wherever she goes," he said, pointing to the car he was still following, the car Roberta was riding in.

"I have a few things to say to her, as do you, I'm sure. If she thinks this is just that easy, she is in for one big surprise reunion," Jag added.

While continuing to sit quietly, Sam took advantage of the short time she had left with Dillon.

CHAPTER 64

▼

"What a stupid little boy he is," Roberta said with a chuckle. The case was calling out to her from the backseat of O'Mally's Pontiac.

"Have you *ever* had a soul?" O'Mally asked as he flung his baseball hat off.

"Don't tell me you're going soft on me now," Roberta said as she rolled her devilish eyes.

"No, I could care less about Jorge, or even you for that matter. I just didn't expect you to be so nonchalant about the whole thing. I figured you would have some internal struggle or momentary feeling of guilt about cheating your own flesh and blood."

"Well, ya figured wrong," Roberta smiled. "And don't get any ideas about cutting me out, I'll slice your throat before you have time to beg me for mercy." She paused for a moment and then continued, "I mean it, you're just like every other man out there, and it wouldn't take an ounce of thought to dispose of ya one way or the other."

"Wow, your charm is overwhelming," O'Mally replied.

"Let's just get to our destination and be done with it already. The sooner you are a distant memory, the better," Roberta snapped. She lowered the window slightly and lit up one of her Pall Mall nonfiltered smokes.

"The first drag is always the best."

O'Mally pulled off after one hundred and fifty miles for fuel and caffeine. Roberta had needed to go to the restroom for at least the past forty miles, but would never admit that she needed him to pull over for her. She'd just as soon wait it out. He stretched his legs while the gas pumped itself into his car as he dreaded the remainder of the car ride with Roberta. She exited the car with her case in tow to take care of her personal business before ordering two corn dogs and a cherry red Slurpee. She flagged at O'Mally to come inside, insisting he pay.

"Well, since you already inhaled half of it, I guess I have no choice."

Roberta cocked her head and smiled.

"You have mustard on your face," he grumbled.

Sam, Jag, and Dillon camouflaged themselves next to a large semi.

"Who were you talking to when I waved at ya from the store?" Roberta asked as they departed the BP Station.

"Hmmm?" he asked.

"Who were you on your cell phone with?"

"Oh, just somebody asking for someone named Caroline. I didn't catch his name," he said smartly.

They pulled into traffic and continued south, as scarce raindrops splashed their front window.

"You know, Roberta, I don't get it. I have heard the way you have talked about Jorge over the past year. You spoke highly of him; you defended his vulnerability; you protected him from Charlie and everyone else in the world. Then all of a sudden you turn on him as if it is nothing. Why? Why put so much effort into raising him and protecting him only to cheat him and, basically, throw him out into the cold? What kind of twisted behavior is that?"

"I was done with him," she replied, casually.

"Done with him? What do you mean done with him?"

"I mean done with him. He ain't no innocent boy no more. He's a man, and I ain't met no man I could trust. Growing up he didn't know any better than to trust and love me. It was pure and honest. Now the world got a hold of him. He's tainted. I could tell just by talking with him. It disgusted me. It was only a matter of time before he was gonna turn on me. I just beat him to the punch."

"So, if men are so evil and unworthy of you, what the hell are you doing here with me?"

"I need something from you, it is as simple as that," she said.

"Once we're done tonight, you'll be a memory that ain't gonna be hard to forget, just like Jorgie."

"You're certifiable," he said.

A look of disgust appeared on Roberta's face. She didn't know if she'd be able to last another second with him sitting next to her. She searched through her denim purse, pulled out a crimson-colored nail polish, and began painting her fingernails.

"Don't get any of that on my seat, Roberta."

"We have millions in the back. You could buy yourself a hundred new seats if you want. Relax."

With a push of a button, she turned the radio on and continued with her distraction.

"How long until we get there?"

"About five hours," O'Mally answered.

CHAPTER 65

───────────── ▼ ─────────────

"We're out enjoying life; leave a message."

Beep.

"Hi, Angel. Well, I have had some car trouble. The mechanics said it would only take an hour or so, but that hour has stretched into three. If I had known, I would have taken a cab home forever ago. I hope you got all your loose ends tied up. I'll be home as soon as I can. The battery in my cell phone is about dead, so if I have any more problems, I'll call you on a landline. Love ya."

Jag closed his flip phone just as O'Mally's car stopped. The streets were cobblestoned, with business after business lining the two-lane road. The sun beamed through the windows warming their legs as they parked one block behind Roberta and her apparent accomplice.

"It's pretty interesting that we ended up here," Jag said.

"Why? What is the significance about Napa?"

"You were mugged here a couple years back. Your wallet was taken, and since then you ironically used the experience to help protect your fortune. Your banking PIN code corresponded with the numbers on the phone that correspond to the letters in the word Napa; the safe in your home had the same combination. Oh, and your safety-deposit box; same thing," Jag said. "Do you think the mugging is somehow linked? Damn, I bet it is!"

"Hopefully we'll find out soon enough," Dillon replied.

Their car doors opened. Sam didn't move. She couldn't let Roberta see her, at least not yet.

"Hey guys? I think I am going to wait here, and watch from a distance. There is bound to be some trouble, and if and when it happens, I can be the element of surprise to step in and catch them off guard."

"You know, that's a good idea. Watch our backs, and if anything funny happens we'll know you're out here and that you'll figure something out," Jag said.

Dillon took a moment to embrace Sam with a loving touch. She knew it might be the last tender moment they were going to have together, so she held on for dear life.

"I'll be back, sweetie; don't worry. I'll be back," Dillon promised.

Jag watched the tender moment. It gave him a glimmer of hope that maybe he could be the one to end up with Lanie. Maybe, just maybe, Dillon didn't want to fight for her. After all, Dillon was obviously in love with Samantha. They released their embrace and each sensed the other's worry about what the day would bring.

Jag and Dillon watched as Roberta and her accomplice parked their car. They locked the case in the trunk before walking quickly and purposefully across a large field of manicured grass. They stopped at a wooden bench that faced a stone statue of a mother and child.

"What on earth are they doing?"

"Interesting that they would leave the case in the trunk and just walk away."

The two brothers hunkered down behind a large bush, watching to see what would happen next. A cool breeze brushed by them as the sun began to disappear.

"Something will happen pretty soon. I am sure of it," Dillon said.

The smell of pizza and fresh-baked bread floated through the air as Jag inhaled deeply for another delicious whiff. His stomach yelled at him. Dillon and Jag continued to watch Roberta and her male friend's uneventful show. Although they occupied the same bench, they failed to interact on any level. The show bored them, but the anticipation more than made up for it. Without warning, a piercing pain seared through Dillon's head. He buckled down and clenched his eyes closed, trying to combat the unexpected surge of agony.

"You all right? Dillon? Dillon?" Jag alternated his stare between Dillon and their mother.

"What's the matter, Dillon?" He continued asking. Jag couldn't lose sight of their target and chance missing their next move, but at the same time, he felt a sense of obligation toward his twin brother.

"I'm fine. I'm fine."

The pain dissipated as quickly as it had attacked, and Dillon, for the first time, had a jolt of memory, a true and honest glimpse into his past.

"Jag, I remember. I remember being here … with Lanie," Dillon whispered. "Man, it's so vivid, as if it just happened."

"What was it? What was the memory?" Jag asked while maintaining a visual of Roberta's backside.

"I remembered that I wore an orange jacket and a black hat. It was cold out, and Lanie and I sat there. We sat right there on that very bench. This is amazing."

"What were you doing? Maybe it has something to do with today. What were you two doing there? What were you talking about?"

He thought hard and tried to grab onto the memory as effectively as he could.

"I can't recall what we were talking about, but I remember feeling happy. I was smiling and so was she. Then something inspired me to look over my shoulder. There was a man in a black ski mask. He charged up behind me carrying a lead pipe of some sort. It all happened so fast, but I think he hit me with it. I just remember falling to the ground. What you said was true, I was mugged right here in this very place," Dillon said as he tried to keep his excited voice low.

He raised his hand up to the back of his head and felt around. Sure enough, there was a slight indention, a tangible scar. His memory brought with it the warm and intense feelings of love that he felt for Lanie that day. He kept that part to himself, but realized that his feelings for her were still alive and kicking somewhere inside of him.

The sound of a cell phone ringing brought Dillon and Jag back to the task at hand. Roberta's partner answered it. He began quickly jolting his head in all directions. Clearly looking around in a state of worry.

"Had someone just warned them of onlookers? Who? No one else knows that we're here," Dillon asked himself as he looked back toward the car. Sam was gone.

"What the hell is going on?" Jag asked. "Do you think they know we are watching them?"

"Where is Sam?" Jag asked. They both looked around, still seeing no evidence of her. "Maybe Sam is the one they are meeting. Maybe Sam has been working with Roberta all this time," Jag guessed.

"That is ridiculous! Sam and I are in love. She is the one who helped me find you; she is the one who helped me figure this whole thing out," Dillon said in her defense.

"Did she help you, or did she lead you exactly where she wanted you to be?" Jag asked. "What made you think you even had a twin brother? How did you know how to get to me?"

Dillon quickly thought back to the heat of the moment.

"Sam helped me. She helped me with all of that. She was able to get phone records for us, and she matched up the phone numbers to addresses. She got information from her connection about Roberta being pregnant and hearing two heartbeats." Dillon's mind traveled back in time, thinking about all of the unselfish help that Sam had offered.

"Why on earth would she help you so much? What was in it for her?" Jag asked.

"Because she cares for me," Dillon responded, but he couldn't help but wonder if he was being foolish.

"Something is about to go down. I can feel it. Everything seems off. I say we just approach and confront them both. We need to get them in our company before they have a chance to disappear," Jag insisted.

They began moving quickly toward the bench. They got closer and then even closer. Their adrenaline soared. Once and for all, the guessing game would end. Soon, only fifteen feet separated their reunion. Without warning, O'Mally darted up. He was unmistakably making a beeline for the getaway car. Roberta remained on the bench, just as still as she had been from the moment the pair had sat down. Jag and Dillon stopped. They were confused, and finally panicked.

Roberta appeared frozen. Her accomplice traveled at full sprint.

"What is going on? Something is going down!" Dillon said, worried.

"I'll go after him, you get Mama," Jag said.

Their eyes locked for a millisecond before they split up to conquer their individual quests.

CHAPTER 66

▼

"Freeze! All of you freeze!" Lieutenant Steele ordered viciously.

Everyone, except O'Mally, halted. His getaway car taunted his continuance. The idea of millions clouded his senses. As an officer himself, he knew it would be a political nightmare to fire shots in a public area.

Dillon stopped dead in his tracks, raised his hands into the air and waited for further instruction. Jag did the same as he furiously watched the unknown man run farther and farther from his grasp. Roberta held her position.

Things were happening in a muffled, slow motion. There were so many officers running about, securing the area and those within it. Jag and Dillon's faces kissed the cool grass in their respective areas. Each had been cuffed and patted down by local officers.

"We need immediate medical attention! Hurry, hurry!" The officer shouted loudly.

A medical team stampeded past Dillon.

"We have a fresh gunshot wound to the side. It's a close-range shot. Let's go, let's go, let's go," the officer yelled out to the approaching medics.

"Mama! Mama!" Jag yelled frantically from across the grass. He instinctively pocketed the hate and disappointment that dwelled within him.

"Is she alive? Is she going to make it?" No one responded to his loud cries. "Answer me damn it! That's my mama. Someone answer me," he continued.

A female officer approached him and said, "We don't know anything yet. You need to be quiet. Yelling will only distract them." Her tone was firm but compassionate.

"I have a pulse!" someone shouted. "Then on the count of three, one … two … three," the medical personnel on the scene hoisted Roberta's limp body onto the stretcher and efficiently carried her to the ambulance.

It zoomed off within seconds.

Dillon remained handcuffed, waiting for further instruction. Despite the problems that faced him now, all he could think about was Sam. Had he been deceived by the one person he counted on, just as Jag had been? Were they both in the same sinking ship? He could see Jag in the distance, sitting in the grass with his head bowed. He was obviously in pain over the condition of his mother; *their* mother. Dillon didn't feel much sorrow for her, but he did feel bad for the pain she'd inflicted on his brother. It surprised him.

CHAPTER 67

▼

Before Roberta was shot, before the guns were drawn, and even before the twins darted toward the bench, Sam had positioned herself in the backseat of the getaway car. She yanked back on the long, flowing hair of Lanie Andresen. Securing her head against the headrest, Sam had held a pocketknife up to the side of her throat. Sweet little Lanie was actually the scheming sister of Officer Tate O'Mally. The two women were able to spend a solid fifteen minutes together before O'Mally received the phone call that had triggered his sprint to the getaway car.

Upon their recent arrival in Napa Valley, Sam noticed the light-haired beauty standing on the side of the road, next to a telephone pole. It was right then and there that Sam knew the scheme went a lot deeper than anyone had realized. She was actually impressed with the evident cleverness, but more so with herself for discovering it.

While the boys were watching Roberta, she slipped away and found out some very interesting information about the not-so-lovely Lanie.

"All I want is Dillon, and with you out of the picture, I can have him all to myself. So, you can leave either one of two ways. You can simply drive away in this car, money and all, never to return again, or you can look forward to life behind bars. The choice is obvious," Sam said, aggressively.

"What's the catch?" Lanie asked.

"You have to answer some questions for me. I want to know how this all got started, and why on earth you need Jag to smuggle money for you when you married into it? You have ten minutes."

Her watch beeped after she set the timer for exactly that, ten minutes. "Go!"

Lanie found herself at the mercy of a stranger.

"We are going to get along just fine," Lanie continued, "If you are willing to push me and the millions out of your life for the love of a broken man, then I am happy to oblige you."

Lanie began, "It's simple, really. A few years ago my parents met Mr. and Mrs. Andresen at some benefit or luncheon or whatnot. Obviously, both couples had something in common, unmarried kids. Dillon and I were considered high-class, so they wanted nothing more than for us to hit it off and become some perfect little couple. He basically repulsed me. Dillon was way too metrosexual for my taste. I prefer the rocker type, the bad boy. To make a long story short, I discovered some papers in my father's office. He is a lawyer. I'd stumbled on a gold mine. There were pages and pages of legal documents: secret adoption information, medical reports, and more importantly, a will. It was the will of none other than Mr. and Mrs. Cliff Andresen, and their net worth was quite impressive. Dillon was the sole beneficiary. So, the wheels in my clever brain started turning. I knew an opportunity when one presented itself. It was no secret that once college was over, my parents were going to cut me off, just like they did when my brother graduated from the academy. So, my sweet little Lanie personality emerged. I was just so damn irresistible and delightful; Dillon didn't have a chance. It was ridiculous how easy it was. After about a year of pretending to be this wonderful and perfect girlfriend, he finally popped the question. We had our big wedding with frilly lace and pathetic toasts and then, shortly after, the most tragic thing happened. His parents died in an unexpected accident." Lanie smiled with a devilish grin. "So, it looked like I was going to be sitting pretty with an astronomical fortune under my belt."

"You murdered his parents?" Sam asked as disgust overwhelmed her.

"How on earth did you arrange a train accident?"

"I don't know what you mean," she smirked.

"Just get back to the story. Time is running out," Sam said. "You have about four minutes to go."

"Well, it turned out that the joke was on me because just days before we'd gotten married, Dillon's parents had changed lawyers over some goddamn conflict of interest. So my parents no longer held a relevant copy of their will. Dillon's mother was a psychotherapist or something like that. She was basically a shrink."

"I thought she was a nurse?" Sam interrupted.

"She was back in the day; she went back to school. Now can I finish my story and get the hell out of here?" Lanie asked.

"Anyway, it was no secret that Mrs. Andresen quickly regretted setting the two of us up. She psychoanalyzed me to death and basically tried to turn Dillon against me. She said I wasn't trustworthy, or some crap like that."

"Hmm, I can't imagine why she felt that way," Sam said sarcastically.

"Oh, shut up! You're infringing on my last, what … two minutes of airtime," she responded, curtly.

"So, at the reading of the will, it was discovered that one third of the money went to various charities and the rest of it went to Dillon. However, the will had a stipulation which was surely a stab at me from his dead mother. You know she was the only one who ever saw through me. The only one."

"Get on with it!" Sam yelled.

"The beneficiary account was in his name and his name only. It was specifically written with an order that forbid anyone else from ever being added to the account. Plus, his mother had requested that he not withdraw any of the money until after he had reached all of his goals in life and retired. You see, Dillon is all about business, taking risks, playing the market, succeeding. His mother's will stated that if he received a fortune before he made his mark on the world, he chanced losing his ambition for personal success. So, all in all, the money would have just sat there, pretty much forever. Dillon would never have been done challenging himself; he's just too damn determined. His mother went on and on about how proud she was of him; it was nauseating. Dillon was such a damn mama's boy; he would never have gone against her precious wishes. So, since there was no chance of him withdrawing the money before he turned like one hundred, I found someone who could. My brother moved to Emmett, approached Roberta, preyed on her needs, and the rest is history."

"So, if Dillon was loaded, why did he embezzle money? Why resort to criminal activity? It doesn't add up," Sam questioned.

"You're such an imbecile," Lanie responded. "It is all fake. Your precious boyfriend is as straitlaced as Mother Teresa was. Roberta and I planted it all. It was all bogus, an illusion created for poor, pathetic Jorgie so that he would go along with the plan."

The news of this blew Sam's mind. It was sheer brilliance. She had to give credit where credit was due.

"So, from day one, Jag was being set up? Used?"

"Oh, don't sound so judgmental. You're the one threatening my life, holding a knife to my throat," she pointed out. "It was the simplest part of the plan. Roberta made him believe his quest was of good intention. He was to save their pathetic world from falling apart and to give them a better life. It is quite pitiful really. His empty little mind was so easily filled with our own agenda. You couldn't help but laugh about it," Lanie chuckled.

Beep, beep, beep.

"Our time is up, lady. We had a deal. Take that knife away from my neck and get the hell out of this car," Lanie demanded.

"Just one more thing. Does your brother have a cell phone?"

"Yes. Why?"

"I don't want him anywhere near Dillon or Jag. Call him now! Tell him that he is being watched and to get back to the car," Sam ordered.

"That wasn't part of ..."

"Now!"

Sam pressed the cold plate of the knife even harder against Lanie's flesh.

Lanie made the call. She was optimistic that Sam's ridiculous love for Dillon would inspire her to honor their agreement.

"Now get the hell out of here," Lanie said to Sam. "If my brother sees you, you're as good as dead."

"Shut up! You can't manipulate me, little girl. I hold the cards now," Sam responded. "It's over; it's just simply over."

"We had a deal! Get out!" Lanie yelled.

"I don't make deals with the devil," Sam responded with satisfaction. She continued, "It looks like the master manipulator got a dose of her own medicine. It is quite pathetic, really. Your empty little mind was so easily filled with my agenda, I can't help but laugh about it," Sam said, repeating the words Lanie had recently spoke in reference to Jag.

Her prisoner was infuriated.

O'Mally ran frantically toward the car screaming, "Start the car! Start the car!" He crossed the road, slid across the slick hood, and rushed into the passenger side door. The police remained hot on his tail.

"Let's go!"

Sam's presence confused him. She still had a knife to his sister's throat. "Roll down your window, put the safety on your gun, and toss it into the street between the car and the curb," Sam said calmly to O'Mally.

Soon, the car would be surrounded.

"No way! What insurance will I have that you won't kill Lanie?" he asked.

"None!"

O'Mally watched as a drop of fresh blood bubbled out of Lanie's neck. This triggered his instant compliance.

"There, the gun is gone!"

The three of them sat quietly, aware of the inevitable outcome. The windows were tinted, forcing the police officers to approach with trained caution. Samantha maintained a hold on Lanie's hair as she folded up the knife using her knee as support. She then lowered her window to give the officers a glimpse inside the car. Lanie and her brother had met their match. The truth was recorded onto the trusted little tape recorder Sam had learned to never leave home without. It is just one of those things a reporter knows.

CHAPTER 68

▼

As the arrests of Lanie Andresen and Tate O'Mally were taking place, Jag caught a glimpse that warranted a double take.

"That's Angel. What on earth is she doing here?" he wondered.

He couldn't take another betrayal, he just couldn't.

"Lanie?" he hollered.

She ignored his attempt at contact, and tears rushed into his eyes.

"Lanie?"

He dropped. His knees crashed into the thick grass. A full sob poured out of him. He felt like a weak little boy, just as he always had. He didn't care though; he wasn't able to care. He was instead, destroyed. His world had been torn apart, not once, but twice, in the same day even. Uncertainty screamed from his soul.

"Will I ever find peace? Will I ever find love?" he wondered.

The past few months flashed through his memory. Everything remained in question. In the midst of his breakdown, Lanie sauntered past him, escorted by police. He watched her strut by, and asked with a desperate glimmer of hope, "This is a mistake, right? I don't understand."

She turned her nose to him and continued on her way.

"Help me understand!"

His voice quavered with each plea. Without even so much as an acknowledgment, she disappeared into the back of the police car.

Within the hour, Lanie, O'Mally, Samantha, Dillon, and Jag were all on their way to the local police department. The authorities had quite a puzzle to assemble, and although the mood was a somber for most, Sam beamed on the inside.

She knew that everything was going to be just fine, at least for Dillon and Jag, the two people who deserved happiness the most.

CHAPTER 69

▼

His grieving eyes looked at her through the plate glass as she annoyingly picked up her telephone receiver.

"I thought we connected. I thought you loved me. I felt it every time we touched. How could I have imagined that?" Jag asked.

"Do we really have to go through this?" Lanie asked in a stern voice. "I am sure Sam filled you in."

"I need to hear it from you," Jag pleaded with some desperate hope that she would somehow make it all better. He hoped that maybe she really did love him and would declare her love at any moment. He needed something in his life to be real.

"We never connected. I don't have feelings for you, and I never did."

"I don't believe you. I was there, remember? For all those weeks, I watched you nurse me back to health, listened to you pray for me when you thought I was asleep. I felt your emotion when we made love. It was real, it had to have been."

"Like I told that bitch Samantha, I was playing a part. I didn't love you or Dillon. And you know you are not as clever as you might think, Jag. Even if I didn't know your true identity when all of this started, which I did, you gave yourself away over and over again."

Jag looked at her perplexed, "What are you talking about?"

"Do you honestly think I wouldn't know the difference between you and Dillon? You two are twins, not clones," she said sarcastically. "How dumb do you think I am?" Lanie meanly said. "For one, you have a mole on your left shoulder, Dillon doesn't. You also have a scar on your left shin, and to your apparent surprise, Dillon doesn't. You take your coffee black; he takes his with milk. There are dozens of inconsistencies. You just simply insult my intelligence," she added. "You obviously didn't do your homework."

Jag couldn't feel any worse about himself. Everything she said made perfect sense, but he did not understand how she'd done this. How had she pulled off the act?

"You loved me more than the real Dillon, though; you had to have. I was the perfect guy."

"Oh, Jag, it kills me. You look so much like a man, but yet you think so much like a child."

He wanted to run and hide, yet couldn't find the courage to leave.

"I messed with your mind. I did what I had to do. You know I talked to Roberta almost weekly. I planted those letters in the safety-deposit box; Roberta doesn't even know they exist," she continued.

"Why would you do that?" Jag asked.

"To get you to turn on your precious mama. It meant more money for me."

"You mean she never wrote those letters?" Jag asked.

"Nope. It worked though. You were going to leave her behind just as I had hoped."

"How could I have been so wrong about you? You're no better than she is."

"Hey, I did you a favor. She was trying to double-cross you, and I was trying to get you to double-cross her back. Oh, and for the record, Dillon isn't allergic to cheese. That was just another way to entertain myself. Damn, it got so boring playing the nice, sweet, free-spirited gal. But I did it, and I did it perfectly, without waiver."

"So, the moving, the packing, the riding off into the sunset with me, it was all bullshit?"

"I would have gone wherever the money went, and I'd have stayed until I could break away as a rich woman. It was as simple as that."

"Did you know about the cameras I planted?"

"Of course. I bought them, mailed them to Roberta, and then she gave them to you. I knew you were watching Dillon and I making love too. It actually kind of turned me on. That was the best sex I had had in a while." Lanie smiled rudely.

"If you and Roberta were in on it together, why couldn't she see the footage? Or could she?" Jag asked with confusion.

"She is about as smart as you are. Those receivers only work if they are within around two hundred feet from the camera. She was too dumb to realize that. I actually told her you had probably disconnected them. That really shot up her suspicions."

Jag stared at her through the slightly smeared glass. She appeared to be enjoying every minute of her devastating revelation. His stomach burned. His blood boiled.

"This conversation is getting tiresome. I have said all I am going to say to you, Jorge."

She went to hang up the prison phone, but paused, bringing it back up to her ear for one more moment.

"For the record, I didn't like you better than Dillon. I may have hated him, but I despised you. Do you know how irritating it was to be so damn nice and sensitive all of the time? At least Dillon had a bit of an edge to him."

She slammed the phone into its holder and the guard escorted her away. Jag was unable to peel himself out of the chair, although he desperately needed to get far, far away. He wondered how he would ever recover and where he could possibly go from here. He had nowhere that he belonged and no one to trust. He wiped the drippings from his nose and closed his eyes. His right hand webbed his face.

"What now?" he asked himself. Numbness paralyzed him.

The sound of a metal chair scraping across the cement floor distracted him from his depression. His quiet eyes looked around at the other visitors. Once again he was the outcast. The one who was rejected. Everyone else seemed to be enjoying their visits and receiving love and sincerity from those behind the glass. His was the exception. He always seemed to be the exception. He peeled his strong body and weak mind out of the chair and slowly departed. On the long drive back to the motel, Jag's emotions were all over the place. He had plenty of time to think about the past and the present, and after about an hour of explosive anger and white knuckles, his rage began to diminish. Before he even realized, the transformation had occurred. The window had been lowered in his rented Malibu, and the hot wind shuffled across his unshaven face. The chaotic breeze weaved in and out of his hair as he caught himself admiring the hills surrounding the freeway. He took a moment to acknowledge this barely recognizable feeling of peacefulness and wondered if he had, in fact, found the very thing he had searched for all of his life. He thought about how he had survived an ordeal, many ordeals, that would send most over the edge: a major car accident, a new secret life, a mother's betrayal, a father's death, meeting a new, mysterious brother, and suffering a devastating heartbreak. Yet there he was still standing strong and somehow feeling content. At that very moment, he learned that Jag Alvin Grapler didn't have to be weak, little Jorgie. Nor did he have to be the untouchable Jag. He could simply be himself, which was somewhere in the middle. And that was exactly where Alvin wanted to be.

CHAPTER 70

▼

Roberta Grapler

Once the bullet wound healed and Roberta was back to her old self, she was left to face prosecution for her crimes. She pled guilty by reason of insanity to the charges of kidnapping, armed robbery, aiding and abetting, and the murder of her husband, Charlie. It was the best option she had to avoid jail time and get back to her way of life. She decided a few years in an asylum was a decent trade for her husband's demise. However, Roberta was outraged when the judge sentenced her to a minimum of thirty years in the state's mental health facility, where she was eventually diagnosed with a severe case of paranoid personality disorder, in addition to having delusional and narcissistic tendencies. The judge made it clear that if she was insane enough to commit so many crimes without remorse, then she needed nothing less than a lifetime of medical attention. Roberta, of course, blamed the judge when her plan backfired. After all, he was a man, and to her, all men were out to get her.

Her psychiatrist is none other than Dr. Alice Bombay, who has eagerly accepted the challenge to try to treat Roberta once again. And although Roberta still firmly denies having an illness, every night she can be seen unfolding an old, worn-out piece of paper and reading it silently to herself. A tear usually streams down her cheek as she finishes reading Charlie's last journal entry—the heartfelt letter he wrote to her, but had never planned on sharing.

Dillon Andresen

Dillon and his brother were both able to find closure when it came to the death of their father. They arranged a proper burial for the man and invited anyone and everyone who wanted to pay their respects. The funeral was packed, which they thought only validated the kind of man their father had actually been. Dillon's memory was never restored. However, he was very content with his new life and happy to have forgotten his old one. Never again did he want to put a price tag on his worth.

He dropped all charges against his brother, and he treasured his new life and his new outlook. He decided to take early retirement and knew his adoptive mother would approve. After all, he had a new family now. Dillon shared his new life with his brother, Alvin, and their son, Charlie. Yep, Lanie had in fact been pregnant, proving to quite possibly be the only thing she hadn't lied about. No one will ever know which brother actually fathered the baby, and that is just the way they wanted it.

Jorge/Jag/and Alvin Grapler

Alvin put his devastation onto paper and single-handedly created a best-selling book of poetry titled *In the Eyes of My Shadow*. It took the loss of everyone he thought he loved to finally learn that no one is better suited to guide him than he is.

Because of his mother's illness, Alvin sold much of the property surrounding their run-down two-bedroom domicile in Emmett, Idaho. There were too many bad memories there, and Alvin had no intention of leaving Oregon or his new family. He and Dillon wholeheartedly agreed that the little log cabin in the woods, and the three surrounding acres should be given to the one person who had served as a common denominator in both their lives—Boyd, the man from the motel parking lot near room 119. He may not have been the most tactful acquaintance, but he was a straight shooter, and Alvin and Dillon had a new-found appreciation for that very trait.

Tate O'Mally

Tate is in custody at the Pelican Bay State Prison, near the California and Oregon border. He was convicted on a long list of crimes, including: attempted murder in the first degree, conspiracy to commit murder, embezzlement, theft, aiding and abetting a known killer, and inappropriate conduct for an officer. He is an obvious favorite of the inmates; after all, he was a policeman.

Lanie Andresen

Lanie wasn't quite as lucky. She went down as the mastermind of the entire plan. Her daddy washed his hands of the matter and left the verdict in the hands of the judge, just as he had done with Tate.

Her future is grim. Most who know her agree that life in prison without the possibility of parole isn't nearly long enough to pay for the murders of Sharon and Cliff Andresen, her conspiracy to commit murder, the attempted theft of a man's fortune, and the heartbreak of a boy named Jorge.

Samantha

To the surprise of most, the money never actually made it into the metal box that was planted in the ceiling above the toilet at the motel. The police were shocked, and slightly amused, to find the box full of *Playboy* magazines—an added bonus brought to them by Dillon's recruited friend, Boyd. The money, not nearly as much as Jag had let on to his mama, had remained in a locker at the YMCA, exactly where Jag had left it. It was returned to Dillon without incident.

The question still remains, why Napa?

The answer is, it all began there, and therefore, that was where it was all supposed to end. Tate O'Mally proved to Lanie that he was up to the task of being her true partner in crime as the mystery mugger. She was impressed at his aggressiveness and the rest is, well, history.

"So, this month my sentence is up. I managed to get off a bit easy because of the help that I provided to the police department and have since been on my best behavior at the minimum-security prison I was assigned. Dillon, the love of my life, has forgiven me for withholding the secret of the whereabouts of Charlie Grapler's body. Once it was all said and done, he understood that my heart was always in the right place. Dillon and I will soon be married and all four of us, Dillon, Alvin, Charlie, and myself, will live happily ever after in our blue house on the hill.

"Years ago, I bought a small house in the woods near a quiet stream. I gazed upon glowing sunsets and attentively listened to the songs of birds, all in the hope of finding my inspiration to greatness. However, it wasn't until I heard the echoing slams of the iron bars and felt the true solitude of loneliness that my search truly began. Inspiration wasn't flowing in the trickling stream or flying high with the peaceful birds; it was just simply within me the entire time. I just wasn't able to see it. And although prison has been the worst experience of my life, I can honestly say it has also been the best, for it brought me to the completion of my very first novel, *Twin Conspiracies*. The book may be categorized as fiction to the rest of the world, but to the others and myself, it is nothing short of our reality."

Signed,
Samantha

Printed in the United States
By Bookmasters